HASHTAG

Also by David Wake

NOVELS
I, Phone
The Derring-Do Club and the Empire of the Dead
The Derring-Do Club and the Year of the Chrononauts
The Derring-Do Club and the Invasion of the Grey
Crossing the Bridge
Atcode

NOVELLAS
The Other Christmas Carol

ONE-ACT PLAYS
Hen and Fox
Down the Hole
Flowers
Stockholm
Groom

NON-FICTION
Punk Publishing (*with Andy Conway*)

HASHTAG

BOOK ONE IN THE **THINKERSPHERE** SERIES

DAVID WAKE

WATLEDGE BOOKS

This is a work of fiction. Names, characters, places, and incidents either are the product of the author's imagination or are used fictitiously, and any resemblance to any persons, living or dead, business establishments, events, or locales is entirely coincidental.

First published in Great Britain by
Watledge Books
Copyright © 2014 David Wake
All rights reserved

This paperback edition 2019
2

ISBN: 978-1-78996-017-4

Cover art by Sean Strong
www.seanstrong.com

What hath god wrought!
> First telegram, 1844
> Samuel B. Morse

Mr Watson, come here, I want to see you.
> First telephone call, 1876
> Alexander Graham Bell

QWERTYUIOP or something similar
> First email, 1971
> Ray Tomlinson

Merry Christmas
> First SMS text message, 1992
> Neil Papworth

just setting up my twttr
> First tweet, 2006
> Oliver Dorsey

Woah, at@bill £bill #weird ah, ah, get it out, get it out!
> First thought, 2018
> Edwin Rallinson

WEEK ONE

SUNDAY

The riot shield's slippery and the bloody baton's awkward, Oliver thought, *stupid kit, designed for gorillas.*

Six of his colleagues liked this: *Gorillas, too right.*

Put it down then, you fascist, the woman opposite, Martha_556, thought back.

Cease and desist... but Oliver hummed the tune, not wanting to be trolled at this point: *pa-pah pa-pah pa-pah...*

Childish.

Oliver rolled forward on the balls of his feet, squeaking his combat boots. It was an irritating tune: *I don't want to get my head kicked in with this nonsense going round and round inside. And it was childish.*

Told you.

He felt hot under his stab vest.

Wasn't this all due to some Jay's thought stream?

Fascist Tepee.

Oliver glanced at the crowd facing him and tried to pick out the woman chiding him, but he couldn't. All their angry faces were directed at individual policemen, but they were probably flaming another cop entirely.

Why he was picking her out of the interminable stream, he didn't know, so he forced himself to focus, deliberately concentrating on one set of thoughts from the feed: *...bastards, bastards, bastards... fascist pig.* He'd slipped back to Martha_556 again, but then Target Four's mental chanting was god awfully tedious. The man must know they were after him. He was using a stooge to rethink his thoughts, after all.

God, I've had a thought-full of this.

The two sides kept their distance, just beyond the recognition range like armies of old staying two spear lengths apart. The rioters were mostly youths, but some of the police were even younger. It was a diversion, creating havoc so that others could loot the shops. Some of these had taken their turn already and they'd tucked all sorts of fashionable clothing under black coats and silver scarves. They looked like fat sports fans topped off with baseball caps. There were a few with tin foil hats showing a contingent from the nutter brigade, and all those grinning plastic masks were creepy.

The Sergeant actually shouted aloud, "Rip!"

Oliver ripped the paper seal off the notice taped to the back of his shield. A sound, like unzipping, went down the line.

'#96jf76tt' it said.

It took a moment for Oliver to follow the hashtag – *Hash 96jf76tt Alpha go left, Charlie go right, Foxtrot front.*

Foxtrot front, he thought. He couldn't help himself.

The rest of the snatch squad were already charging forward: Chen and Mox in the lead. They'd be beyond recognition range any moment if he didn't look lively himself.

Shit, thought Martha_556 opposite, *here they come!*

Bastards, bast- Scatter, thought Target Four – theirs. The delay was due to the stooge, some kid in foreign climes on pay-as-you-think, needing time to rethink. He was probably taken by surprise by the sudden change.

Oliver glanced through the Perspex visor at the colourful movement of rioters going left and right. One was Target Four, but which one was impossible to tell.

"Arrghh, phase two!" the Sergeant shouted, clearly overloaded by the trolling he was sustaining. He was the obvious target – they always went for the leader – but the other Sergeant, who had kept his head down and his thoughts on other things, would take over now.

One of the constables to Oliver's left engaged, slamming his shield forward and up so that he could swipe low with his baton. The rioter yelped and went down as his leg twisted under the blow. Oliver held back, unused to this work and to uniform in general. With all the clamour and confusion, he could barely follow the thoughts of the Sergeant; others jumped out at him demanding his attention and he had the distracting flicker of recognition as the rioters came into range.

Bog.

Bog the fascists!

They're bogging.

"What?" Oliver said, more of a swear word than a question.

Damn jargon, Chen thought, *all these code words are designed to confuse and—*

Take this you bastard.

Hash 96jf76tt switch to squad hashtags.

Hash Foxtrot, phase three.

Something heavy went crump to his left and Oliver glanced up just in time to see something large arcing down towards him. He ducked behind his shield which took the impact, yanking his arm around.

A chant went up: "Pa-pah! Pa-pah!"

God, we're using the tune as a battle cry.

Battle, see. You fascist.

Tepee pig.

Hash Foxtrot, Point Alpha.

There was only '...*run, run, run*...' from Target Four.

Oliver jogged with his colleagues, who knew what was what and where was where. Point Alpha was a street corner.

You'll just be making up the numbers, Inspector Dartford had thought, *fill in to help uniform. Don't worry.*

Useful experience before your Sergeant's exam, Freya had added.

Welcome aboard, Mox had thought, when he thumped him on the back.

Strange how those giving the orders were never, ever actually present. *Mustn't think that... pa-pah, pa-pah! Too late.*

Just following orders were you, Martha_556 thought, *you fascist Tepee.*

Oliver ignored her: *Stay at the back, don't get drawn in,* he thought.

Coward.

That woman who'd zeroed him was really getting on his tits, but he refused to give her the satisfaction of knowing it: *Pa-pah, pa-pah...* "Pa-pah!"

He swung rather savagely at a rioter as his section charged past. He might have connected, or probably hit Chen's riot shield, but they all thundered on around the street corner.

Scatter!

That had been stooge's rethink; so Target Four was responding to their movements, which meant he had to be nearby.

Oliver took two steps to slow down so he could scan the area.

The street was full of dropped shoes taken from one of the looted shops. A few rioters saw them and fled up the High Street or along St. Thomas Street. Others came out of a newsagents, their feet kicking up the shattered glass as they came to a halt.

Target Four wouldn't be one of these, but he had responded to their arrival, so probably–

Chen thought so too: *Even go left, odd right.*

Hash Foxtrot, Oliver thought, *what the hell is my number?*

It was on the back of his borrowed riot jacket.

Oliver started running towards the High Street with Target Four's mental chant ironically driving him on: ...*run, run, run...*

Your other left, Ollie.

Shit.

Oliver changed direction.

St. Thomas Street led to some abandoned shops internetted out of existence and now boarded up. There were cobbles between the pavements at the far end. This was where Chen and Oliver headed.

Fascist Tepee! Stop it! I have rights.

Martha_556 had obviously not identified him properly, so whoever she was venting her anger on was blissfully unaware of it. 'Tepee' was irritating: an insult on account of the conical helmet and the initials. Trying to follow the thoughts of the group he was chasing, while another group's intruded was confusing.

Oliver felt wrong footed.

You've got the wrong guy, Oliver thought.

You're not him, Martha_556 thought. *Who's this Tepee then? Fucking Thought Police.*

There were four men in the street: two City fans, a Goth and an orange balaclava, sidestepping to the pavements now the tarmac had run out. They clearly didn't want to turn an ankle on the uneven surface. Odds are Target Four had the mask.

"There, over there!" Chen shouted aloud, wobbling his shield towards the boarded up phone shop. There was a side alley: two youths went down that and Chen clearly wanted to cover all possibilities. Oliver was closer, so he followed, turned sideways to get his shield between the alley wall and a large industrial refuse bin. His colleague, he'd no idea who, bumped him as they went through.

"Ow!"

Oliver recognised him as Mox.

At Ollie, are you all right?

It was his girlfriend, Jasmine, her thoughts coming clearer now that he was out of recognition range of everyone but Mox.

At Jasmine! I'm at work, Oliver thought frantically.

I've changed my status, Jasmine thought back.

The youths were already right down the end of the alley, and would have disappeared into the gloom had the fashion for silver scarves not been so prevalent. Oliver thumped his way down between the high walls, jumped a broken box and skidded to a halt at the far end.

They came out onto Tumney Row – disconcertingly. Oliver was lost. The very thought gave him his co-ordinates, but it didn't mean anything.

He saw a flash of white trainers disappearing over the wire fence opposite. The 'No Trespassing' sign flapped back and forth.

There's no way I can get over that, Oliver thought.

Ollie, you could pass the riot shield over after I've climbed it, Mox thought.

"You're kidding?" Oliver's voice echoed and his visor steamed up.

They both looked at the fence again, gauging its height.

Oliver noodled it: *This alley goes several hundred metres and then out towards the train station*, he thought at Mox, *we'll never catch 'em.*

You're one of those desk jockeys, aren't you?

Detective Constable, Oliver thought, *yes.*

It's not them anyway, it'll be the man wearing the–

"Careful!"

Wearing the pa-pah, pa-pah, Mox thought, waving his hands over his riot helmet to signify the... pa-pah, pa-pah. *Pa-pah hat.*

Oliver laughed aloud and Mox joined in.

Oliver thought: *Let's find Chen.*

Mox nodded.

They jogged back down the alleyway.

"Oi!" Mox yelled.

By the time Oliver got clear of the refuse bin, the rioter had fled.

He went this way, Mox thought, already moving across the cobbles.

Oliver, bent double to get his breath back, straightened and followed, walking. There was no sign of Chen or the balaclava. He was sure the man was Target Four.

Further down, there was a crossroads as Old Tollgate crossed from Chedding to Portman Square. There was a group loitering, probably with intent, but they all had baseball caps or bare heads.

We could ask, Ollie thought.

One of the loiterers, close enough to recognise, gave them the finger: *Piss off.*

Mox jerked into a charge and they scattered.

"No pa-pah," Mox said, coming to a halt.

Oliver thought at Chen: *I'm at... shit.*

"Point er... five!" said Mox.

"Point five..." *I mean*, he thought, *Hash Foxtrot, point five with Mox.*

Some wag thought: *Is that what we're calling point five now?*

Stay there, Chen thought, *he may double back, but he's... oh, to hell with this.*

A rethink: *Is that what we're calling point five now?*

Other thoughts followed.

To hell with what?

Pa-pah, pa-pah.

Point five is called 'shit' now.

Hash Foxtrot, Target Four is wearing an orange balaclava north of Old Tollgate, rethink.

Oliver took Chen's thought, rethinking it to his followers.

Target Four is wearing an orange balaclava, north of Old Tollgate, came Mox's rethink followed by all of Foxtrot squad doing the same.

At Jimmy, you're target four, came the woman who'd called him a fascist, Martha_556.

Someone sprinted from a doorway down towards the old Chedding Shopping Centre.

Not him, Mox thought, but then Oliver saw a flash of orange stuffed in the man's pocket.

Yes, yes, Oliver thought: *Chedding, Chedding! Hash Foxtrot. Rethink.*

Oliver flung his riot shield to one side and accelerated downhill, bringing his arms up and down.

His target quickened his pace too and stayed tantalizingly out of range. Once he was within recognition, the man's stooge would be pointless and they'd be able to pick him up any time, but Oliver couldn't quite close the gap. He felt the merest flicker in his brow, just as the man turned back towards the High Street.

Oliver stumbled, he'd not expected that change of direction: the man was trapped now. He'd been stupid because–

Damn, the door's forced, Oliver thought as he reached the huge, white building at the end.

What door?

Chedding, he's gone into Chedding Shopping Centre.

We're at 'Shit' moving up Old Tollgate now.

Don't be stupid, that's sealed up.

Not anymore, Oliver thought.

He burst through the steel door causing the heavy lock to fall to the ground. It had been sheared with bolt cutters. Concrete stairs led upwards and round, the stairwell making his footsteps, and those of Mox behind him, echo.

He reached a landing.

Up, he thought.

You take this one, Mox thought back.

Oliver tried the door: *Locked.*

Mox had already passed him and turned the corner.

Oliver started after him.

At Ollie, we're outside Chedding now, Chen thought, *where are you?*

Going up, Oliver thought back as he took two steps at a time.

Second is open, Mox thought, *I'll take it, you try three.*

Bloody stairs, Oliver thought, swinging around and continuing up.

The door on the third level was open, the concrete and plaster dust disturbed.

I think he's on my level, Mox thought; just as Oliver was about to think the same.

The floor tiles gave the deserted shopping centre a clinical feel and Oliver's combat boots squeaked as he came in.

I'm hiding, I'm hiding, Target Four's stooge rethought in a mantra beyond maddening. Why couldn't the kid just stop doing it, but then perhaps the stooge didn't even understand English? Back office must have correlated enough phrases to make a search by now.

Perhaps he doesn't know I'm chasing him, Oliver thought.

Filth, Tepee pig, scum, Target Four's stooge repeated. It was very old fashioned, trust the ringleader to have been traditionally educated.

Cleverer than you.

He's following me, Oliver thought. *The change meant he—*

Yea, I am, you scum.

What level?

Piss off.

Oliver only just caught the wisp amongst the chorus of his squad. Everyone had switched to 'pa-pah' to avoid giving anything away and the tune wormed its way firmly into the back of his mind, eclipsing everything else. The melody was supposed to prevent any thoughts leaking out, but counterproductive. Oliver couldn't hear himself think.

He glanced round to clear his head and distract himself from the insidious repetition.

I always liked it here, he thought. His Mum used to bring him here back in the day: *Burger for lunch, lollipop on the way back if I'd been good. Every good boy deserves chocolate. There were toilets on the third level.*

Not near any toilets.

Target Four was getting stressed, his mantra going pear shaped.

Not stressed, Tepee.

I'm leaking too, Oliver thought.

Too right.

Amazing how the man had managed to pick Oliver out of the cacophony of all the police. Oliver was focused now, picking out the man's rethought commentary and ignoring everything else. He went further in, almost on tip-toe, looking round at the whitewashed display windows and the boarded-up doors. This had been a CD shop, over there was once a toy shop and that – *gosh* – a bookshop.

Target Four bolted from the information booth near the old bookshop. He was running on instinct, or Oliver had missed the thought in his rush to give chase. They sprinted down the length of the shopping centre to the far stairs.

Far stairs, Oliver thought as he clattered through the door. He was in a stairwell similar to the one he'd come up in.

Chen's thought was a distinct voice in amongst the maddening tune: *Far from what?*

Far from Old Tollgate.

Ollie, which end?

I don't know.

On your brow.

Oliver checked and rethought the result: *South.*

Hash Foxtrot, converge on the south end of Chedding.

Target Four was nowhere to be seen, but Oliver ran down the stairs. He knew from his training that fugitives tended to run downwards, an instinct to get out of the trees perhaps.

I'm going up, I'm on level four, Target Four's stooge thought, but, even second hand, it included the hint of a basement.

Oliver flung himself around the awkward spiral, grabbing the metal rails for leverage. Without the daylight from the windows, it was dark below ground level. It frightened him, always had from childhood, but at least with his colleagues' thoughts in his head, he wasn't alone.

His eyes didn't adjust fast enough, or his heavy gasps fogged the riot helmet's visor, but he assumed the shape of the turns would be identical and the door to the sub-level in the same place. He got away with it, and he came out in a gloomy underground car park.

There were no cars. *No, wait! One car, there, and pillars holding up the ceiling and the entire abandoned shopping centre above.* Light streamed in weakly from the distant iron shutters.

"Give it up," said Oliver, aloud. His voice echoed like a rethink.

He snapped his torch on and scanned the beam around to be rewarded by a scuffle.

Target Four's thoughts were now distorted by fear with a strange echo. Oliver had him almost on recognition, which meant he must be close, and the stooge's repetition came afterwards.

Perhaps he was behind the abandoned car?

Oliver bent over until he could see under the vehicle.

Or one of these pillars then?

Oliver began to move sideways, deliberately moving around the pillar in a clockwise direction before he flicked the torch's beam off. He paused, waited for his eyes to adjust before moving around anti-clockwise. He thought he might catch the man moving to keep the pillar between them.

No way, came a thought.

Oliver took two strides back the way he'd come, flicked the torch on and jumped around the nearest pillar. Target Four's wide eyes reflected back and Oliver recognised him, a clear signal now there wasn't anything between them, and he knew he was Jimmy Scanlan.

Give it up, Oliver thought.

The man came for him: *Take this!*

Oliver's reflexes took over, his training kicking in, and he flung his torch forward as a distraction. The metal tube bounced and clattered away, but caused something in the man's right hand to glint silver.

Take this, came the stooge's rethink.

Oliver blocked and then twisted so that the blade snagged on his stab vest. They went down, the man landing on top. Oliver was winded, his neck jarred when his helmet struck the concrete floor.

In your guts!

Oliver felt the man shift position, his arm going down to probe below his Kevlar protection.

The stooge: *In your guts!*

Jimmy! Don't!

Their eyes met, he smiled: *Any last request?*

Oliver head-butted him.

Ah! Bast-ak, @£,$%, #mum... mummy...

Oliver did it again and was rewarded with a flaring shutdown.

Any last request... nah, he's toast, the man thought... no, his stooge had thought that. The kid, wherever he was, did know English after all.

For a moment Oliver didn't think, he just lay there, breathing, and glad to be alive.

Chen and the others arrived in a thundering stampede as Oliver pushed the unconscious man off.

Ollie, at Ollie, OK, OK? It was Chen checking.

Oliver undid the strap of his helmet and pulled it off. His head felt suddenly cold without the clammy padding and metal covering. Oliver held his thumb upwards. Chen liked this.

"Jimmy Scanlan," said Chen in a loud and clear voice. "I'm, like, arresting you—"

He's unconscious, Oliver thought, as he tried to swat the light away from his eyes. The others got the hint and pointed their torches downwards.

Which reminds me, Oliver thought, *where's my torch?*

A couple of the police moved their own torches to indicate where a beam of light shone from under the abandoned car.

Thanks.

He called for his Mummy when Ollie smacked him in the head.

Six others in the squad liked this.

Oliver wasn't sure which of them had thought that. They all looked the same in their visors, but he recognised them all from their signals.

You got 'im, Ollie, Mox thought.

Yea, Oliver thought back.

He had really connected with Target Four's forehead with obvious results. It would be a while before the man's iBrow settled and they got any straight thinking out of him. Jimmy Scanlan writhed on the floor as if he was having a fit, a sort of disconnected automaton, disturbingly inhuman due to the lack of thought.

I'd like to read his 'Mummy' thought out in court, thought someone, the idea as clear as day.

Straight away, everyone liked this.

Imagine reading the rest out in court: run, run, run...

Everyone laughed at that, their relief spilling out into the echoing subterranean chamber.

Hash Foxtrot, we deserve to go to the pub now, Chen thought.

Oliver got up and sauntered over to the vehicle, a red Tiger Fire. He reached first, but then had to go down on his hands and knees to retrieve his torch. When he stood up, he flicked it on and off to check it was working properly and, in doing so, shone the beam across the back seat of the car.

"Shit!"

There was a body, quite clearly very dead.

Chen came over: *Is he dead?*

Oliver realised he must have leaked a thought or two unconsciously. *She's seen better days*, he thought in reply.

Chen looked in the car. "Jeez, what a mess," he said. Sometimes thoughts weren't enough. Chen glanced at everyone in turn: *Who's senior officer?*

The others looked at each other, almost shuffling back to avoid volunteering.

Oliver raised his hand: *Detective Constable*, he thought.

Your show then, Chen thought.

Do we need one, Oliver thought.

Murder, Chen thought, *she can't have smashed her head in like that herself.*

Oliver nodded, *OK, OK,* and took charge: *Mox, you're scene of crime officer.*

When he received no reply, Oliver called out, "Mox!"

Mox looked startled: *Sorry, just updating my status.*

Secure the area until forensics gets here.

Mox saluted and stepped forward, holding out his hand to back everyone away from the car, even Oliver. He tilted his head, a sure sign he was noodling something.

It's 2:35pm, Mox thought, *and this is now officially a crime scene: Hash 83,648,819*

Given the situation, Oliver thought, *someone best stay with him.*

Riot's over.

No way.

Overtime?

Oliver considered for a moment, recognizing each of the identically dressed officers: *Tim.*

Ollie!!!

Two paramedics arrived to deal with the injured prisoner, Jimmy Scanlan, who was no longer Target Four but officially an 'alleged' riot jay.

The rest of them went outside.

Beyond the abandoned construction site, its steel reinforcing rods visible sticking up through the concrete dust, a police mini-bus was cruising past collecting the various groups: a clear sign that the flash mob's interest had waned.

Oliver noodled for a situation update and, sure enough, with the ring-leaders bagged and some celebrity event going viral, the streets had turned eerily quiet. There'd be a lot of glass to replace and items to recover, but that was it.

Chen came up beside him: *Can we get across that?*

Oliver checked the construction site: *No, we'll have to go around.*

OK.

Chen led the way to the steel shutters and they found a place where they could climb up to the vehicle access ramp. The mini-bus doubled back when the driver got their thoughts.

Oliver suddenly remembered: *Shield?*

What number?

Oliver tried to pull his police overall round to see the stencil, but he couldn't.

Fifty-three, Chen thought.

Is it in the back?

Yes, here.

Here.

Oliver took the offered hand and jumped into the mini-bus with the others.

At Ollie, Jellicoe wants to see you, Freya thought.

Me?

Yes, in person.

Can he not brief me here, Oliver thought back.

No, he's in the Lamp.

He wants to talk to me in person!?

Yes. Then get the report on my desk about today's operation by 16:30 and one for this new crime, Hash 83,648,819.

Oliver sighed and held the bridge of his nose tightly.

I heard that.

That was from Freya, either she'd replied to someone else or she'd simply assumed he'd thought something sarcastic.

On the way back, Oliver noodled a list of the various interactions over the morning. This he sent to his ancient tablet, so that when he got back to the office and changed out of the riot gear, a rough draft of a report was waiting. He assigned names to thoughts, deleted a few idiotic asides and inserted some hooks for the wiki. It would have to do. He wasn't sure why they used this obsolete technology anyway. Why hot-desk when you can hot-foot? He emailed it to Freya.

The Lamp was the tavern of choice for the Senior Detectives. It was dark, secluded and ancient; their custom all that kept the place going. Oliver was a new breed of detective, he knew, and he wasn't going to end up in this throw-back to the last century. The decor came from an age before the iBrow or the internet even.

In person, honestly.

The pub was guarded by two elderly detectives smoking just outside the doorway. Oliver held his breath as he went past.

When he breathed in again, he smelt the hops and stale beer. Everyone was wearing corduroy and tweed. There was a babble of audible talking as you always had in pubs. Jellicoe was in the third booth along; alone, except for a tumbler of scotch.

I'm here, Sir, Oliver thought.

No reaction.

Sir?

Nothing.

Still nothing.

Oliver coughed deliberately.

Inspector Jellicoe looked up. "Ah, Oliver..." The man consulted a piece of paper. *Oh for... the man uses paper.* "Braddon."

Sir.

"Cat got your tongue?"

"Sir?"

"Sit down, what would you like?"

"I'm fine," Oliver said, squeezing into the booth. His mouth felt dry as it was unused to talking aloud, and he swallowed to relieve his throat.

"I insist."

"Tonic water."

"Just that?"

"I'm on duty."

"So am I."

"Oh. Right. Er... half a lager then."

"Same again," said Jellicoe, showing his glass to Oliver. "Her name's Babs Lamp."

At Babslamp... At Babs_lamp, Oliver thought, *could I have a half of Stella and whatever Jellicoe was having, please.*

Coming up.

Oliver sidled out again and walked to the bar, getting there just as the barmaid topped up the lager. Babs looked fifteen and Oliver wondered about checking her ID.

Gland problem.

Sorry, he thought back.

Oliver waited for the buzz – nine fifty – and reckoned with his bank.

Get me a lawyer, get me a fucking lawyer! Fucking Thought Police.

God, Oliver thought, *I'm still following Jimmy Scanlan and he's come round.* Oliver tweaked his settings as he negotiated his way back with the drinks.

Jellicoe took his glass with a grunt, swirled the neat liquid and then held it to the light. "Hello scotch," he said, "glad to meet you."

He took a sip.

This is going to take all day, Oliver thought.

Better not, Jasmine thought, *we've a date at six.*

Don't worry.

I do.

Thanks.

Booked and asked for our table.

We have a table?

Yes, Ollie, the one–

Jellicoe banged his glass down sharply, shocking Oliver back to the Lamp.

At Jasmine, got to concentrate here – sorry.

Later.

"This body of yours," the Inspector said.

"Not mine."

"It is now, you're assigned."

"Me?"

"You found it."

Jellicoe was old, crumpled, and his nose was marked with a fine tracery of red lines. He was borderline alcoholic: *No*, Oliver thought, *he is alcoholic*. Thin hair, grey and swept back. When the man frowned, the skin of his forehead furrowed to reveal the shape of the iBrow underneath. He represented everything that Oliver hoped never to be. The police force was modern now and didn't need these has-beens. The Inspector wore a uniform of tweed jacket and wrist watch. *Honestly – steampunk – or whatever – was what? Ten years ago, at least.*

"Get it sorted quick, we don't want any hacking group picking it up and making this morning's flash riot political," said Jellicoe.

"It was nothing to do with the riot," Oliver replied.

"Nothing?"

"We found it because Jimmy Scanlan tried to escape through Chedding Shopping Centre. The body was hidden in a car in the underground car park. We found it by pure chance."

"You're sure? Bit of a co-incidence – bodies don't just turn up," said Jellicoe. The Inspector fumbled in his pocket and brought out a bottle of tablets. He spilled three into his palm, took them and washed them down with his whiskey.

Oliver waited for him to finish and then said, "We'll see when the pathologist reports back."

"I'm having the pathologist rush through the autopsy tonight," said Jellicoe. "I'd like you to investigate it now."

"Oh, sure, as soon as the pathologist–"

"Now!"

What honestly was the point? All they had to do was wait for the code and they'd have a proper identification of the victim, otherwise it was endless searches.

Jellicoe's expression brooked no argument.

"OK," Oliver said.

Oliver noodled missing persons and was momentarily overwhelmed when he remembered the list of 158,912 missing persons worldwide. He narrowed the search both in the time parameters and geographically. Jellicoe sipped his scotch, so Oliver took a mouthful of his drink. It was refreshing, it had been a day of running about, and he needed it. All this actual talking had made his throat dry.

"Well?"

"I remember about 700 odd. I'll narrow it once more people wake up or," he added, pointedly, "sober up."

"Hmmm... I've a gut feeling about this one," said Jellicoe, continuing to talk aloud.

"Why don't you use thinking, Sir?"

"I prefer my thoughts to be my own."

"People only do that, Sir, if they've something to hide."

"So the slogan says."

"Forensics will tell me who she was, and then we'll noodle her thoughts and know everything there is to know."

"You shouldn't rely on that all the time."

"Why not?"

Jellicoe shrugged.

Oliver had the impression that there was more that Jellicoe wanted to say, but, without a proper chain of thought to follow, it was impossible to guess. Usually, once he'd parsed a chain, Oliver could pretty much predict the next few thoughts as, he knew, could everyone.

"Is that all, Sir?"

Jellicoe nodded and waited until Oliver had extracted himself from the booth, before calling him back, "Braddon, you could make a good detective."

"I will Sir," Oliver replied. *But not like you.*

The number of applicable missing persons was down to 451. This was from the official list. Anybody who wasn't thinking was missing in a way: in any instant that was 16 billion, but as people thought every six seconds or so, that quickly dropped by around a billion every second, levelling off quickly. After a minute, that bottomed out at around 5 billion, those people asleep.

Why are you thinking about populations?

Sorry, Jas, work – it's on my mind. I'll be there in ten. If I can get a cab.

He checked up and down the street.

Hash cab, hash cab, he thought.

One pulled over and Oliver got in.

A Missing Person didn't become a police matter until there had been no thoughts for forty-eight hours. Hence the 441, reducing as more possibilities were eliminated, on the list.

The taxi driver pulled out into the passing traffic. Oliver recognised him and then thought at him about the Palatine Restaurant. They skirted the High Street where clean-up crews were working already, brushing away the shattered glass and hammering boards over the broken windows.

It was getting late: 6pm here was 10am in Los Angeles, so the whole of the Americas was awake now, so... this was stupid. Jellicoe had got him trying to second guess the pathologist. Tomorrow morning, first thing, they would get the iBrow code and then they'd know the registered owner – done. Unless the owner hadn't thought about her attacker in which case there'd be a lot of fiddly searches to find who was responsible. So, evening off, glass of wine, chance to unwind.

Too right... woo hoo.

Jasmine's train of thought was breaking up. She must be having a drink while she waited. *And why not?* He would too. *Off duty was off call.*

By the time Oliver reached the restaurant, he was late, but luckily, he had worried enough about arriving on time so his thoughts had mollified Jasmine. The Palatine was a classy Italian restaurant with a large open plan space, split into two levels by a step. Jasmine waved as Oliver tried to link with the waiter. Instead, seeing her, Oliver pointed, and the waiter nodded.

"Hi," she said. They air-kissed.

Sorry, I'm late, Oliver thought.

"It's OK."

Work, you know.

"No problemo."

Oliver fussed with the menu and realised that he hadn't worked out who the waiter was. He tried to find the restaurant's hashtag on the back, but Jasmine raised her arm and clicked her fingers. Her bangles clattered down her wrist.

A waitress came over.

I'd like... "I'd like a Stella... OK, that's fine," said Oliver.

Jasmine circled her wine glass with her finger and the waitress nodded. Oliver didn't pick up any thought.

He glanced across the table: *Have you decided?*

"Yes, the pasta."

Oliver checked the choices, and glanced up at the specials board, but all it had was the restaurant's hashtag. He noodled their site and remembered the day's specials. He picked the spaghetti bolognese.

"I ordered nibbles for starters," Jasmine said.

Great.

The list was down to 112 and beginning to reduce as A&E staff thought about recent deaths, car accidents, heart attacks and so on. *Perhaps...* but Oliver's drink arrived along with a large white wine for Jasmine.

Cheers.

"Bottoms up."

He drank, a good gulp feeling he ought to be catching up. The fizz went down, slightly gassy and, along with the half of lager in the afternoon, the alcohol leached into his blood supply. A spreading prickling sensation, entirely psychosomatic he knew, told him that his inebriation safety had cut in.

"So," he said aloud, "how was your day?"

"Ah, you know," said Jasmine, casually.

He did know, of course, although he'd missed a lot of her thoughts because of the riot.

"Well?" she asked.

"Er..."

The waitress arrived, and they ordered.

Oliver remembered that the search list was now 85.

"Can you not think about work?"

"I'm not thinking," Oliver replied.

Jasmine was angry: she didn't push her long black hair back behind her ear and instead let it gather like a storm cloud around her face. Even without a thought to underline it, it was a clear sign.

"I've every right to be," Jasmine said.

Oliver was thrown as he clearly hadn't thought that explicitly. Perhaps she'd read his body language, or something involved female intuition.

"Sorry," Oliver said. He waved his drink in front of her. "I can't switch it off."

It was now 80.

"You have my full attention," said Oliver.

78.

"I'm not cross," Jasmine said, leaning forward, her long fingers pushing her hair back.

The pathologist was getting ready to do the autopsy and Oliver knew because he was following the case hashtag.

"What is it?" Oliver asked.

"I changed my status."

"Right, of course."

Oliver noodled her status changes and, perhaps because he was befuddled, he remembered all of them, but the pathologist's thoughts intruded: ...*female, mid-thirties, extreme trauma to the face and head, signs of decomposition.*

Why was he doing the autopsy now? Ghoulish at this time of night. Ignore him, concentrate... and Oliver got a hint of a migraine shadow as his thoughts backed up due to the inebriation safety.

Jasmine flicked her finger back and forth between them: "We're in a relationship."

"Yes."

"I changed my status!"

"Oh, right."

The list was 37... 36.

Making the first incision, thought Doctor Ridge, *to examine the guts now.*

Oliver's spaghetti bolognese arrived, its strands curling in a rich red meaty sauce.

I'm not really that hungry, Oliver tried thinking, but his brow didn't respond.

He twirled his fork in the tomato covered intertwined strands.

"Oliver!"

He noodled her current status again and remembered that she was in a relationship with 'Oliver Braddon'.

Examining the heart now, Doctor Ridge thought.

Oliver felt lost, he always did when he was drinking. It wasn't the alcohol itself, he'd barely had any: it was because he wasn't able to trace the steps of his own thoughts and so make the next one. Perhaps he should write them down – *oh, what a ridiculous idea.* That did give him a migraine shadow.

"That's nice," he said, aloud.

Moving to the head, Doctor Ridge thought.

Jasmine glared, full on, but no thought came through.

Doctor Ridge's next thought was a removed expletive.

"Ollie," Jasmine insisted. "I changed my status!"

"Yes."

"And you haven't."

"Oh, well, I've been busy."

As if on cue, he remembered that the list was now 23.

"Too busy for us," she leaned forward and hissed, "My friends all know."

"I don't follow all your friends."

"If you did, you know how people feel about someone who doesn't update his relationship after his supposed girlfriend has updated hers."

"Sorry, of course, I'll–"

"It's been six hours!"

"Yes."

"My friends will think I'm some sort of slapper."

This is a bombshell, Doctor Ridge thought, *a right mess – a definite Red Indian.*

What's a Red Indian? These Doctors and their jargon.

Never you mind what a Red Indian is, Doctor Ridge thought.

Oliver hadn't thought anything, so clearly others were following the autopsy. These Doctors must be specifically trained at medical school to substitute gibberish for medical jargon.

"You've still not done it!"

"Done what?"

It was something about her friends and he tried to remember: the list was 11.

Detective Constable Oliver Braddon – at Ollie, Doctor Ridge thought, *you'd better get down here.*

In person!? Migraine shadow. *Bloody drink*, he finished his drink and put the glass down.

Jasmine slapped him, hard across the face.

The restaurant's audible hubbub of conversation stopped abruptly.

Oliver felt his face burning, he could almost feel everyone's attention turning to him, passing on the recognition to those further away and the riffling down of his, and Jasmine's, thoughts.

Now Ollie, Doctor Ridge insisted.

"I have to go," Oliver said, woodenly.

He stood up and without another word walked to the doorway. Irritatingly there were a few customers arriving, so he had to wait. As they came in, their eyes widened as they recognised him and then the salacious smile appeared as they realised this was the man who'd been slapped. A few stray thoughts flickered onto his stream as they swept in and out of recognition range.

She changed her status, he didn't.
Bastard.
Policeman.
Six hours and he did nothing.
Stupid Tepee.
Is she ugly?
Where is she?

The waiter caught him and showed him the Palatine Restaurant's teller machine. He waited for the buzz and opened a reckoning with his bank.

"Ollie! Don't walk away from me when I'm talking!"

It was cold outside, sharp on his slapped cheek, and he made his way down the road threading through the throng.

He thought about a cab, an error which affected his head.

It was a long walk back to the station. As he reached Old Tollgate, someone thought he was a wanker.

At Ollie, what did you say to Jasmine?

Men are such bastards.

Jasmine has talked to one of us and she's crying.

I hope you're happy Ollie, upsetting poor Jasmine like that.

No-one liked it.

"Shut up, shut up!" he said aloud.

Passers-by glanced at him and moved aside.

Oliver put his hand to his forehead, his fingers touching the skin a centimetre away from his iBrow. He let it wash over him, there was after all no choice.

You should apologise to Jasmine right away.

Sober up and think good thoughts.

The list dropped to zero – no missing people matched the description. That was impossible, so how much had he had to drink?

At Ollie, where are you? Now means now.

There was no way he could go in now.

Do you realise how upset she is, wanker?

Two-for-one on drinks with your next visit to the Palatine.

As soon as the coffee takes effect, Jasmine's going to make you history.

Hasqueth Finest is the best – it tastes so good.

Jellicoe insists you get over to the pathologist in person.

Special thoughts, just a reckon away.

At Ollie, you are a wanker.

Hi, I'm Mithering: did you find a body in a car park?

MONDAY

Oliver dreamt of wandering around lost in an underground concrete maze. He found a body trapped in a car, and then another in a fridge and a third in a locker, before his alarm thought intruded. He woke bewildered, unable to open his eyes, and his mouth tasted disgusting. He wanted desperately to brush his teeth, but instead he pulled off his head band charger, rolled over and tried to ignore the appointment with Doctor Ridge, but it continuously popped to the top of his thoughts. He wasn't going to get any peace, so he thought about the lights.

"Ah!"

Dazzled, he thought about darkness and stumbled from his bed to the bathroom, which was preferable to being dazzled. Once he'd splashed water on his face and brushed his teeth, he allowed himself to skim along all the thoughts he'd picked up during the night. There weren't too many, so he must be up early. He noodled: *God, six o'clock*, he thought. Few of those he followed were up yet, so it only took ten minutes to process everything, and by that time the kettle had boiled.

This coffee doesn't taste so good, he thought. He remembered that others of his friends drank Hasqueth

Finest, and a delivery was just a thought away. Others who ordered it liked Milton Luxury Biscuits.

I must be tired, he thought, *if the spam's gaining my attention. Energy drinks came in several isotonic flavours and—*

Oliver shook head, downed his coffee and went back to the bedroom to find some clothes.

At the door, he noodled for his checklist and then made sure he had his keys and warrant card.

It was bracing outside: Noodle put it at 11 degrees, but it felt colder. For Oliver, it was like stepping into the Arctic. He should have had some breakfast, so he noodled the available options and thought about pastries. They were ready on the counter when he reached the bakery by the train station. At the buzz, he reckoned with his bank and then thought his thanks to the shop assistant, who must have been in the back baking fresh produce.

He ate on the station platform, shaking the crumbs off his fingers as the commuter train pulled in. The sunlight flickered off the windows causing him to squint and the flash of recognition for every passenger as they zipped past was disconcerting. He thought at the door and remembered the start of his journey along with the various options of return, on-going and so forth. He was registered, so whatever the day's travel turned out to be, his bank would pay for the cheapest deal.

As the train pulled into the terminus, he noodled the time and then thought he'd be with Doctor Ridge in about ten minutes. He remembered some taxi offers, because he must have leaked about leaving the train station, but he ignored them and walked instead. It wasn't far, and he needed to clear his head.

At Ollie, did you know that people think that someone was killed in the riot and that the police are covering it up?

It's Mithering, Oliver thought. *Why couldn't people use their own names?*

Privacy, Mithering thought.

Do you have something to hide?

No – do you?
No.
Sure?
Yes, Oliver insisted.
So did the police kill that woman during the riot?
No, Oliver thought back, *we didn't. I was there.*
You're a policeman, perhaps you're in on it.
You can noodle my thoughts.
I have, perhaps you're a patsy too.

Oliver arrived at the police station, thought his way in and nodded to the Desk Sergeant, recognising Draith, who he already knew. The man was drinking a mug of Hasqueth Finest, which was so good. Oliver could see the coffee machine behind him and the distinctive packaging.

At Ollie, Doctor Ridge wants to see you, Sergeant Draith thought, without looking up, when he recognised Oliver.

On my way, Oliver thought back, and then he rethought it to Doctor Ridge.

Chen was in the office, twitching as he played a cerebral, and oblivious to everything.

Oliver checked his locker, but he had nothing to put in or get out.

At Ollie, autopsy report for Hash 83,648,819 ready, Doctor Ridge thought.

OK.

I can give it to you now.

OK.

Best if you come down here.

In person!?

There was no follow up from Doctor Ridge. Nothing, which was strange, because following him ought to have given him some idle thought. People tended to think every six seconds, so it was strange for someone to go blank.

"Oh god," he mumbled under his breath, *another pissed dinosaur.*

It was a long way down into the basement and then another long walk along a white tiled corridor. It didn't help his mood. He disliked underground places.

Cheer up, Mithering thought.

Oliver had never been to the morgue before: it hadn't been part of the tour when he'd been transferred. But why should it? There was no need. Once the pathologist, Doctor Ridge or Doctor Hassan, thought they were finished, everyone just noodled the summary. Oliver couldn't actually remember having to check a path lab report in detail, except for the carbon monoxide case last year. Carbon monoxide makes thinking sluggish, so the victims hadn't thought they were in any trouble until it had been too late. The landlord was up for negligence, and they'd worked out the man's slang and could prove that he'd been aware of the issue. He went down for manslaughter, five years.

As the hospital smell hit him, Oliver felt a growing sense of foreboding as if his soul was leaching away from him. He felt small, infantile, like a schoolboy sent to the headmaster's study in some tbook.

Morgues are dreadful places, he thought, *really awful.*

He felt a presence, someone breathing down his neck, but when he jerked his head around there was no-one there. Someone had been there, and now they were gone.

"You coming?"

Doctor Ridge was standing holding one of the double doors open. He smiled; not pleasantly, but as if he knew something. Oliver still felt strange as if he had been left alone somewhere, lost as a child when he was young. His impulse was to run to catch up, but he walked as normal.

The morgue was a big room, cold and grim, with large black and white squares on the floor. One wall was devoted to column after column of oversized filing cabinets. Oliver realised that these were the drawers they kept the bodies in. Each was numbered.

Doctor Ridge was tall, cold and grim too, his eyes sunk back into his sockets. Oliver stepped closer until he recognised him.

"Oliver Braddon." It was a statement.

"Ollie."

"You're here for Unknown 271."

Oliver noodled: *Who is Unknown 271?*

Nothing, except a headache.

"Don't think, talk aloud?"

"Er... why?"

"You'll see, humour me."

"OK," said Oliver. *Another speaker*, he thought, and his head ached again in response.

Doctor Ridge went over to the fourth section along and picked the bottom drawer.

"Number thirteen," the man said, aloud. "If there's family, we don't use it in case. Superstition. You understand?"

Oliver didn't: *Of course.*

Ridge grimaced.

"Of course," Oliver repeated.

Ridge grasped the handle and pulled, it boomed like a large kettle drum. There was a shape in heavy black plastic.

"You want?"

"I'm fine."

"You need to see," Ridge said; *I'll give him a shock.*

Oliver realised that the man had thought brow-to-brow only.

The Pathologist fiddled at one corner and then unzipped the body bag, and then he flipped the corner away to reveal—

"Jesus!"

Ridge reached for a bucket, but it was too far away. Oliver missed it, and instead vomited what looked like pulped spaghetti bolognese onto the polished concrete.

"Shit – ah – sorry."

"No worries." *Pathetic, where do they find these boys.*

"I'll–"

"Don't worry, sit there. It's not just the body, it's a communications black spot here."

Oliver was shocked: *That's illegal!*

In a police station?

But it's against the Communications Act.

Report it then.

I can't, Oliver thought as he'd switched modes properly. "How come I've your thoughts?"

Please save me from babes and innocents, Ridge thought, but aloud he said, "We're close enough for recognition, it's brow-to-brow."

"Oh... of course."

"Just sit down."

Oliver did as he was told, scraping the plastic chair away from the wall to avoid the fire extinguisher.

He sat, feeling guilty about throwing up, particularly when the eminent Doctor fetched a bucket and mop.

"Sorry," Oliver said.

Ridge shrugged: "Happens all the time."

Oliver closed his eyes.

It was cold and quiet, creepily so, as somehow Ridge's splash-squidge accentuated the silence in between. The man's thoughts were clear: *What's he been eating?* However, it was the lack of clamour in Oliver's brain that disturbed him. It was frightening, like staring over a high parapet into nothingness.

Test, he thought. "Ow!"

"No thinking via the network," said Ridge. *They never listen.*

So, the man had been right, this was a communications black spot. Rare: you heard of them in the Sahara, Antarctica, down a mine or... well, did you? *How many places were officially communications black spots,* he thought. They were illegal, once they were found, they were filled in with a thought repeater.

The dull feeling, not exactly a pain as such, came back to him.

"It's an error message," said Ridge, who went back to his cleaning.

Oliver was very conscious of his breathing, deeper than usual, and he tried slowing it down, but his heart started to race. With his hand to his head he realised that he hadn't felt this vacuous since he was eleven and he'd gone, nervously holding his Mother's hand, to hospital to have his iBrow installed. Now he was a big boy. *Every good boy deserves chocolate.* They used general anaesthetic and, as he'd counted backwards and gone under, the surgical team had loomed over him in masks. He'd been frightened: the stuff of nightmares, and that had been his last non-augmented memory.

Count backwards: ten, nine... and then he'd woken up with a desperate thirst and a feeling of something pushing on his forehead. There had been a tingling, a crawling sensation as if there were spiders on his face, but it was just the links sliding along the pinholes drilled through his skull to his frontal lobe. Soon his nerves learnt what this strange intrusion was and how it opened up the world.

"Don't think with your tongue hanging out," his Mother had insisted. But it had been hard to form the thoughts at first and then he was thinking to his school friends, wondering what all the fuss had been about. It had been easy, apart from all the choir practice needed to keep his vocal chords working, and he couldn't remember when he'd had to form the special characters before a person or the hashtag for a subject. Months later he'd fallen over in the playground and been bombarded with abusive thoughts about calling for his Mother. When he'd formed the thought, he turned 'Mother' into '@elenor3941' automatically: it was second nature. He hadn't been aware of the hashes and ampersands for years now.

"Woah!" he said aloud, leaning forward to put his head between his legs.

Doctor Ridge paused in his mopping. "Scary eh?" *Idiot*, he thought.

"I'm fine."

"Careful you don't buffer too many worries."

"No, er... I'll not think."

Oliver leant back, closing his eyes. It felt like he was falling forward.

"It's the roof," said the Doctor.

"I didn't think..."

"No, but I can guess your... hmmm..." Ridge circled his temple with a finger to signify a mental process. *God, he's slow*, the man thought.

"I guess the language has changed somewhat. Before thought, mental processes were called... er..."

"Hmmm..."

Ridge went back to his work, realised he'd finished and propped the mop and bucket against the wall.

"The roof?" Oliver asked.

"Lead, cables – something to do with too much copper – or just that we're a long way down."

"But your thinking during the autopsy was clear."

"The cutting room's down there, there's a skylight," said Ridge. "Not here though. We probably don't want to encourage people to hang around down here anyway. Too many ghosts."

"I wish I could ask her ghost," said Oliver, signifying the corpse drawer with a hand gesture.

"Aye. We could hold a séance. They used to do that."

"Did it work?"

"What do you think?" *What a moron, you can't talk to the dead.*

"She was murdered."

"You don't say?" *State the obvious, why don't you?*

The man's thoughts were very clear because Oliver's Thinkerfeed was otherwise completely empty, even so Oliver ignored the jibes.

"Why did you do the autopsy so late?"

Doctor Ridge waggled his left hand at Oliver to show his blank wrist. "Can't noodle in here, so I lose track of time."

"Difficult to kill yourself by smashing your face in," Oliver said.

"Even more difficult to scalp yourself, post-mortem."

"Scalp!?"

"You know, Red Indian style," said Ridge, and he unnecessarily lifted his slight fringe and mimed cutting his forehead off.

"Maybe that was someone else?" said Oliver, losing his way in his chain of reasoning. "Except that an iBrow isn't worth anything, a bit of iridium and gold, I suppose, but it's too small to be worth... the bother. Simpler..."

"Drink of water?"

"Please... simpler to consider the death and the scalping as one event with one culprit."

Ridge turned on the tap at the basin in the corner, swilled out a cup and brought it over to Oliver.

"Thanks."

Oliver drank, cooling his raw throat and taking the unpleasantness away. He was glad to be rid of the taste of vomit.

Murdered or not murdered, he thought. *Murdered... ah, buffered, damn.*

"Talking, stops thinking," said Ridge.

"Are you psychic or something?"

The Doctor pointed two fingers at his own eyes as if he was going to gouge them out, but he just wiggled his hand side to side. "I saw your eyes move."

"Who was she?"

"No idea."

"The code?"

"She's been scalped, her iBrow removed."

"Oh, but perhaps she didn't have one."

"There are lesions in the frontal lobe and cerebralisation strands left over. It was a five series, the shape's unmistakable."

"But no-one's missing," Oliver insisted. *That was a stupid thing to say*: whether or not the iBrow was removed didn't make any difference to the missing person status.

"Yes, it was a stupid thing to say," Doctor Ridge snapped. "What was your time parameter?"

"Last week."

"Earlier than that, she's been dead for three to four weeks, a month."

"No!"

That meant he'd wasted all that time: he noodled a new list with an adjusted time parameter to include those missing weeks.

Nothing.

"Damn!"

"Buffered?"

"Yes."

"Ever deleted?"

"No," said Oliver, genuinely puzzled. *What was the man talking about*, he thought – he was getting a headache.

"Bring up your recent thoughts."

Oliver did: what was the man talking about? The extended Noodle search. Murdered or not murdered, murdered... ah, buffered, damn. How many places were officially communications black spots? Test. Another speaker. Who is Unknown 271? Morgues are dreadful places, really awful.

"Now, poke it."

"Sorry?"

"With your mind."

"Oh, right... er... ah..."

The floating thoughts stabilised, and he had a hint of 'rethink' as usual.

"There's just rethink," but then Oliver realised that there was also 'edit' and 'delete'. He jogged at 'delete' and 'what was the man talking about' – suddenly he couldn't remember what had been there.

"People just think and don't realise that there's delete," said Doctor Ridge, "though to be fair, there aren't many places where it's possible."

"You can, er... set a delay," said Oliver, vaguely aware that he'd heard of the possibility.

"You need your remote," said Ridge, now wiggling an imaginary gadget near his forehead. "And your pin code and password."

Every good pa-pah... "Yes," Oliver said aloud, "How come you don't get a headache?"

"I've a lot of time down here, so I played with all the settings, not just the spam filters. Did you know you can switch from network to recognition modes entirely?"

"Can you?"

"I can."

Deleting is weird enough, I'll never get the hang of that – ouch!

Ridge smirked, then said, "He made a mess of her forehead."

Oliver felt bile rising again.

"You'd need an electric saw or something for that."

The iBrow filaments would have intertwined with the neurons of the frontal lobe, brain matter twisting and contorting like spaghetti around growing ivy. Oliver realised his metaphors were all over the place, but his head felt very strange, almost loose as if he was cut adrift. How could you follow a chain of thought when you couldn't store the first links? And the lack of other people's thoughts in his head made him both euphoric and desperately lonely.

"Jellicoe will want an update," Ridge said.

At Jellicoe, Oliver started thinking, but then he realised. He fancied a drink anyway.

"Thanks," said Oliver.

"You're welcome." *Idiot.*

"I don't like your tone."

"I've been polite," said Ridge; *here we go.*

"Your thoughts are insulting," Oliver said. "You say one thing, you think another, it's hypocritical."

"Do you judge a man by his thoughts or his words?"

"His thoughts... words... I don't know."

"You judge a man by his actions." *Something to think about, sonny.*

Oliver was glad to get out. The corridor seemed wider and then suddenly the cacophony of thoughts returned like a comforting blanket. Once he felt a faint network signal, he ran the last few paces until he was completely reconnected with everyone he knew.

At Ollie, you've to see Jellicoe, Freya thought.

New menu at the Palatine.

Hash Charlie, Hash Foxtrot, Snatch Squad Charlie is having a beer and skittles evening, all welcome.

Five members of Snatch Squad Charlie liked this.

Special thoughts for special people.

Chen, Sasha and Vincent have birthdays this month.

Don't forget your Sergeant's Exam this Thursday.

Surprise Me for that special present.

It settled down and only those threads that interested him became apparent.

Hash Charlie, what time is the beer and skittles?

Except for some intrusions.

He remembered that Unknown 271 was unknown, a more solid memory than the fleeting words and thoughts of Doctor Ridge, and then recalled the obvious missing persons list: no missing persons in the last six months.

At Ollie, did you understand that you have to see Jellicoe, Freya thought.

Square one, he thought. *At Freya, yes, sorry, thought problem.*

No luck, Mithering thought.

I'm afraid not.

Oh, you saw Doctor Ridge, Freya thought, *or Doctor Hassan?*

That's it, Ridge, Oliver thought back, *on my way now.*

Jellicoe was in the same booth in the Lamp. It was as if he hadn't moved. *If this is going to be the regular haunt for my meetings with my line-manager, then it's going to be expensive*, Oliver thought.

Special thoughts, only £9.50 a month.

Hash Charlie, Hash Foxtrot, beer and skittles, 7:30.

"My round," Jellicoe said. There were two pints on the table. "An Inspector's salary is more than a Detective Constable's after all."

This is totally against regulations–

Jellicoe held his finger up: "Ah!"

Oliver hadn't finished the thought: *Another psychic.*

Once he was settled, Oliver picked up his glass and acknowledged Jellicoe's generosity with a 'cheers'. He took a sip, it was horrible.

"When's your Sergeant's Exam?"

Oliver didn't need to noodle that one. "Thursday."

Hash Charlie, Hash Foxtrot, 7:30 on what day?

Jellicoe grunted, "Anyone take an interest in the case?"

You, Oliver thought.

"Apart from me."

So you can hear thoughts when you want to.

"When I want to, yes," said Jellicoe. "Go on."

"Er... Freya–"

"Chief Superintendent Turner?"

"Yes, and my girlfriend... well, not recently... and Chen, Mox, someone called Mithering."

"You'll get more of that when the papers come out."

"Papers?"

"It's an expression. All the vultures will descend to pick at the bones as it were. Drink up."

Oliver was not happy. He wanted to be somewhere else and the beer and skittles conversation jumped to the fore.

7:30pm this evening, stupid! Hash Charlie, Hash Foxtrot.

"Freya doesn't come down here," Jellicoe said.

Oliver couldn't imagine the Super down in this dive. "No."

"Too good for the likes of us."

"She's uniform, so... it's not... she can't, you know, er... drink."

"Don't mind if I do – same again."

Jellicoe had downed his. Oliver did the same and felt himself go off-line.

At Babs_lamp, can I... oh, damn.

Oliver dragged himself over to the bar and waited to be served. Eventually he was. Pubs were the one place that had stayed stuck in the last century, if not earlier; full of those stupefied into thoughtlessness.

Oliver spilt most of one pint when he turned round and so placed that one in front of himself. Jellicoe swapped them over, his little finger raised in a strangely polite manner for someone so crumpled in appearance.

"Why did he scalp her then?" Jellicoe asked.

"Oh, well, maybe he took the iBrow as a trophy," Oliver said, and then, warming to the idea, "they do that – serial killers. I've seen it in profiling: trophy collection. The killer wants something to remind him about it, so he can, er... relive the experience."

"Why not just remember the thoughts?"

"In public?"

"Reliving the experience without a thought would be tricky."

Oliver nodded as he realised that was true. "Not many serial killers now."

"No," said Jellicoe. "Can't really stalk prostitutes broadcasting your intentions to all and sundry, can you?"

Oliver nodded in agreement. "One victim doesn't make a serial killer."

"How do you know there's only one victim?"

"Only one body."

"We didn't know about that one, except by accident. There could be many, many more."

"No-one's missing."

"This one isn't missing."

Oliver felt flummoxed: he noodled why people might not be registered as missing.

"We should examine the scene of the crime," Jellicoe said.

Oliver remembered that to be an 'officially missing person' the last thought had to be more than 48 hours old, or a non-thinking individual who was reported as missing.

"Did you hear what I said?"

"Sorry," said Oliver. "I was just... we've got a body with no possible missing person to match. Well, that's, er... impossible."

"At least she wasn't killed in a locked room."

"What?"

"Drink up."

Jellicoe led the way outside, stopping to whisper to one of the detectives smoking at the doorway. Oliver didn't know who they were. He recognised them as he walked past when their iBrows came into range, of course, but he was none the wiser. When the conversation was over, Jellicoe and Oliver walked towards the police station. A car rolled up and stopped: the driver was Chen. It was strange that Jellicoe was too drunk to think at Chen and yet here was a car on cue.

Jellicoe got in the back and Oliver in the front.

You're not thinking, Chen thought.

Oliver made a drinking motion with his hand and rolled his eyes in the direction of the back seat.

"Chedding car park, James," said Jellicoe.

"It's Chen, Sir."

"Thank you, James."

They drove in silence, which gave Oliver a chance to check up on some thoughts: Jasmine had asked him to unfollow her, he was a git and other variations from her friends, Mithering wondered why he'd gone quiet, a DC had killed a woman in the car park apparently (*where do these ideas come from – ouch!*), Chen had warned Mox of their impending arrival, Mox was complaining about the interface to the fingerprint machine at the scene of the crime and Oliver was to drop by Freya's office when he had the chance.

Mox had the security shutters up, so Chen was able to drive straight into Chedding's car park. They descended and drove between the empty bays towards a bright light. Chen brought the car to a slow crawl, indicated and then parked neatly between the white lines.

They got out, Jellicoe signalled Chen to stay in the car. Chen nodded and glazed over, a sure sign that he was surfing the Thinkersphere.

The scene was the same as before, except for the lamps set up on stands around the vehicle to illuminate it and the quaint finger print dust over the door handles.

Jellicoe leant against a pillar, his arm out to hold the concrete to support himself.

"Fancy a snifter," Jellicoe said. He held out a hip flask.

Not on duty, Oliver thought. *Ow!*

He was still technically drunk. Two pints and he realised he'd need the loo soon.

Jellicoe wiggled the hip flask, sloshing the contents suggestively.

Oliver shook his head: he checked, poking his thoughts, and he'd not buffered that one. Of course, you wouldn't want all your drunken thoughts to fly off once you sobered up. The trick only worked in black spots, he realised.

"Suit yourself." The man lurched himself away from the pillar and secreted the hip flask back in his pocket. "Well?"

Oliver looked at the crime scene. He was too used to examining the thoughts of suspects and victims to have ever really worried about physical evidence.

"It's a car," he said.

"Come on."

It was a four-door Tiger Fire, neatly parked, although he wasn't sure how anyone had managed to drive it past the barriers and into the abandoned car park. He opened the driver's door and got in. Comfortable, although he shivered when he imagined the presence of the late passenger lying behind him.

Looking round he examined the rear view mirror, the back seat empty and blood stained. There was the steering wheel and the autopilot. He checked the vehicle was in 'safe' and thought for a pairing.

Nothing: flat as a pancake.

It ought to have tried to boot up. Modern batteries last... he noodled, the Tiger Fire used Benning Supers, so two years would be perfectly reasonable according to the advertising. Maybe not to drive it far, but the CPU ought to have thought back at least.

Looking again, more carefully, he saw it: the colour e-ink display still showed the aircon settings. It was 'on' and 'cool' with the fan to 'mild'. It had obviously run until the battery gave out. Whatever else, the car must have sent a reminder that the aircon was on when the door was closed. The driver must have synced with the on-board computer to have thought these aircon settings in the first place.

Oliver sat back and brought his forefingers up to his pursed lips: *At Doctor Ridge, would an aircon setting of cool change your prognosis about the time of death?* But all he got was a dull ache; good enough reason not to drink on duty.

Mox thought that it had been a glorious waste of time because the dead woman's fingerprints hadn't been on the database or on any of the car's controls.

The car ceiling boomed: Oliver jumped. Jellicoe had banged his hands on the roof. He leaned in, leering.

"Well?" he asked.

"I'm not sure what to look for," Oliver admitted.

"Did you notice that the car was unlocked?"

"Yes!"

Oliver noodled the list and set the time parameters from when they found the body back to the beginning of time.

"Come on, come on – detect!" Jellicoe demanded.

I am thinking, Oliver thought, only to get an error because of the alcohol still in his blood stream.

Oliver remembered what he knew anyway: there were no missing persons unaccounted for. He noodled for any exceptions and there were some people 'lost at sea', 'down a sink hole' and so on. He noodled to check them against the body they'd found, and then, after an exasperating wait, he remembered that there wasn't a match. She could be the body of someone before the thought revolution... no, she'd had an iBrow, Series 5.

Oliver rubbed the skin above his: *I'm getting a hangover*, he thought and then realised that his iBrow had detected he was sober. He could think at the car and drive it now... if it had had battery power.

He rethought to Doctor Ridge: *At Doctor Ridge, would an aircon setting of cool change your prognosis about the time of death?*

There was a sloshing noise by his ear. Jellicoe was shaking his hip flask at him.

"No! Thanks."

Jellicoe put it away. "Tricky," he said.

"Yes," Oliver admitted.

"You'll have to do some old-fashioned police work."

Doctor Ridge thought he was busy and yes, it would alter the time of death: a week earlier maybe.

Jellicoe opened the back door.

Oliver hadn't got a clue what Jellicoe was talking about, so he noodled, of course, and remembered tall helmets, buttoned jackets, 'evening all' and 'hello, hello, hello', Peelers and members of the public asking for the time and directions. *Everyone knew the time or directions nowadays*, he thought.

At Ollie, people without iBrows, Mox thought.

Mithering's thought intruded: *At Ollie, what have you found?*

Give me time.

Jellicoe unscrewed the hip flask cap and poured some amber liquid onto the back seat, wetting the upholstery where the body had been.

"Hey?" said Oliver.

"Smell it."

"Pardon?"

"Smell it."

"I will not."

"Smell it, that's an order."

"Sir, I er... oh... fine."

Oliver shuffled round and leaned over the back.

"All the way down, properly."

Oliver did so, leaning right down and putting his nose almost against the seat.

"What do you smell?"

Nothing for it, Oliver breathed in through his nose.

"Whiskey," he said.

"Any particularly variety?"

"The variety in your hip flask."

"But not steak?"

Oliver shuffled upright. "No!"

"So she wasn't killed here, not enough blood."

"But forensics..."

Oliver hadn't read the report. A quick noodle and he remembered that there weren't any substantial blood stains; some, enough to look nasty, but not the four or five litres that ought to have soaked into the seat. It was all there, clearly in his memory.

So... she wasn't killed here, he thought, *or scalped here.*

"If it wasn't such a new car," Jellicoe said, "we could have examined the sat nav and found out where it had been."

New car!? The Tiger Fire's hardly new, but to have a sat nav, it'd be positively ancient.

"Inspector–" Oliver began, but the man wasn't behind him anymore. Oliver struggled in the awkward space to see where he'd gone.

Chen pointed: *That way.*

Jellicoe had stepped away and was calling him out of the car with a curling forefinger. Oliver got out and followed him around to the front of the vehicle.

The Inspector waved his hand down towards the radiator grill.

It was a Tiger Fire – obviously. Oliver shrugged.

"The registration," Jellicoe said.

Just below the radiator grill was a plate with letters and numbers.

"Ah!" said Oliver.

He noodled the car registration's owner.

Finally, progress, he thought.

Mithering liked this.

Jessica Stenson, Oliver remembered, owned the car and another noodle meant he knew her address.

At Jessica Stenson, he thought, *are you alive?*

You think the body is Jessica Stenson, Mithering thought, *but there aren't any of the murder victim's fingerprints on the car's controls.*

What sort of stupid question is that, thought Jessica Stenson.

Police, Ma'am, Oliver thought, *we've located your car.*

What! My car's on the drive.

The Tiger Fire?

That thing! It was stolen months ago. Have you only just got round to checking?

Oliver was surprised and noodled about the car registration.

Our taxes pay your salary, you know, thought Jessica Stenson.

Oliver remembered Mrs Stenson's original thoughts on the stealing of her car, its inconvenience above anything else and that it had only just been serviced. They were new tires.

The trouble we had registering the crime, Jessica Stenson added: *You had to do it on-line with a computer, I ask you. It'll be paper forms next.*

Oliver took a deep breath, but caught sight of Jellicoe. The old man shook his head and mouthed, as if Mrs Jessica Stenson could overhear, 'go and talk to her' while he held up his hand and did a walking gesture with his first two fingers.

Ma'am, Oliver thought, *I shall be coming round to interview you.*

A house call?

Yes, Ma'am.

Whatever for? Do you do those? Why? Oh, this is just ridiculous.

Which it was really.

Chen had already started the car when Oliver reached him. He got in and set off; obviously he'd followed enough of their thoughts to know the next destination. Oliver didn't know where Mallard Drive was, exactly, but Chen would have noodled it.

Oliver settled down to go through the recent thoughts in his Thinkerfeed to make sure he hadn't missed anything important.

Freya thought the report was fine, so that was a relief.

Mithering was curious about what Jessica Stenson could add to the enquiry.

Snatch Squad Charlie were having their beer and skittles on Friday now.

Jasmine was really upset and wanted to make things work.

The Palatine Restaurant was changing its menu.

Perhaps he should combine those two–

"What the hell!" Jellicoe shouted.

Oliver panicked: he'd missed whatever had happened – a bang, an explosion, something had hit the car.

Ahead, and to the right, a group of protesters had gathered, yelling, throwing–

Oliver caught something on recognition: *Bog 'em* and *Take this, you Tepee bastards!*

Chen saw it first: "Incom–"

Another missile arced through the air, almost leisurely, and landed on the bonnet with sudden, shocking solidity.

Their car swerved.

"Shut up, shut up!" Chen shouted as he thought, *Bloody auto-pilot.* The drive would cut out if he hit the kerb, but instead Chen swerved back and put his foot down. The engine blurted a revving noise through its external speakers and the pedestrian alarm went off, but the group scattered before it affected the drive. Or perhaps Chen had activated the override.

Fascist Tepee pigs, murderers, came a thought at Oliver. It was the woman, Martha_556, from the riot; he'd recognised her when she got close to the car.

He thought back: *What?*

At Ollie, you killed a woman protester in Chedding car park.

We did not.

Lying pig!

Why hasn't she been picked up?

I'm too clever for you, Tepee.

Oliver looked back through the rear window and saw the figures coming back together, too far away now for his iBrow to recognise, and to his eyes they were just black shadows in the glare of the sunlight. Another object came towards them, but they had accelerated away. It split on the ground: a brick.

She's a martyr, Martha_556 thought.

We did not kill anyone, he thought back.

Murderers.

"Bloody hell, bloody hell," Chen repeated and then he laughed, relief rather than humour.

For a moment, Oliver didn't know what to think and then thought: *Hash 999, officers attacked on Stephenson Street, corner of...*

"Radley," Jellicoe said.

Radley Street.

No-one had any real coherent thoughts for the rest of the journey. Oliver let the police feed, friend updates and anything else slip by. Everything from the Thinkersphere he followed was there, of course, but only so much came to the attention of the conscious mind. He was aware, in a non-thinking sense, of his breathing, deep and ragged, and of a sting in his blood caused by stale adrenalin and alcohol derivatives.

Mallard Drive was in suburbia, full of triple glazed semi-detached houses dating from the previous century.

"I'll stay here," said Jellicoe.

"Chen?" Oliver asked.

"What?" *Why are we talking,* Chen thought.

"It's..." *never mind,* Oliver thought.

Oliver got out and walked across the tarmac of the pavement and up the brick laid driveway passing alongside a fancy, dark green car as he did so. Someone was gardening, he recognised her name as he passed, but she looked like hired help rather than the owner.

Oliver rang the doorbell and waited.

Presently, a woman appeared in the distorted glass and he recognised Jessie. When the door opened, Oliver saw that she was wearing a pinafore over an expensive designer dress, and she had flour dusted over her hands and wrists.

Yes?

Police, Oliver thought, *Detective Oliver Braddon.*

I know, I recognised you, thought the woman, *but show me your warrant card.*

You're not being very helpful.

Warrant card.

Oliver fished it out and opened his identification. The woman peered at it, her eyes quivering as she remembered his details.

You were involved in the riot.

Yes, Ma'am.

Give 'em what for, I say, she thought.

About your stolen car, there's been a development.

Come in, tea, coffee, left... yes, that door.

The lounge was clean and pristine, more of a drawing room. *Clearly she has money,* he thought.

Mrs Stenson continued on to the kitchen: *My husband works in the building trade.*

Mrs Jessica Stenson was alive, so one particular theory, which didn't fit the facts, was shot down in flames.

We found your car, he thought.

Yes, but it's the insurance company's problem now, I have the new Leopard Supra.

Oliver sat, awkwardly, because the sofa seemed to try and envelop him. He perched on the edge, feeling off-balance. He had no idea what to ask her. He knew it was her car, when it was stolen and what was done to find it (not much when the initial thought search brought up nothing). And that was more or less it.

Have any of your friends gone missing?

Missing, what do you mean?

Missing as in... missing.

The woman clattered in with a tray, placed it on a glass coffee table and then poured a cup of tea from a tea pot. Oliver took the cup and saucer, and sipped from the light brown, almost beige liquid.

"Lovely," he said.

You wouldn't have said it if you'd meant it.

We found a body in the back seat of your car.

Really, the woman thought, sipping her tea without any change of expression, *hopefully one of the youths who stole it.*

We don't know.

An Unbrow... that'll be an immigrant then – typical.

No, Madam.
So they had an iBrow?
Yes.
And the victim hasn't been identified.
No.
And they had an iBrow?
Yes.
I pay my taxes, do you know that? What for, I ask you?
At Ollie, ask her about her husband, Mithering thought.

Oliver ignored her. "We do our duty fully and responsibly," he said to Mrs Stenson.

Just incompetently.
Ma'am—
It's taken you two months to find a car.

Mithering rethought: *Ask her about—*
Tell me about your husband.
We don't follow each other anymore.

Oliver noodled for her husband and then for John Stenson. He remembered that he ran Stenson Supplies for the building trade. He specialised in steel reinforcement, copper cabling and aluminium cladding. Oliver followed him only to see that he was making apologies for having to miss some sailing club get-together, because he was at a trade event in the States.

Oliver thought the obvious: *Why?*

"This interview is over," said Mrs Stenson.

If you'd just tell—

"Over, out! Otherwise you are trespassing."

"I'm sorry."

Oliver stood, and Mrs Stenson ushered him out quickly, saying "out, out, out" almost like a mantra.

That was pointless, Oliver thought as he made his way down the garden path back to the car. *And embarrassing.*

Yes, you should be ashamed.

Jessica Stenson was still following him.

He reached the car: Chen was nodding his head, clearly following some music, and Jellicoe was flicking through a something. It took Oliver a few moments to realise what the black card-and-white lined paper object actually was. It was a notebook.

It was like the whole world was slipping back in time, he thought.

"Tried and trusted method," said Jellicoe.

Really?

Oliver looked at the man, but he was concentrating on his scribbles.

"Really?" Oliver said, deliberately trying to squeeze as much sarcasm as he could into the two syllables.

"It means you don't forget something."

This is beyond a joke, Oliver thought, *when you can noodle the sum total of human knowledge in an instant. What was two dozen small pages of illegible handwriting in comparison?*

"You'd be surprised."

Must be home time now, Oliver thought at Chen.

Chen laughed.

"Just one more thing," Jellicoe said. "Milltown, James."

"Sir," said Chen: *That is so irritating*, he thought.

Don't let him know, Oliver thought.

He knows.

Oliver looked at the Inspector patiently pencilling in his notebook. Potentially he was following them and knew of all their exchanges and opinions. They could follow him, but considering the man's alcohol intake there wasn't anything to follow. The man's liver must be a wreck, and without accessing social thinking properly he couldn't have any friends, could he?

Jellicoe looked up at Oliver, either in whatever passed as thought for such a man or because he knew Oliver's point-of-view.

Let him, thought Oliver.

Milltown was a posh suburb, sprawling as more and more streets on the edges claimed the heritage, so it stretched, it was said, from one red light district to another. Oliver didn't know for sure as he'd never worked vice, and noodling it produced an awful lot of hearsay and twaddle.

"Left there," said Jellicoe. "And then there."

They reached Almond Drive and came to a rest at a spot Jellicoe called 'here'. Jellicoe leaned back, examined the street up and down before producing a pair of binoculars. He hummed and harred under his breath.

Oliver noodled his location and then found that Number 37, the one under Jellicoe's gaze, belonged to Alfred Westbourne. It looked boarded up to Oliver.

"Westbourne?" said Oliver, by way of trying to elicit a reason for this visit.

"Nasty piece of work," said Jellicoe, not looking round.

Oliver noodled and remembered the libel action that a newspaper had paid out to Westbourne when a report had claimed he was the head of an organised crime syndicate. He'd been able to afford some pretty strong lawyers.

"Newspaper!" said Chen. Clearly, he'd noodled the same thing.

"This is old news," Oliver agreed. "Very old news if it was in a newspaper."

"Never caught him," said Jellicoe.

"No?"

"Disappeared."

"Presumed dead or dead?" Oliver asked.

"Disappeared."

"Disappeared with a brow?"

Jellicoe hummed in reply: yes.

"Is he, er... thinking?"

"Yes, not much... Alzheimer's, tends to think he's in the South of France."

"Is he?"

"Not according to our colleagues in the Nationale."

"Right."

"And his son has disappeared too... not Alzheimer's."

"Son? The body in the morgue is a woman."

"Yes, but interesting that he's 'disappeared' and she's 'appeared'."

"He had a sex change," said Chen.

Jellicoe spat his answer, "Don't be facetious!"

"Sir."

"Does he think?" Oliver asked.

"Yes," said Jellicoe and he lowered his binoculars. "But he doesn't think about his location – ever."

"That's impossible."

"You'd think."

"Do you think the, er... cases are connected?"

Jellicoe put the binoculars back to his eyes and gazed out. "He's got to be up to something."

The Inspector believed Westbourne was behind the Peters case, Chen thought, *and the Fletcher and the Oscart and–*

"Sooner or later," said Jellicoe, "we'll find something that he is connected to, and then I'll have him."

Sir, thought Chen.

The Inspector didn't react: perhaps he wasn't following them. It was hard to say. Perhaps he drifted in and out adjusting who he was following all the time, but his eyes didn't flicker like someone changing their mind.

"He's done people in, for sure," Jellicoe said. "Sooner or later, he'll make a mistake."

"But how does he do people in?" Chen asked.

"It's a right Chinese Puzzle, all right," said Jellicoe. "I've seen enough James, let's take this Detective Constable home."

The area around Oliver's apartments was paved in bricks with bollards to stop any vehicle ruining it. Chen dropped him off at the corner.

Thanks Chen, Oliver thought. "Sir," he said aloud.

"Braddon," said Jellicoe, and then "home James."

I'm not James, Chen thought, *how many times?*

As the car pulled away, Oliver saw the damage to the bonnet of the Panther Elite.

Nasty dent there, he thought, and then Oliver wondered where Jellicoe lived: *Probably in a museum.*

You're not far wrong, Chen thought, although whether he was referring to the dent or Jellicoe's home wasn't clear.

Standing between the bollards, wearing a sandwich board topped off with a silver hat, was a crazy man, shouting at the passing cars.

"They control your mind!" he yelled, gesticulating to slow the traffic down. One car swerved dangerously to avoid him. "Mind control!"

The front board had the legend: 'The End of the World' and when he turned, Oliver saw that the reverse had 'Fight the Thought Police'.

Despite the tin foil headgear, Oliver recognised him as 'Daniel', and a noodle revealed that he'd once been a city trader who had suffered a nervous breakdown.

You don't say, Oliver thought.

Aye, Daniel thought, *they got to me with their mind waves... they'll get to you.*

Not me.

You... my friend, Oliver, because... you're one of them, one of the Thought Police.

Me, Thought Police – you're the one in my mind.

And you're not in mine.

Oliver shook his head and walked away: *foil hat brigade, unbelievable.*

"There's one, there's one," the man shouted.

People looked and stared, but not at him, or if they did it was out of pity for someone being picked on by a nutter.

Oliver thought at the outer door of the complex and it buzzed as it unlocked. Finally, up the lift and through his own buzzing door, he was in his own space. He dumped his jacket over the sofa. He thought about the lights and then made his way to the kitchen. It was late: he noodled what he had in the fridge and cupboards, and when he remembered, he noodled what was easy to make. He remembered that he could make a ham sandwich. The instructions were easy to follow, although he had to noodle where he'd left the pickle, and he selected a beer from the fridge. Back in the lounge, he sat down.

His flat was sparse, minimalist, with all the seating arranged in a square. He tended to choose his armchair as he could put a plate on the armrest and he wasn't distracted by the view.

He flicked down his Thinkerfeed, tracking along to see what he'd missed, but his heart wasn't in it. He wanted his girlfriend back. He ended up in Mindstore perusing the latest cerebrals: special thoughts and he deserved to feel special. There was Soulmate or Corinthian: a chance to have the thoughts of ardent lovers thinking sweet nothings into his brow. Or various Rock Star options with devoted groupies or Secret Agents, who get the girl.

Sweet nothings, he thought and blinked himself back to his Thinkersphere Home: *Keep it real.*

He took a bite from his sandwich.

At Jasmine, he thought, *I'm sorry, it was work. Can we do something?*

He found his favourite podcast and let the thoughts wash over him as he ate. There were a few intrusions from Hasqueth Coffee, but not enough to break the law, technically.

I am too, Jasmine thought back.

He was tired, rubbed his forehead and eyes, getting crumbs into the latter. He thought the podcast off.

What was it, Jasmine thought.

Nothing, just... Oliver couldn't even remember and didn't care enough to noodle it. *Nothing.*

Miss you, Ollie.

Miss you too, Jas.

Thanks.

What can we do to make it up, Oliver thought, *anything you want?*

Anything?

Anything.

I'd like to go to the theatre.

"Pa-pah! Pa-pah!" he said aloud. *That would be great*, he thought.

OK, Jasmine thought, *I've taken a tablet, so... tomorrow then.*

Tomorrow, he thought back, *and best I go to bed too.*

Sweet dreams, Mithering thought.

He thought the shower on, dropped his clothes on the floor on the way to the bathroom, and after that, he finally got into bed.

He couldn't sleep: his, and a lot of other people's thoughts, seemed to circle in his head. The iBrow charger made his head feel warm and clammy.

Who killed the woman?

Who was she?

How could they not know?

Sleep tight, Mithering thought, or perhaps he just imagined it as he drifted off. His iBrow registered unconsciousness and his thoughts, if he had any, were his own.

TUESDAY

The next morning, back at the police station, his colleagues had already brought in suspects for formal identification and charging. They divided into the two usual groups: those full of false bravado and those tearfully racked with guilt and regret. Lawyers chimed on about the right to remain silent. There wasn't any talking, but the appropriate hashtags of the Thinkersphere hummed. They were caught, that was all there was to it, and their confessions, which were their own contemporaneous thoughts, were a matter of public record.

There was some movement, when Oliver came in, as people recognised him and noodled that he was something to do with the body in the car park. Oliver didn't bother following it.

Mox stood against the wall, idling tapping his baton against his gloved hand. Whenever he detected any arsey thought, he'd glance in their direction.

"This the brick thrower?" the Desk Sergeant asked.

Oliver was puzzled before he realised that it was a formal request for the records. He looked, but obviously he'd not seen the man clearly; however, after noodling, he remembered the suspect's thoughts at the time: *Take this, you Tepee bastards!*

"Yes, that's him," he said.

"OK, matey, in the cell with you."

At Ollie, where are you, Freya thought.

On my way.

Woo hoo, Chen thought, and it jumped to the fore.

Oliver looked quizzically at Mox. He'd not recognised Chen since coming into the station.

One of them ran, Mox thought back, *and Chen's chasing him.*

In the fast car?

Mox nodded: *Oh yes.*

Oliver laughed imagining Chen zooming around the city in the Panther Elite, noodling the fugitive's location to every panicked thought from the desperate runner. It was ludicrous, but every now and then someone ran. He couldn't remember the last time someone had 'got away', perhaps no-one ever had.

Oliver found his way up to the first-floor offices. Chief Superintendent Turner's was at the far end with prints of landscapes on the walls.

Go straight in, Max thought even before Oliver had reached the PA's desk.

Hi, there, Oliver thought, but Max had a vague look and was probably doing some complicated analysis.

Oliver knocked formally.

Oliver, Freya thought.

Freya.

Oliver went in. Freya signalled to a chair. It was comfortable, a grey upholstered bucket shape held aloft by thin steel tubes. Freya's desk had an executive toy, a Newton's cradle, and a picture. Oliver had only ever seen the back of the picture, black with a fold out stand. There were several pieces of paper in a neat pile, which always amused Oliver. The word 'paperwork' now referred to something quite unrelated to ink stained white sheets. She also had a tablet computer currently acting as a paperweight. Behind him was a set of wooden shelves with a set of hardback books and a framed photograph of an extremely youthful looking Freya graduating from Police College.

Tea?

No, thank you Ma'am.

"Freya!" *No Ma'am, please.*

Oliver bowed slightly: *Freya.*

When's your Sergeant's Exam? A formality, I know, but we can't fast track you to Inspector without it.

The no-noodling one's Thursday, day after tomorrow.

That's the beast.

What's the point?

"You must be well aware," she said, "that sometimes we have to do things the old-fashioned way."

Point taken.

They're like the old no-calculator exams in Maths.

Oliver noodled this and remembered what she was talking about, although it was hard to believe people once had to press buttons to add up numbers.

How are things, Oliver, the case?

Everything's fine, Oliver thought, *Jellicoe has taken me under his wing with the murder enquiry.*

"Murder!"

Yes.

And you've not solved it.

No, we can't identify the victim.

A non-brow?

That's the problem, the victim's iBrow was removed – scalped.

Freya's nose wrinkled at this: *Unpleasant.*

Very.

Jellicoe looking after you, though?

Yes, but he's a little... old fashioned.

"Ha!"

I'll get used to him.

Freya took a moment to look out of her window at the white clouds scudding along, waved on by a flapping

English flag. Oliver followed her example and thought that it was a nice day.

It is, Freya thought, tapping her desk with her index finger.

Oliver straightened in the chair and thought: *Anything else?*

No, so I guess that counts as our one-to-one.

It does.

One-to-one with DC Oliver Braddon, concluded today at... Freya closed her eyes momentarily as she checked: *...nine twenty-two.*

Thank you, Ma'am.

Less of the Ma'am, if you don't mind.

Oliver got out of his chair, always unsure of how to leave such a meeting, and then made his way past Max.

Oh, at Ollie, one more thing, Freya thought to him before he was half way down the corridor. *That police murder allegation in the car park – anything in that?*

No, it's just some conspiracy nonsense.

Just the same, keep an eye on it.

Will do.

Briefing at ten, isn't it?

That's right.

The rethinking around the station was about the runner. Chen had caught him on some waste ground. Oliver missed the arrival and processing, but apparently, he looked like a half-witted dork. He'd been wearing a balaclava even when he knew the police were onto him.

Once we were following his thoughts, Chen thought, what was the use of hiding his identity? Unless he doesn't even know who he is.

Oliver smiled, liked it and rethought it.

Several others liked it straight away.

It was strange how these disguises kept on appearing, almost like a uniform, when all you had to do was put your forehead within recognition distance to know who they were, and from there you could surf their entire life history on Noodle. But still the balaclavas, Guy Fawkes disguises and dead president masks kept appearing.

There was no-one in the meeting room at 10:00, when Oliver glanced in, and the discussion was held in the Thinkersphere. Or rather not. Oliver, like all the police, skimmed Maxine's thoughts and noodled the results. There were no comments. It had been called by Maxine, and everyone knew what that meant. She enjoyed the drama. Oliver met the others in the parking area at the back of the station at 10:15.

There was the usual group: Mike, Zack, Mox, Bob, Chen and Oliver. DS Mike Milton was nominally in charge, but they all waited for Maxine.

Chen was ready to drive again. The dent in the bonnet of the Panther Elite was still there along with churned up mud stains around the wheel arches.

Oliver tried to think about his case, noodling in different ways to see if he could identify the victim, but it came out the same every time. He was getting heartily fed up of it and Maxine's lecture, which they had to follow. She went on about how sick and twisted some individuals were. At least he wasn't in the same car as the police psychologist herself, so there was no need to nod and smile.

They pulled up outside a terrace in Donald Street. There was no rush, DS Mike Milton had been following the suspect and knew that the man had no idea what was about to hit him.

Oliver ended up at the front.

He rang the doorbell.

There was no answer.

Chen rethought something from the suspect about beans, and it gave Oliver his identity. Oliver followed him and then thought at the man directly: *At Jürgens, Police, open up.*

Oh shit, my stuff, the man thought.

The light in the frosted window changed as a figure inside ran past.

Mike responded: *In, upstairs, go, go, go!*

Oliver, get out of the way, thought Zack.

Oliver stepped smartly to one side and DC Zack and DC Mox came up the path with the heavy ram. They smashed into the lock section causing the frosted glass to crack and their second charge smashed it completely. The door hung at an angle on the hinge, and still connected by a chain, but Oliver used his baton to clear the glass. Zack and Bob went in, upstairs as directed by DS Mike.

Oliver followed.

They all went up into the back bedroom.

When Oliver reached the squad, the man was held down on a single bed by Zack. The grubby carpet was awash with photographs, most badly focused and blurred, but clearly all of the same woman. A few had been used to jam a shredding machine.

Someone nudged Oliver forward and he went in.

Maxine stood at the door in her designer suit.

"You pervert," she said aloud, "you rapist, you piece of shit."

I didn't do anything, the man thought.

You wanted to. We've your thoughts on record, Maxine thought, *category five, planned sexual offence.*

I didn't do anything.

Officer, do your duty, Maxine thought.

DS Mike Milton stepped up smartly and thought: *Carl Jürgens–*

"Aloud!" said Maxine. "I don't want any legal cock-ups."

Mike coughed, then spoke aloud, "Carl Jürgens, I'm um... arresting you on suspicion of stalking and category – let's see – five, planned sexual offence. You do not have to say anything, but it may harm your defence if you do not mention, when questioned, something which you later rely on in court. Anything you do say or think may be given in evidence."

Thank you, Mike, Maxine thought.

Carl Jürgens thoughts were insistent: *I didn't do anything.*

The man was on his knees, his wispy long hair combed over his baldness fooling no-one, and his cardigan was buttoned-up askew.

"Look, mate," said Mike aloud, "you've been following this woman's thoughts, stalking her, taking pictures and imagining all sorts of weird shit, so best get you down to a clinic for a little re-education."

I didn't do anything, Jürgens thought, *you fucking Thought Police!*

"Now, now."

The Chinese Box, oh God no, Jürgens thought. He glanced at his wardrobe.

Zack and Bob hauled the man to his feet and marched him off down the stairs.

Mike responded: *What did he mean by the Chinese Box?*

Dunno, Oliver thought, *but he looked over here.*

Where?

Oliver went over to the wardrobe and opened it: *Here.*

There were some sad shirts hanging there, shoes littering the base and a smart black case.

No box here, Oliver thought.

My door! You bastards, Jürgens thought, *I didn't do anyth—*

Oliver stopped following the prisoner and instead knelt down to help Mike collect the pictures.

Oliver wondered about the victim: *Does she know?*

No, thought Mike, *so we can't do him for mental assault.*

She's attractive.

I'll get jealous, Mithering thought.

I have a girlfriend.

Mike looked at Oliver: *What?*

Someone else, Oliver thought waving his hand by his forehead.

Mike nodded without thinking.

Oliver found a flat box under the bed that still had some photographs in it, and then gathered it all together. They double-checked they had everything and then they looked over the house. The man didn't clean, the only things they found with any gloss were the photographs they took with them.

"What do you know about Westbourne?" Mike asked aloud.

"Er..."

"Without noodling."

"Without noodling – er... bugger all," Oliver said; *Why are we talking?*

"Just tell me."

"Inspector Jellicoe has a thing about it, probably he got a 'case that haunts because he was the one that got away' complex."

"Careful of Jellicoe, more likely to hold you back than help you forward."

"I will."

Downstairs and back outside, they met two WPCs from uniform, who had arrived to guard the premises until it was secured. Oliver recognised Laura and Zoe when they walked up.

Zoe saw him first: *You catch the bastard?*

Oliver nodded.

"Yay!"

Hope they castrate the pervert, Laura thought.

Zoe liked this.

Oliver stopped: *Pardon?*

In a liberal, reforming way, Laura thought back, *while strung up by the goolies.*

Zoe laughed and lolled.

Others started liking this too.

Oliver left them to it.

Chen had stayed in the car the whole time noodling music by the sound of his hand beating a rhythm on the steering wheel. They had to tap the window to rouse him to think about unlocking the doors.

Back at the station, Oliver joined Zack and Bob in the observation room. There was a pot of coffee ready, but it wasn't Hasqueth Finest, so Oliver gave it a miss. Carl Jürgens was already seated at the table in the interview room. Oliver could see him through the one-way mirror, but by standing at the back he was beyond the recognition range. Max stood on guard by the door, his arms folded and his scowl directed down towards the suspect.

Lawyer, Jürgens demanded.

Mox showed him five fingers and then added in thought, *if you're lucky*.

The door to the interview room opened and in rushed a middle-aged man wearing a formal suit that was more of a uniform than the uniform division wore. Oliver recognised him as Mellors_Jnr from Mellors, Mellors and Smyth. Strange that a lawyer would have an underscore in his recognition. The man put his briefcase down on the table.

"I'm..."

Yes, I recognised you, Jürgens thought.

"For the record," Mellors_Jnr said, pointedly. "I'm your court appointed lawyer."

Mellors_Jnr glanced at the CCTV camera in the corner of the room. Those in the observation room looked up at it too, despite knowing that they were invisible behind the one-way mirror. The lawyer stepped up to the window.

"I recognise that we have a lot of police observing," said Mellors_Jnr to his own reflection, before he pulled a chair to the table, so he could sit closer to his client. He leant in to whisper. Despite the amplification from the microphones in the interview room, none of them could hear what he was saying.

I understand, Jürgens thought, *don't say anything, don't think about that piece of arse, don't let them rile you, don't react, don't say anything... I understand. Yes, I understand, I do—*

"I do understand," Jürgens said.

Mox suddenly opened the door and Maxine walked in. Clearly Mox had been following Maxine.

"I see your brief has finally arrived," said Maxine as she glanced pointedly at the camera.

"You're the one who was late," said Mellors_Jnr. "For the record."

Maxine took a seat opposite Jürgens, like chess players, with Mellors_Jnr to his client's right. Mox stood back.

"Jürgens, Carl," said Maxine. "Stalking... planned sexual offence."

"That remains to be proven," said Mellors_Jnr.

"I didn't do anything," said Jürgens.

"Please, Mr Jürgens, Carl, I advise you to remain silent," said Mellors_Jnr. The lawyer turned to Maxine. "He has that right."

"Of course," said Maxine. "He doesn't have to talk."

"Thank you."

"I can still ask questions though."

"Yes," Mellors_Jnr admitted.

Maxine stared at Jürgens: that playground game of trying to make the other child think something.

"Mum's the word," said Jürgens, smiling. *You're not getting me*, he thought, which left a self-satisfied and confident aftertaste.

Maxine looked at him closely and then smiled. Oliver didn't catch her thought as Jürgens' reaction was so strong.

No, she isn't!!! She gorgeous, a fucking gorgeous piece of arse, which I'd like to f—

Oliver unfollowed: he knew where this was going and didn't want to accidentally rethink any of it to his own friends.

There was a general outflow of breath in the observation room.

What a fucking pervert, Zack thought.

"I heard that!" Jürgens screamed in their direction.

"Admissible in court," said Maxine, scraping her chair back and making for the door.

Jürgens turned his attention to Maxine: *You bitch! I'll get the Chinese Room onto you. I will. I've got the Chinese Box. They owe me. Then you'll be sorry. Do you hear!*

Mox stepped in front of Jürgens, his hand out, and the man sat down.

Maxine didn't even turn round, but simply stepped through the door and let it close.

Mellors_Jnr put his head in his hands, crinkling his smart suit around his shoulders.

"I said nothing!" Jürgens shouted.

"It's..." but Mellors_Jnr couldn't articulate, and Oliver wasn't following his thoughts.

Result, Zack thought.

Everyone else in the observation room liked this.

She just thought of the victim's name, Bob thought, *that's not leading him on. You've got to admit she's good.*

They filed out and their thoughts turned to coffee: Hasqueth Finest, tastes so good.

What kind of sick bastard stalks women, Mike thought.

What kind indeed, Oliver thought back, but he had other things on his mind: *At Jasmine, looking forward to tonight*, Oliver thought.

He didn't receive a reply and noodled her recent thoughts: she'd been thinking with her friend Cheryl, they were planning a trip to Norway, and with her boss about some report. She'd booked the tickets for the evening. While he drank his coffee, he skimmed up and down the record as if caressing her. It made Oliver feel warm and happy. *Who needs special thoughts?* So good.

He sipped his coffee.

I wonder if this is contentment, he thought.

Damn right, thought Zack, *we got the bastard*.

Good result, team, Freya thought, *please pass on my congratulations. Hash Foxtrot*.

Chen clinked a spoon in his mug: *I wonder what that Chinese Box was?*

DS Mike Milton rethought Freya's congratulations.

Probably nothing, Mox thought.

Oliver was inclined to agree and didn't want the case to develop any complications. He was going out after all. Even so, it nagged as he packed away his kit into his locker, and then made his way home to shower and change.

So Oliver did think about it: *What could a Chinese Box be?*

It could be pretty, Mithering thought.

Oliver checked himself in the mirror as he left his apartment for the evening. *All right*, he thought.

On the way, Oliver passed a *Surprise Me!* store and on a whim, popped in. The assistant looked very smart in her crisp blouse and smiled as Oliver approached. He recognised her as Matilda long before he read the name on her name badge.

"Lovely day," said Matilda aloud.

"It is," said Oliver, falling into the conversational pattern. "My er... girlfriend."

"Lovely," she replied, "and..."

"I'm Oliver Braddon," he said, even though she was close enough to recognise him.

She arched her well-groomed eyebrow: "Excellent... one moment – oh, you're not in a relationship."

"No. I mean, yes; I forgot to change it: she's Jasmine."

"Wait a sec... oh yes, here she is."

"Something..." said Oliver and he held his hands as if he was holding a small box. "In her handbag."

"I see. Price?"

Oliver indicated on the chart and suspected he'd seen a disapproving look on the Matilda's face, not enough to distort her forehead and reveal her brow, but fleetingly there.

"I won't be a moment," she said. "Perhaps you'd like to peruse the distractions."

Oliver went over to some quaint old-fashioned video screens and watched the images flicker. They were enough to generate a few thoughts, although if any of his followers were paying attention, they'd know what he was up to. He saw the assistant standing with her arms folded, her weight on one leg so that her hip was pushed to one side. She was noodling, probably tracking down Jasmine's trains of thoughts. Suddenly, she smiled, and then went back to tidying her counter.

Oliver wondered if she'd forgotten and, after a noodle, he remembered the time and how long it would take to walk to the bar where he'd agreed to meet Jasmine; but then another assistant, who he recognised as Tammy when she was in range, arrived with a brightly wrapped present.

Oliver went back: "Excellent, thank you."

Matilda indicated the till and Oliver waited for the buzz.

God, it's at the top end of my price range, he thought.

He reckoned with his bank all the same, because there was no way he could argue the bill without a thought escaping.

He took the present and went back into the pedestrianised area, walking quickly to make up time. He noodled and remembered that he had five minutes to spare at least. He felt foolish carrying the fancy package.

Bar Terrific was in the trendy part of town, just by *Tony's Restaurant*, and it opened out onto the canals. There were high rise apartments towering overhead, Delaware Towers and the West District Spires. Oliver was five minutes early, but knew from Jasmine's thoughts that she was going to be ten minutes late. She'd thought to her friend Cheryl about making him wait.

And he did wait by the door until his hearing adjusted to the ear-splitting volume of the music, and then he thought about getting a drink.

Yes, Jasmine thought, *I'll have a white wine.*

Large?

Yes.

Oliver had been to the wine bar before, so he had it in his favourites and ordered his drinks before he managed to push his way through the throng to the bar. It was packed, the sheer number of recognitions disquieting. His drinks were waiting for him when he finally got there, and there was only a short queue for the till: buzz, reckon, all very quick. There was a lot of shouting from those whose alcohol intake meant they couldn't think their order ahead and, even though it was early evening, the queuing was two tiers already.

Jasmine had arrived by this stage, her cab being so quick that her fashionably late stance was ruined.

Oliver worked his way back to the door, awkwardly holding a white wine, a bottle of lager and the present. The sound system was playing something phasial, full of drum beats and wailing sequences. As he walked past a speaker, he could feel the beat vibrating the skin on the side of his face. He felt deaf.

He saw Jasmine come in. She looked smart, still in her work clothes, with her long black hair framing her face. She winced at the volume.

You look nice, Oliver thought.

Thanks.

Here, he thought as he reached her, and she took her glass.

And here.

Oliver gave Jasmine the present.

Oh lovely, she thought, *and at the top end of your price range too.*

I hope it's good, Oliver thought.

I'm sure it will be.

She began opening the wrapping, tearing it apart and then she gave a little squeal of delight.

It is!

You like it?

Yes.

Good.

She started to tuck it away in her handbag.

Oliver thought: *what is it?*

Never you mind, Jasmine thought with a smile: *It's the thought that counts.*

The present disappeared, secreted in Jasmine's bag, and Oliver resigned himself to never knowing. He'd just been the messenger. It reminded him of something, a package going from A to B, but the–

Oliver was jostled by some new arrivals, so he and Jasmine shuffled away from the door. Oliver didn't know them, had never met them, but as they rushed past he recognised them as Bill, Nancy, Tom and Kenton. They soon disappeared into the maelstrom of other names jostling in the crowd.

Oliver drank for a while looking at the apartment lights reflected in the canal outside. *There must be a spectacular view from up there*, he thought.

Shall we buy one?

On my salary?

If you pass your Sergeant's Exam?

It's in two days' time.

I know.

God, it's the day after tomorrow.

Don't worry, you'll be fine.

She put her hand on his shoulder and somehow it turned into an awkward kiss.

Shall we go, Jasmine thought, *the music is so loud I can hardly hear myself think?*

It was cool outside, refreshing, and they walked along the canal side enjoying the night air and the quiet. Oliver's ears still felt like they were hissing. He and Jasmine held hands as they took the long way around to the theatre.

I've got tickets reserved, Jasmine thought.

I know, Oliver thought back and then he realised that she was communicating with the box office. As they came in, their tickets were being held out by someone Oliver recognised once they were inside.

"Doors are open," said a front-of-house staff member, an old chap, Macduff, holding the door to the auditorium open.

The Menagerie Theatre was a fringe venue, maybe sixty seats, arranged on three sides of a dark, black box of a room. Bizarrely, there were actual programmes. These had been laid out on the seats and gave the event a wonderfully quaint feel. Oliver picked his up when he took his place in the second row. Jasmine sidled in beside him. The programme itself looked neat and sparse, most of its information being given in the form of a hashtag. Oliver accessed it to follow the evening's events, luckily just in time, as the lights dimmed making any further reading impossible.

There were two pieces: a Souza, which was short, obviously, and consisted of an extract from *The Deep Castle* with live commentary from the director and, after the interval, there was to be a mask work. The cast list had been rethought about half an hour ago, so he skimmed down that to see if he knew anyone and then set up the recommended follows for the actual show.

This was all done easily, which left Oliver fiddling with the paper programme unsure what he was supposed to do with it. Finally, he folded it and slipped it into his pocket.

A few stage hands came on with some furniture before a man in a tweed jacket, Adamson, stood to one side and addressed the audience.

"Ladies and Gentlemen," he said, "this is a full Souza, so please noodle us and follow the proceedings. You can either follow the characters or my commentary or both."

He bowed to faint applause and then stepped smartly into the shadows.

The hashtag was rethought by the director and Oliver then unfollowed the commentary as he didn't care much for pretentious opinions and instead decided to focus on the thoughts of the actors. They were already in character, somewhere in the wings, thinking about the relationships and improvising a preamble to the famous opening of *The Deep Castle*. It meant that the first entrance wasn't much of a surprise and the lead wasn't what Oliver had expected from the actor's thoughts. He was too thin, whereas his thinking had a weight. Some of the dialogue had been replaced by thought and when this first happened, there was an "Eh?" from someone sitting behind Oliver: he'd obviously just been watching it or rudely checking personal thoughts.

The Noodle version of the programme pointed out that the Director had wanted it to be like a foreign film without subtitles – whatever that was.

Oliver knew the story, as it had been taught at school, and he'd thought it deep and meaningful then, but now he thought it trite. It was rarely performed in full nowadays as people didn't have the attention spans to last the whole fifty-five minutes. The convoluted plot depended on the two main leads not knowing the other's opinion. It was technically farce, each misunderstanding leading to inevitable confusion and finally tragedy, but it was ridiculous – people, not knowing what others thought. It might work set in the Dark Ages as some historical curiosity, but not as a modern piece, which this production was most assuredly trying to be with its costumes firmly in latest fashions, full of silver scarves, and the comedy character was portrayed in a tin foil hat, but the director had replaced lines of dialogue with thoughts, just to make it a Souza.

At the end, the main character went from person to person trying to get them to understand.

"Listen to me," he said, and he thought: *Listen to me, listen to me.*

It was a real blunder that the man didn't simply follow their thoughts to find out why they weren't listening.

Unbelievable.

And the whole point of *The Deep Castle*, at least according to his English teacher, was that the lead didn't know why they didn't listen to him. So, doing a Souza by having the other actors improvise their reasons in clear thoughts defeated the whole purpose.

I wish you'd keep your opinions to yourself, Jasmine thought, but not harshly.

The blackout was sudden and then the applause started before the lights came up. The cast stood in a row, bowed, and one of them kept thinking that they'd done it, *done it, actually done it.*

Thirty-one people in the audience liked it.

The lead was still in character despite bowing and walking off.

The theatre's stream had a prominent rethought of the reviewer's opinion. Oliver, like others, glanced round to see if they could work out who the reviewer was, but he only recognised names.

You can stop now, the director thought to the hashtag.

Oliver thought: *What would you like to drink?*

Gin and tonic, Jasmine thought.

By the time they got to the bar, their drinks were ready on a tray, but Olivier still had to go to the bar to feel the buzz and then reckon with his bank.

They drank in silence thinking about the first half to each other, and to the director, others in the room and with members of the cast still changing somewhere behind the stage. And indeed, to all their followers.

Come on, come on, you were fine, thought Adamson.

Oliver noodled: they could take their drinks in, so he liked this.

Jasmine nudged him.

Sorry, he thought.

She looked at him as if he was–

"Ah... sorry, my brow's shut down," she said.

"Oh, right."

A couple of gulps later, Oliver's did the same.

The stage darkened, and shadowy figures emerged, their faces shining and bland. For something devoid of facial expression, they conjured up a disturbing impression, and Oliver didn't recognise any of them!

He was shocked.

The audience shifted uncomfortably. Without being able to recognise them, no-one could follow their thoughts. It was as if they weren't there.

He heard an audible whisper behind him, "Copper wire in the masks."

Something masking... he noodled. A mesh of copper wire, he remembered, would interfere with the iBrow signal. It was called a Faraday Cage. However, the technical explanation didn't alleviate any of the disturbing effect and it was sobering.

A thought escaped, suddenly: *What's this all about?*

"Shhh..." Jasmine hissed.

Shhh?

She jabbed him with her elbow.

The characters on stage moved, gesticulating with their fingers all the time, but the strangest part was that they talked aloud without the usual pauses for thought. *This must be how people were before the invention of brows*, Oliver thought, *strange and unknowable*.

I don't like it, Jasmine thought.

Oliver reached across in the dark and squeezed her hand.

At one point, the actors stood in a line, one holding their hand cupped to hide their non-existent lips as they whispered in the ear of the next person. The motion went down the line, each passing on a message that the audience could not perceive in thought or word.

Towards the end, the creatures, Oliver could no longer think of the blank shapes as human, turned on the hero, ripping him limb from limb. They were so alien, utterly unlike individuals and more like a flash mob acting out its own collective impulses. They tore away the man's face and body until there was... nothing there.

The lights dimmed: the audience clapped anxiously.

Fifteen liked this.

The strange beings came on again, the lights on full as they bowed and then they pulled off their masks. There was a general sigh of relief: Oliver recognised them and suddenly they were human beings after all, smiling and relieved that the show had gone well. They bowed again and ran off.

Five more liked this.

Afterwards Oliver and Jasmine had another drink in the bar, they felt they needed it.

"That was amazing," Jasmine said: *Creepy though*.

One bottle of lager and Oliver's iBrow turned off his thinking. Luckily Jasmine sobered enough to think for a taxi.

They went outside briefly. It had turned chilly and Jasmine thought she was cold. Oliver slipped off his jacket and put it around her shoulders. She smiled at him. When the cab came, Oliver got in after her as Jasmine thought about home. They sat in silence, unthinking, as Oliver let the images of the masked performance flit through his mind like a waking dream.

When they pulled up at Tensing Row, Jasmine put her hand on Oliver's hand: *Come up*, she thought.

Oliver nodded.

"Oh shut up, you wanker!" she shouted at the cab driver.

Jasmine stormed off.

Oliver hadn't followed the driver, so he'd no idea what the man had thought. He went after Jasmine, who was failing to open her door, she was that upset. She dropped her keys and Oliver bent down to retrieve them.

Calm down, Oliver tried to think, but it didn't work as he was still over the limit, so he said, "Calm... it's OK."

The door jerked open and Jasmine went in. Oliver followed. When he got into her apartment the wrong lights came on giving the open plan space the sense of a stage, lit here and there with spotlights.

I didn't pay, Jasmine thought.

"Neither did I."

Oh God.

"Don't worry."

Jasmine exploded with laughter: "I didn't pay."

I won't arrest you. He probably deserved it.

Damn right, Jasmine thought.

She returned his jacket and he put it neatly over the back of a chair.

Coffee, she thought. *Hasqueth Finest tastes so good.*

Hmmm... Oliver thought back, *or...*

I've got brandy.

Jasmine fumbled around in the kitchen and came back with a bottle and two glasses. She put them on the table and Oliver took the bottle up. He pulled the cork out with a satisfying pop, but Jasmine had her hand over his glass.

"Not too much," she said, and thought, *God, I want him.*

"Afterwards," he suggested, and slipped the cork back.

Now.

OK.

He realised that the excitement had sobered him. Oliver put the bottle down and followed her, thinking about the way her hips moved. As he did so, she swayed more, overdoing it, but it was still provocative.

Follow or not follow?

Follow.

She reached the landing and turned into her bedroom, dropping some clothing on the floor.

You look gorgeous, he thought, *so good.*

Thank you.

Now?

Jasmine turned round, unbuttoning her blouse. She tilted her head back, letting her long black hair cascade behind her, her eyes half closed and somehow she was beyond thought, acting instinctively.

Oliver unbuttoned his shirt. He couldn't remember where he'd taken his jacket off. Had he left it in the cab?

It's on the sofa, Jasmine thought, *forget it.*

He took his shirt off, took hold of Jasmine and ran his fingers through her hair, down her back, held her, kissed her.

Again!

Was that her thought or his, or both?

They fumbled to the bed, somehow managed to divest themselves of their clothing without the inevitable worry of creases and mess ruining the moment.

They were in bed.

God, she is beautiful, felt great, just there and there.

Get in there my—

Oliver cut the incoming thought off with an angry unfollow.

"What?"

"Some—"

Don't worry, let me.

She snuggled herself under him, shuffled him around until he was in the right position. He dipped his head until their foreheads touched, almost as close as the mixing of their thoughts.

Careful.

He was, tried to be...

Yes.

"Ah!" *Deeper.*

They moved together, their monosyllabic thoughts tuning-in to each other until each wasn't sure which thought was their own or which was superimposed. The tempo built, their bodies wanting to be as close and intertwined as their thinking, and built; so Oliver tried to think about his taxes, the cleaning lady at work, anything–

No, no, don't ruin it, Jasmine thought, *just – yes, yes...*

And then Oliver was somewhere beyond thought, his own and everyone else's.

Afterwards, he didn't care about the clamour for attention in his brain. It was all sort of out-of-focus.

Yes, it was lovely, Cheryl, Jasmine thought, *now go away.*

Seventeen of Jasmine's friends liked this.

Oliver rolled off and over to lie on his back feeling peaceful, although he couldn't help wondering how many people had been following his progress. Jasmine cuddled up, put her arm over his chest and nestled into the dip by his shoulder. Oliver shifted, making himself comfortable.

You OK?

"Don't worry..." *...about it... mmm... love you.*

She was asleep.

So was he, really.

WEDNESDAY

Oliver poured himself an orange juice, having to get some paper towels to mop up a spillage. His iBrow was at 60% as he'd not charged overnight, and physically he felt fuzzy headed, dehydrated, and–

Better have coffee, he thought.

Me too, Jasmine thought.

He glanced at the ceiling: *You're awake then.*

Hmmm.

He remembered that tomorrow was his Sergeant's Exam.

Of course, it was 8am exactly and so the reminder had popped into his head.

"Oh Shit." *Shit, shit.*

What have you broken?

Nothing, just remembered my exam.

Stop worrying, you'll be fine.

He found the machine and checked the cupboards for coffee. On the second, more careful, search, Jasmine rethought that the tin was in the fridge, which it was: Hasqueth Finest.

As the machine percolated, Oliver noodled his revision notes, remembering it all. The trouble was he wouldn't be able to do that in the exam and it was very difficult to separate out what he remembered from what he really knew. It was all becoming one mass of trite nonsense. He had a day spare, so there was plenty of time.

Shall I bring your coffee up?

I'll come down.

OK.

You scored then, Chen thought.

Oliver tried to ignore him: *None of your business*, he thought.

Whose business, Jasmine thought.

Nothing... Chen.

Chen is a dirty sod and he must be breaking some law.

Oliver rethought that at him.

Just friendly interest, Chen thought.

Oliver ignored him: *This coffee smells so good.*

Hmm, it does, Jasmine thought coming into the kitchen.

She leant over and kissed him, it was pleasant, minty from her toothpaste.

That's lovely, he thought.

"Thanks."

What's lovely, Chen thought.

The coffee, Oliver thought back: *He'll know that was fake.*

Lucky sod, Chen thought.

Go away, Oliver thought, unfollowing him. *I might as well start now*, he thought, *as I have the non-Noodle exam tomorrow.*

Best to be prepared, Jasmine thought, taking a sip of her coffee.

She did look lovely in her pyjamas and robe, her face pretty and her long dark hair delightfully tousled. *Gorgeous.*

Thank you, she thought.

Oliver came over and sat at the table too. His coffee was strong, beginning to have an effect and bringing him round.

When's your meeting?

Oliver noodled and remembered that it was 11:30. He rethought it.

Plenty of time then?

Yes, he thought, nodding. *We could go to bed.*

"No!" And then she thought about her work, meetings in the morning and the client's specification to go through.

Can't you just noodle it.

There was a pause as Jasmine received a thought.

If we could just noodle it, she thought back, *then the client would just noodle it. It's bespoke. We still have to do the drawings on the computer.*

Fair enough. Oliver sniffed his shirt.

Yes, rank, Jasmine thought.

I better have a shower.

At yours, I need to shower here.

We could shower together.

You need a change of clothes.

Yes, I do.

Let yourself out.

At the sound of falling water, Oliver did.

He made it home, showered and changed, before rushing back to work. While he did all this, he exchanged some thoughts with Freya. She was concerned about this 'Chinese Box'. It had taken Oliver a moment to noodle about the case and remember that it was DS Mike Milton who was assisting. Maxine had moved upstairs to review the next potential culprit. It needed another noodle to remember that the Chinese Box and the Chinese Room had been something that Carl Jürgens, now the 'alleged' stalker as the case had been turned over to the Crown Prosecution Service, had threatened during yesterday's interrogation.

It's nothing, Oliver thought. That nagged him slightly.

Whatever, I want you to check it out, Freya thought. *We don't want anything crawling out of the woodwork to mess up the case.*

Damn right, Zack thought.

Oliver thought about the Chedding murder enquiry.

Freya must have been following him, because she had a question straight away: *At Ollie, are you making any progress?*

Not really, Oliver had to admit.

See Jellicoe then, she thought. *And, if you aren't making any progress, then check out this Jürgens case and find this box.*

OK, Oliver thought. *I'm everybody's dogsbody.*

It'll be different once you've passed your Sergeant's Exam, Mike thought.

In what way?

All your slave drivers will be Inspectors.

They already are.

Jellicoe will come up with his Westbourne theory.

Oh God.

Oliver's particular slave driver was already ensconced in his booth in the Lamp. The man had had something to drink already. Oliver ordered a coffee.

"I think it might be Westbourne," said Jellicoe.

Oh God, you were right, at Mike, Oliver thought. He said, "Behind the Chedding murder?"

"Yes."

"Who's Westbourne?"

Jellicoe gave him a sour look and so Oliver noodled, filtering to crime only when he remembered too much. Westbourne was a crime boss back in the day, apparently, a 'Jay', someone whose thoughts influenced others. A trendsetter just like Jimmy Scanlan, the man who'd orchestrated the recent riot. Apparently, people were such sheep, even back in Westbourne's day.

"Old though," Oliver said.

Jellicoe nodded: "It's got his hall marks. I'm sure he's done people in, but we can't locate him."

"We can't locate him?"

"No, Stevens follows him closely, and we know he's organising, using every trick to get around our investigations and then some. It's the 'and then some' that's worrying."

"Surely..." but Oliver couldn't develop the idea further.

"He's playing Chinese Whispers."

"Eh?"

"You stand in a line and the person on the far left thinks of a phrase, he whispers to the person to his right, who whispers it to the next person and so on until it reaches the far end. That person says what they think it is and everyone laughs, because it never is."

"Surely the person at the far end simply follows the thoughts of the person on the other end and–"

"I can tell you never had any good birthday parties as a kid."

"We didn't play stupid games."

"Westbourne is doing the same thing, only with thoughts... he passes his instruction on, so does someone else – with someone who doesn't understand what's going on and substitutes word – and we lose track. We know Westbourne started it, but not where he is, but we don't know who's carrying out the crimes."

"That makes no sense," said Oliver, seeing the flaw straight away. "Rethinking is completely accurate."

"They don't..." Jellicoe held his fingers up to make a quote sign, "'rethink', they think it again."

"But that's... oh, right."

"Some of the heists go wrong, of course. The idiots didn't understand the instructions, or all the smoke and mirrors gets in the way, but enough for Westbourne to pocket a tidy sum."

"He'd still think where he was, surely?"

"He doesn't."

"Lives in a cave?"

Jellicoe nodded: "A cave he doesn't think about."

"But he does think."

Jellicoe nodded again.

"OK, so we do... what?"

Jellicoe shrugged.

"Great."

"It's always the brick wall: we follow a trail but come across a thinker who doesn't leave location traces."

Oliver noodled his own thoughts for the previous few days: most were just trivial when he mentally stepped back to look at them, but a lot were specific to named individuals, Jasmine, Chen, Mox, Mike, Freya... but not Jellicoe, whom he talked to aloud. He could also tell he'd been to the theatre, which one, when, what he'd thought of the show, the taxi ordered, a pretty good hint of Jasmine's part of town and so on.

He was sitting in the third booth in the Lamp – would anyone else know?

He noodled his own location and remembered, like an echo, that he was sitting in the third booth in the Lamp. Of course, he'd just thought that, and it was therefore available on Noodle to anyone. However, there were also some idle thoughts he'd had walking to the Lamp, so he'd left an easy trail to follow.

"You could get someone to put a bag over your head, dump you in the boot of the car and drive you somewhere," said Jellicoe.

"Is that what happened to Westbourne?"

"If it did, he had no thoughts on the matter."

Oliver's coffee arrived: Jellicoe turned his nose up at the idea. Oliver added milk and too much sugar in an attempt to get himself started. It tasted bitter, he so much preferred Hasqueth's.

"Chinese Whispers, eh?" Oliver said.

"That's what we think."

"Freya has asked me to look into the Chinese Box... and, come to think of it, Jürgens–"

"Who?"

"Category Five Stalker we arrested yesterday. He threatened Maxine with this Chinese Box or something."

"How exactly?"

"You know, shouted, nasty thoughts – the usual."

"How exactly?" Jellicoe said sharply. Oliver regretted chasing the Target at the weekend riot, regretted looking in the car and seeing the body, and most of all regretted being assigned to Jellicoe.

"Let me noodle it," Oliver said. "Can you follow me?"

Jellicoe nodded, so Oliver thought it all through.

Jürgens: *I didn't do anything.*

Maxine: *We've your thoughts on record, category five, planned sexual offence.*

Jürgens: *I didn't do anything.*

Maxine: *Officer, do your duty.*

Mike: *Carl Jürgens—*

Jellicoe interrupted, "Why did he stop?"

"Maxine wanted his rights read aloud; you know, proper procedure. Dumb really because someone has to think that it's been done to create a proper thought trail and—"

"Yes, fine, I get the point. Go on."

Maxine: *Thank you, Mike.*

Jürgens: *I didn't do anything. I didn't do anything. You fucking Thought Police! The Chinese Box, oh God no!*

Mike: *What did he mean by the Chinese Box?*

Oliver: *Dunno, but he looked over here.*

"Where?"

"The er... wardrobe... it's not much further."

Mike: *Where?*

Oliver: *Here…. No box here.*

Jürgens: *My door! You bastards, I didn't do anyth—*

"Why did it stop then?"

"I stopped following him," Oliver admitted.

"There was more though."

"Later, in the interview… here it is."

Jürgens: *You bitch! I'll get the Chinese Room onto you. I will. I've got the Chinese Box. They owe me. Do you hear!*

"Chinese Room, not Box," said Jellicoe. "I've heard of that before. A meeting place."

"For?"

"Criminal organisations, conspiracies, the Tongs."

"Tongs!?"

"The word 'tong' means 'meeting hall' in Cantonese, it's a literal Chinese Room."

"Right."

"Who was the bitch?"

"Maxine... it's a common reaction."

"Maybe it wasn't a box, but a code word for something else. What was in the wardrobe?"

"Let me see," Oliver said. He tried to picture himself back in the bedroom, the photographs littering the floor, the single bed, the shredding machine, the mirror on the wall, the door, the police, the wardrobe. *Here*, he'd thought, *no box here*. Unconsciously Oliver held his hand up, echoing the move he'd made to pull the wardrobe door open: *shirts*, he thought, *shoes... a case.*

Jellicoe picked up on the word: "Case?"

"Black, shiny, one of those er... attaché cases."

"Something Jürgens would have?"

"No, it was... clean."

"Made in China perhaps."

"I better go and see what's inside it."

"I'll come," said Jellicoe. "I need the exercise."

Oliver wasn't sure whether he was being sarcastic: it was difficult to tell with speech.

Chen was ready with the car and they sped back to the Jürgens' place. Chen parked in the same spot he had the first time around. Oliver went up, Jellicoe with him. The door had been repaired, the new wood looking stark and unpainted against the old rotten frame. There was blue and white police tape lying on the floor, damp and forlorn.

"Locked," said Oliver: *Damn, I forgot to get the keys from the Duty Sergeant.*

"Let's have a look round the back," said Jellicoe.

There was a path round the house and they went past some bins and piles of bricks. Jellicoe picked one up.

"What's that for?"

"A key."

They reached an over-grown garden.

"I'm not sure I agree with this," said Oliver, but then he saw the back kitchen door. It had been forced.

"What do you say?" Jellicoe said.

They went in – *Officers suspecting a crime,* Oliver thought for the record – and upstairs. The bedroom was exactly how Oliver had left it. The floor cleaned of photographs.

"Here," said Oliver.

He opened the wardrobe: shirts, down at the floor shoes and a smart attaché case. He picked that up, it felt light, but something moved inside it. Oliver glanced at Jellicoe and it was clear from the man's expression that he too had heard the hollow bump. Oliver put it down on the bed and pulled the clasps, but it wouldn't open.

"Combination," he said.

"What are the numbers now?"

Oliver checked: '000' and '010'. He moved the wheels and they caught at zero.

"Damn," said Oliver.

"A proper Chinese Puzzle," said Jellicoe, "although rather more modern than the traditional push here, pull there."

"We'll have to ask Jürgens."

"Don't be so wet," said Jellicoe, "it's only six numbers. Solve one and you'll probably be able to deduce the other. Come on."

Oliver set the left set to '000' and then advanced it to '001'. It didn't open. He started to add one, '002', '003' and so on, getting the rhythm of it reasonably quickly.

"That's it," said Jellicoe. "One a second is only…"

Oliver noodled it and remembered that 1,000 seconds divided by 60 was 16 minutes and 40 seconds. "This'll take over a quarter of an hour!" he complained.

"Get on with it," said Jellicoe. "You do to 300 and I'll take over."

Jellicoe sat on the bed.

Using both hands, Oliver found he could move the lower digit with one finger and the other two dials with the other. At '300', he passed it over. Jellicoe grunted and, all fingers and thumbs, he took over. Oliver eased his fingers and took the opportunity to look around the room.

"We only came for the stalking case," Oliver said. "It never crossed anyone's mind that there was another case involved."

"I suspect the one led to the other."

"What do you mean?"

"I've found – bugger, this is fiddly – that those who break the law tend to find themselves victims of bigger sharks. If he was a stalker; well, we found him via Noodle, so others may have found him first in the same way. He was open to persuasion, I'm sure. Do this, or we'll turn you in. Your go."

Oliver took back the case: it was only on '500'. He started advancing through the numbers. It became mechanical for him, '0' to '9', move the other dial, '0' to '9' and make sure that he spotted when the hundreds had to go up.

"Westbourne was never involved with the Chinese," Jellicoe said, more to himself than anything.

"Perhaps these cases aren't related."

"Did you ever play that game?"

"I need slightly more than that."

"Children's game: rubbing your tummy while patting you head."

"No."

"Did you have a childhood?"

"Yes."

"Happy?"

"Yes."

"Likely story."

"Why do you say that?"

"You joined the police."

Oliver lost position and so moved back a hundred.

"If you could rub your tummy and pat your head," Jellicoe continued, "then maybe you can do one thing, while thinking something else."

"You'd have to do something while thinking about it, while you thought about something else."

"Perhaps. You're a machine on that."

"Yes, well, practice makes – ah ha!"

It had opened: quite a sudden jolt as the clasp leapt up.

"What's the number?"

Oliver checked: '888'.

Jellicoe had seen it too. "Go on," he said.

Oliver flicked the right-hand set to all the eights and – click – it opened.

"Eight's a lucky number for the Chinese," Jellicoe said.

"Let's see," said Oliver and he opened it.

Inside, there was a rectangular box, beautifully lacquered in a deep red, and Oriental in design. Oliver took it out gently and carefully. It was light, airy, and he flipped the catch almost reverentially.

It was empty.

What does this mean?

"Hidden base?" Jellicoe suggested.

Oliver checked, top, bottom, sides, but it was a normal box with no obvious surprises.

"Bugger," said Jellicoe.

Oliver went back to the attaché case and double checked it. There wasn't anything tucked in any of the interior pockets of the lid. It was empty now, and had only contained an empty box.

"A Chinese Puzzle in a Chinese Puzzle," said Jellicoe.

Oliver pressed his thumbs against the lacquered box checking the surface for anything that might slide. Nothing did. He opened it again and smelt the interior. It didn't smell of anything. On a whim he did the same with the case, but that had the overpowering aroma of new leather.

"Let me see," said Jellicoe.

Olivier handed them over and then sat down to concentrate on some serious noodling: who had bought a box recently, who sold these boxes, who had given one recently. The trouble was that all the various refinements in his searches either meant he remembered nothing or he remembered far, far too much. With Noodle, it was either straight away or never.

"Check the man's thoughts," said Jellicoe, shaking the case and listening to it.

Olivier noodled Jürgens' thoughts, skimming around the perversions and focusing on anything to do with the Chinese Box.

He was constantly worried about it... and then sometimes not. Ah, sometimes he had it, and therefore worried about it and obsessed about what might be in it, and sometimes he didn't have it and so felt more relaxed, although he worried about having it again. He bought a case recently just for the Chinese Box. He collected it from Tamsin and gave it to Duke. No, Tamsin was a waitress in a coffee chain. He'd ordered hot chocolate and tried to ogle down her cleavage. No, that was a distraction, he was trying not to think about the bins at the back. Between the wall and some wood, they left the box. They? Jürgens didn't know. Sometimes there was an envelope with money in the case. He could look in the case, but not in the box. The black box. *That must be a euphemism*, Oliver thought. Jürgens took it across town and left it in the Duke pub.

"He..." but Oliver found it difficult to explain, so he parcelled it all up and thought it at Jellicoe.

Jellicoe sat. "Hmm... dead letter box."

"He takes it from the café to the pub," said Oliver, "so who..."

He noodled: lots of people went to the café, too many; less to the Duke, but there were plenty of regulars. No-one seemed to go to the bins or the corner seat that you could slide the case behind.

"They must get the case back somehow..." said Jellicoe. "Shit! We need a drink."

"Drink? It's not even lunchtime!"

"To stop the eavesdroppers."

Jellicoe pursed his lips in concentration and then went straight downstairs to the kitchen. By the time Oliver joined him, struggling with the case and box, Jellicoe had filled two mugs from a bottle.

"Sherry," Jellicoe explained.

Oliver sniffed it doubtfully. It looked like piss and tasted of sugar.

Jellicoe topped his up. "I really must carry a bottle of single malt with me."

Oliver felt the prickling sensation in his forehead, thankful that he hadn't had to drink the whole mug.

"They must have some trick like this," Jellicoe said, swilling the sickly-sweet liquid back. "Habit, instinct – these can all be back brain stuff and they don't come forward enough to the brow."

"We'll have to ask Jürgens," Oliver said. "Do a Maxine on him."

"Eh?"

"She says odd things, or uses thoughts, to come at a question sideways. People can avoid thinking about things by thinking about something else, but it always builds up. You can't 'not think' about something without thinking about it at some level. The trick is to find the right cue to get a connection."

"Hmm."

"This is technically stealing," Oliver said putting the mug down.

"Like Jürgens is going to make bail. Even if he does, he's never going to come back here."

"I suppose."

Jellicoe scanned the cupboards, looking along the work surfaces and then across the grimy floor.

"Someone else will have to move the box from Tamsin's café to the Duke."

"We've got the box," said Oliver, holding up the dark red object. "I'll see Jürgens this afternoon."

Chen was waiting for them in the car: he was playing a cerebral or similar and looked vacant when they got in, but he soon came round. They sped through the city back to the station in silence. Chen didn't ask any questions, but then if he'd wanted to know, he would have just followed them; at least until they had the sherry. Oliver wanted to clean his teeth and sober up so that he could think straight. A drink that could both inebriate and rot your teeth seemed doubly immoral.

At the station, Oliver put the case containing the Chinese Box under his desk and waited to sober up. *Was his mind clear?* To answer that, he thought a request to Freya to interview Jürgens.

Why?

Well, there might be something pertinent to the Chedding murder.

Very well.

Oliver didn't want to delve into that man's mind, it would be unpleasant or, even worse, enjoyable. Some people had train wrecks for personalities.

I should do it now, he thought.

That's the spirit, Mithering thought.

He noodled the station log and made his way to the cells. Cell 15, Jürgens, was at the end and the man was on suicide watch. That was a mere precaution. As Oliver passed, the Desk Sergeant thought, *hi*, and Mox was sitting, bored, playing some cerebral.

Just seeing Jürgens, Oliver thought at them both as he passed within recognition range.

Fine, Sergeant Draith thought back.

Mox grunted.

Down the end of the corridor, Oliver thought at the door lock and went in. Jürgens was lying on the bed, contorted like the lunatic he was, and–

"Fuck!"

He was dead, pale and his face pulled back in a rictus.

Er... shit, Oliver thought, *medical emergency, cell fifteen — stat!*

Sergeant Draith reacted at once: *What!?*

Stat, stat!

Oliver put two fingers on Jürgens' neck, but he already knew he was dead. A quick follow revealed that he'd not had a single thought for half an hour. Last thought: *No, no, no...*

And then nothing.

Oliver looked at the man's shirt with a creeping horror and found what he feared. There were two holes, and underneath two pinpricks and bruising. Someone had – but they were banned!

"Oh shit," *oh shit, oh shit.*

Sergeant Draith came in, and thought: *What?*

Dead, Oliver thought back.

Draith leaned over and took the man's pulse too. "Fuck!" he said. *My job.*

"Look at his shirt," Oliver shouted.

Draith looked instead at Oliver: *My pension. Clara will kill me.*

"He's been shot with a Taser," said Oliver. "Someone fried his brow."

"Nasty," said Draith. *Oh, nothing dear, I'll be home at the usual time, don't worry.*

The next 30 minutes were a blur: the number of important thoughts passing into Oliver's brow went up just as his ability to cope with them plummeted. It was shock.

Everyone ended up in Meeting Room Three as other police, brought in to relieve the staff took over the vital functions of the station. Inspector Dartford had taken on the case, and quickly switched from noodling it to coming across in person. Clearly it had become politically wise to be seen to be investigating.

He'd noodled the facts. Everyone had noodled. Oliver too.

So, Oliver remembered where everyone was at the time of the murder: he had been at this desk thinking about Chinese boxes, which now seemed utterly trivial in comparison; Draith had been at his desk; Mox had been on guard and had already apologised about playing a cerebral on duty; Chen had been in the garage fiddling with spark plugs; Freya had been out having a coffee with a colleague, and so on... and on and on, spreading out across the Thinkersphere. The trouble was – the big trouble was – that no-one had thought: *I'm going to kill you, Jürgens*.

Dartford paced up and down in front of them.

They sat like naughty schoolchildren.

Dartford thought of nothing significant. They all had the same information and had each noodled it several different ways.

Basically, no-one had thought it.

An Unbrow couldn't have got past security. There were two doors to think at for starters and Sergeant Draith was at his desk. There wasn't another way in. Everyone else could be accounted for due to their thoughts.

"CCTV," said Chen. "Why don't we check the CCTV?"

Dartford swivelled on the balls of his feet. "For God's sake, don't be such an–", but he thought better of it: *Get the CCTV – now!*

Chen and Mox were on their feet and out of the door.

Oliver thought it was a good idea and wished he'd thought of it.

Yes, thought Dartford, *I wish you had too*.

Zack added an idea: *Do the doors record the opening?*

Don't be stupid, Dartford thought back.

There's no need for the doors to record their openings because the thought to open them is in the Thinkersphere along with the identity of the thinker, Oliver thought.

Thank you, DC Braddon, Dartford thought, *better late than never.*

The next to last thought about opening the cell was Draith when he, Zack and Mox had put the prisoner in his cell. He had been fine, checked by the police surgeon beforehand, then later every fifteen minutes by Draith or Mox. The door wasn't opened again. Food was passed through a special hatch. The man had had a long thought conversation with his brief, Mellors_Jnr. Draith and Mox had continued to look in and think for the record that he was still alive. The last check was by Mox a mere ten minutes before Oliver had arrived.

And he was fine, Mox thought.

Finally, Oliver had thought the cell door open and found the body.

Yes, thank you for that summary, Dartford thought, *all very obvious.*

Clearly Inspector Dartford had been through all the suspects' trains of thought. Oliver was probably the main suspect on most people's list. Except that he'd been dead for more than five minutes when Oliver had thought the door unlocked.

Perhaps it was because of this Chinese Box, Chen thought.

He wouldn't be killed on account of an empty box, Oliver thought.

Dartford was on it in an instant: *What's this Chinese Box?*

It's something that Jürgens had and we wondered if it related to the Chedding car park murder enquiry.

What's that?

Oliver noodled, then thought: *Hash 83,648,819.*

And does it?

Not as far as we can confirm.

And what is it?

It's an empty Chinese Box about yea – Oliver held out his hands as if holding the box *– big, fancy, but not worth anything.*

And what was in it?

Nothing.

Where is this box?
It's by my desk, Oliver thought.
Valuable?
What do you mean?
Antique? Collector's piece?
Nope.
Sounds like a dead end, Inspector Dartford thought.
Everyone back to work and let Inspector Dartford get on with his investigation, Freya thought.

They all stood and filed out with their heads down, each gradually taking over from the relief personnel.

The Chinese Box was waiting for Oliver when he reached his desk as if taunting him to work it out.

He considered it: *What's this about?*

What indeed, Mithering thought.

It might shed light on the Jürgens stalking case (although that wouldn't come to court now), the Jürgens murder or the Chedding car park murder.

Any would be progress, Mithering agreed.

Once he'd had a coffee, so good, Oliver noodled Jürgens' thoughts, skimming down and seeing what jumped out.

He collected the Chinese Box from behind the café and took it across town and left it under a seat in a pub. It was confusing, full of euphemism and distraction, but that seemed the gist of it. After that Jürgens always thought about a summer's day in Oxford. He wasn't in Oxford, so this was a coded message. As Jellicoe had guessed, it was a dead letter box. Spies used them in the olden days. Jürgens had been tempted to look inside, but he hadn't; if he had, his thoughts would have betrayed him, and he was very frightened of the Chinese Room. Those in the Chinese Room would know about it. They could noodle his thoughts as much as anyone and probably knew his movements.

Oliver noodled various hashtags: the café, the Duke, Chinese Rooms; but without any joy.

Dead letter boxes meant that messages could be passed and if they were intercepted, as this communication route had been, then the rest of the spy cell wouldn't be compromised. This was nonsense, because to plan all this, you had to think and that would be in the Thinkersphere.

Except it wasn't.

Someone Unbrow could do it, but it was too interlinked with thought. You'd need to pick up Jürgens' opinion of the weather in Oxford, after all. The thoughtless were involved in muggings, but nothing complicated. You couldn't do anything complicated in the modern world without thought.

And this was complicated.

Planned.

Thought through.

Oliver noodled a summer's day in Oxford and remembered some bed and breakfast places and hotel deals along with a t-book novel. He refined his search and cross-referenced it with Jürgens' followers. He had a lot of followers, probably full of those who wanted the vicarious thrill of stalking without actually doing it themselves. Second-hand stalking – was that better or worse? None of them thought about a summer's day in Oxford, no-one rethought it, no-one paid it any attention. And yet, clearly, it was a signal: 'box moved'.

And it was empty.

Maybe, maybe, he had to move it at set times – Oliver noodled and remembered that Jürgens didn't have a schedule as such. He followed a hashtag: York_spring.

Maybe, just maybe, they – whoever they were – occasionally tested him by getting him to move an empty box. Jellicoe and himself had simply been unlucky and found the box during one of these dummy runs.

Maybe the message had been delivered, Mithering thought, *and the… envelope needs to be returned.*

Yes, Oliver thought, *it had been dealt with before they arrived?*

Jürgens' house had been broken into.

Or the message stolen?

Yes, but that could have been last week, Oliver thought, *or by Jürgens himself if he'd forgotten his key.*

A co-incidence, Mithering thought.

Oliver ignored that, he felt a chain developing: *Those in the Chinese Room would know about it.* Now that was an interesting thought: plural, more than one, a conspiratorial gathering in Chinatown maybe.

Maybe.

This could be some Tong?

Perhaps some ninja had sneaked into the police station and murdered Jürgens in his locked cell.

Oliver considered Mithering's thought, detecting some humour there. It was slightly ludicrous.

Perhaps a snake: two puncture marks and a death like a Taser shock, venom rather than electricity.

Now you are just being silly, Oliver thought back.

It matches the facts.

Facts! Oliver thought. He noodled the pathologist's report. Doctor Hassan had finished, an extraordinarily quick turnaround, but unsurprising considering. The summary was death by brain haemorrhage caused by electrocution of the synaptic filament connections.

Locked door mystery, illegal weapon, suspects all pah "-pah, pa-pah... police."

What was that?

Nothing, mustn't think about it, Oliver thought.

Think about what?

Just worried about the Sergeant's Exam tomorrow.

It's a doddle, Sergeant Draith thought back, *except for the loneliness.*

I need a drink, Oliver thought.

As Oliver expected, Jellicoe was in the Lamp sitting in the third booth along.

"This Chinese Box business," Oliver said. "Could it be, er... the Tongs?"

Jellicoe practically spat out his whiskey.

"Chinese Room, Chinese Whispers, Chinese Box," Oliver insisted. "There are immigrants here, a lot of poor people from the East don't have brows."

"They stay in Chinatown," said Jellicoe.

"But Jürgens moved the box from a café... someone had to have brought it to café, and regularly."

"So the tentacles of this conspiracy of yours–"

"Not my conspiracy."

"Granted, so these tentacles spread out."

"That's the idea."

"To do what?"

"I thought you were the conspiracy..." Oliver searched for a word other than 'nutcase'. "Expert."

"Nutcase is it?"

"I meant–"

"You might be right," said Jellicoe. He wiped his chin with a handkerchief. "There are shops on the East Side that sell imports. Lacquered boxes might well be bought there and not via brows."

"How do they pay for it?"

"Something old and untraceable like cash, gold or bitcoins," said Jellicoe. "While you are there, you could pop into the Duck."

The Duck?

"The Peking Duck in Chinatown," Jellicoe explained. "And ask for Zhaodi. If there's anything in this Chinese Room business, then that's where you'll find the answer. Nothing goes on in Chinatown without Zhaodi knowing."

Oliver looked Jellicoe in the eye: "You're kidding."

"Say Jellicoe sends his regards."

"The Tongs? This is the Triad, the Chinese Mafia? There's no such thing."

Jellicoe tapped the side of his nose.

"I can't," Oliver realised. "It's my exam tomorrow."

"Afterwards."

"I've enough to worry about with the exam and being investigated over the Jürgens death."

"As I said, afterwards," said Jellicoe. "And good luck with your exam."

"Thanks."

"Good night."

Oliver left: he hadn't had a drink.

THURSDAY

Oliver had tried to sleep, but his thoughts, and those of many others, just went round and round in his head. He'd noodled his revision notes, but they no longer made any sense. He kept thinking of Jürgens lying dead, impossibly murdered in his locked cell. He and Jasmine had decided that as his Sergeant's Exam was so important, he should stay over at his apartment to get some rest.

Like that worked, he thought.

At least his iBrow was fully charged. *On the only day I can't use it!*

Her thought wishing him luck arrived as he was having coffee in the morning.

Thanks, he thought back.

Don't forget to turn me on, Jasmine thought: *Following, I mean.*

I promise, Oliver thought back, lolling to all at her Freudian slip.

See you on the other side, Freya thought at him, *you'll be fine.*

Aye, thanks, Oliver thought back.

Break a leg, Mithering thought.

The examination centre was in the suburbs, a college specialising in those few non-Noodle exams that certain professions insisted upon. It was a converted Edwardian house on three floors although most of it had been modernised back at the turn of the twenty first century, so there was an open lobby with comfortable chairs. Oliver had noodled their hashtag, so he was able to check-in as he waited to be buzzed through the front door.

The receptionist thought back to him a welcome as soon as he was within recognition range and reminded him to sever all his social networking. There were very few exams like this now, and Oliver was grateful because it was such an extraordinary faff. Freya herself had briefed him on it months ago.

So, gradually, as the other constables gathered to sit uncomfortably with a cup of tea, Oliver began to unfollow everyone he knew. He'd arrived early, warned that this took longer than expected, and he did need plenty of time to pick his way through it all. No-one was really consciously aware of all the thoughts that passed through their iBrow, only those that piqued their interest, so it was always a surprise to come across any real statistics: thousands a second. As he unfollowed, the steady stream of thoughts wavered and slowed. Their increasing rarity giving them importance and odd juxtapositions of ideas jumped to his attention. Instead of being, for all intents and purposes, a mostly anonymous stream, every thought now had an individual thinker. People he'd not met in years, friends from his University days that he'd become too used to skipping, became so loud and clear.

Finally, he was down to the Duty Sergeant, which he kept bubbling away; both in case there was an emergency and also for the background hubbub that kept him feeling included. Even so, it was like he was at the end of a party and all the guests had left.

As there were fewer thoughts in his head, Oliver became aware of his fellow examinees. He'd recognised them all as the room wasn't that large. There were seven of them, in suits, all looking nervous. Four of them clutched small bags like talismans, and one, Adams, was a burly looking bloke, a rugby player of a man, who fiddled with his tie.

They smiled at each other awkwardly.

A secretary came in. "Everyone! Time to unfollow. Candidates, if you'd please unfriend everyone."

Cheerio, Oliver thought and then he unfollowed the Duty Sergeant.

He felt strangely euphoric as he made his way to the exam hall with the others. They didn't know each other and were, of course, strictly forbidden to think to each other, so none of them had followed the others. It reminded him of his experience in the morgue when he met Doctor Ridge. Without thoughts, they were like walking corpses or those actors in masks.

Hello, Oliver thought as he saw the Invigilator. The woman nodded, and her eyes flickered as she discontinued whatever she'd been doing. He was allowed to transmit, impossible not to, but receiving was against the regulations. She was sticking to the rules by not replying brow-to-brow.

There were rows of school desks and chairs, Oliver felt lost and wanted to noodle which desk was his, but he saw 'Adams' and then easily found 'Braddon' on the second desk on the first row. They were all spread far apart, beyond recognition range, so suddenly Oliver felt very alone, aware of the wind in the trees outside.

"This is a non-brow exam," said the man who'd showed them in, "so no use of Noodle allowed from now on! Please fill in your details on the cover, but don't open your exam book until instructed." He sat down by the Invigilator.

Oliver, settled, saw that he had to fill in his name, police number and the centre number.

What was the centre number, he thought.

There was a distracting knocking sound.

Centre number... can't noodle.

Knocking and a cough.

Oliver looked up: the Invigilator was tapping the whiteboard. It had 'Centre number: HF 923' in writing on it.

Thanks, Oliver thought.

He returned his attention to the paper: no pen!

He hadn't brought a pen.

I've no pen, he thought.

The woman sighed: "Pens?"

Oliver wasn't the only one to raise his hand.

The woman took her time going up and down almost as if she was trying to demonstrate her disapproval and contempt.

Every time, she thought as she briefly stepped into recognition range.

Thank you, Oliver thought as he took a black biro off her.

She gave a pen to each of the men.

Pencil cases! They had been holding pencil cases.

He wrote his name out, added the centre number and then his police number. He breathed a sigh of relief that he'd known his police number, but his hand felt cramped. He flexed it a few times. It was completely psychosomatic, he knew, but that didn't stop it hurting. He wasn't used to handwriting, always considered it stupid and pointless at school, because when was he ever going to use such a skill. Now, obviously. This was the dark ages reborn.

The Invigilator addressed them aloud, "You have forty-five minutes starting from... now!"

Oliver opened the paper.

Out of the corner of his eye, he noticed the Invigilator blinking. She was probably checking down a list of their names, noodling their last noodle no doubt, and she'd probably passed 'B' by now. She'd check again at the end.

Oliver was suddenly unsure if he could read anymore, but obviously he could, although the challenge made him feel dizzy.

The first question was an ethics one. Follow your gut, but quote something official sounding had been the advice on that. Liberal values.

He felt cold and giddy, which he knew was a side-effect of being alone.

Another ethics question, this time about cerebrals. 'What happens in a cerebral, stays in a cerebral', he knew, but there was a more official and technical way of putting that. Oh, the quip would have to do. What people did in the privacy of their own private part of their head was their own concern. If people wanted to be a celebrity, rock star, rapper, gangster, fashionista, film star or whatever, that was their own concern, so long as it didn't affect anyone else and wasn't a Category 5.

Ah ha, that would be on the mark scheme, definitely.

He wondered if anyone following him would be keeping count of his score. Chen perhaps.

He was getting distracted: *must concentrate.* He looked round.

The room seemed empty with everyone so far apart, the gaze of the Invigilator fell upon him occasionally, but she seemed distant. Because he was no longer following anyone, a type of sensory deprivation closed in. It was a form of torture and indeed there were rules covering it in police custody. He vaguely recalled revising it. You could lock a suspect up in a single cell, but it took a court order to prevent him thinking. Applicable when the suspect might warn accomplices, although in practical terms it was impossible to stop. It was covered in... he could noodle, but he mustn't, and it wasn't a question anyway.

"No use of Noodle," warned the Invigilator. Oliver was sure he hadn't thought about it as such. *Perhaps one of the others?* Adams next to him turned round to see who was looking guilty. *Can you tell from a person's expression?* It was too easy to noodle by accident. Oliver wondered how many failed because of it and realised that he could easily remember – and that would mean he'd fail too.

He moved through a multiple-choice section easily enough: either he knew, or he guessed.

How long left? He... no!

Oliver looked at the clock on the wall. Half past... when did he start? It was on the white board. Forty-five minus thirty was... the mental arithmetic was hard.

"You have a quarter of an hour left," the Invigilator announced.

Thanks, Oliver thought. *So, fifteen minutes! Jeez, I'm not going to make it.*

He turned over to the last page. Another multiple choice and – God – a half page to write. It was an essay, a bloody novel. His hand was already falling off.

Concentrate.

Oliver wrote, carefully forming each letter.

"Time's up!"

That was quick. He hadn't finished. He quickly shuffled his pen along the line to complete the sentence with a full stop.

"No noodling!" shouted the Invigilator, and then, after a pause, "you are not finished until you have left the examination hall."

Oliver sat back, appreciated the relief. He no longer cared whether he'd passed or failed: it was over – nearly – and that was all that mattered.

"Close your answer books."

Oliver realised he hadn't, so he did so. The cover looked unreal, his handwriting neater than the essay question at the end, but then that had been an age of forty-five minutes earlier when he'd been fresh.

The Invigilator came down the rows, collecting the papers. *Monks used to write out books by hand*, she thought, using a patently practised jibe.

"You may leave," she said, finally.

Oliver and the others picked themselves up and made their way out through the exit.

"Thank God," said the bloke in front.

Once Oliver was through, he followed a few people straight away: Jasmine, the Duty Sergeant, Mithering and felt their thoughts skimming past, comforting and gentle, reminding him he wasn't alone. The man behind bumped into him.

"Come on, come on, keep going."

"Oh. Sorry," said Oliver.

"I'm sorry. I'm just on edge, you know," said the other, his hands up placating.

"I was er... following," said Oliver.

"Oh, yes, we can."

The man stepped to one side, his eyes blinking as he was engrossed in his own mental processes.

Oliver realised that he was still holding the biro: he should have handed it back. It wasn't of anymore use to him. The Inspector Exam didn't require a non-Noodle session. Not that he was going to make Inspector for a long time. He made his way out of the building into the sunlight: '*how did it go?*' summed up a lot of the thoughts pending as if everyone he'd followed had rethought the same thing.

My exam went fine, he thought officially. He wasn't following enough to know how many people liked this. Being honest with himself, he hadn't a clue. It was all a blur and, because he hadn't been able to think about it, there was nothing to noodle into his memory.

Told you, thought Desk Sergeant Draith, *doddle*.

Not really, forty-five minutes is too long.

Hand hurt?

Yes, Oliver thought rubbing his right with his left. The tendons crunched under his pressure.

Wuss.

I am not, Oliver thought back, but he felt weak.

And you forgot your pen!

That was Chen's pearl of wisdom.

Following those doing exams was recommended as a form of preparation, but Oliver guessed Chen had just scanned down his train of thought for something to mock.

"Fancy a drink?"

Oliver turned round: it was the big bloke from the exam hall. He recognised him. "Adams?" he said.

"I can see you'll be a detective."

"I already am."

"A group of us were going for a drink, celebrate, that sort of thing."

"Sure," said Oliver.

The man held out his hand: "Jack."

"Er... Ollie."

They followed each other straight away as a matter of politeness.

In the end there were four of them in the group: Jack Adams, Melissa Trent, Matthew Parker and Oliver himself. They went to the *Beehive*, a wine bar that Melissa suggested, and Adams went to buy the first round.

Melissa had the first thought: *How did you find it?*

Fine, thought Oliver. The others nodded in agreement: *And you?*

Fine too, she agreed, *although the lack of thought was creepy.*

Everyone agreed on that one.

And pointless, Adams thought from over at the bar, *I mean, after all, we can use Thinkersphere and Noodle, so why test our ability without it.*

Maybe it's to discover what we're like underneath, thought Oliver.

Matthew snorted: *You can find that out much better by following a person's thoughts.*

Adams returned with the first two drinks: Oliver's lager and Melissa's white wine.

I know, I know, Oliver agreed. He sipped his lager, enjoying it, pleased to have an afternoon off.

It's a throwback to the new examination system, Melissa thought. *It's to drive standards up by stopping people relying on technology.*

It's a political hot potato, Adams thought as he made the second trip to the bar. *There's a lot of archaic nonsense in policing. Like having to turn up in court. We could be on duty and just follow the case hashtag, think a reply when we're asked something. It would be much more efficient. But justice must be seen to be done, even though a person can control their face when lying, but not their thoughts. So it's hours and hours of waiting around just to have it cancelled. Here you go.*

It must be 'seen' to be done, Melissa thought, *otherwise we are Thought Police.*

I hate being called a Tepee, Adams thought. *'Is your head shaped like a cone? Does it go all the way up your helmet?'*

Thanks, Parker thought. *I had one of those last week. Bloke changed his plea when the prosecution read out his thoughts. Like, he couldn't have noodled that with his lawyer when he was on remand.*

Adams finished his previous thought: *Bloody foil heads.*

Happened to me, Melissa thought.

Me too, thought Adams.

Oliver nodded: *And me.*

They drank for a while in silence, stuck for something to think.

This... Melissa thought and then she said aloud, "This has gone to my head."

"Me too," said Adams.

Orange juice, Parker thought sadly.

I'm fine, Oliver thought, noticing that he'd drunk the most and was still able to think.

"Orange juice?" Adams asked.

I'm driving, Parker thought, *and you lot can't think now, can you?*

"Bit silly following each other really," Melissa said.

They laughed at this – Oliver and Parker liked it – bonding despite the lack of social thinking. The alcohol helped. Oliver finished his first, so he bought the next round: two lagers, a large white wine and Parker had lemonade this time.

On his way to the bar, Oliver felt the familiar prickling sensation across his forehead.

The barmaid gave him a tray for all four drinks.

"Thanks", said Parker and then thought: *I hate lemonade too.* To distract everyone from this he added, aloud, "Look at this." He showed them his hand. It was shaking. "Withdrawal."

"From handwriting!?" said Adams.

"No, from thinking."

Adams nodded, despite the man's obvious machismo style, he too had experienced the awful emptiness. Oliver checked his hand, but it seemed steady enough. Perhaps it had been shaking, but one-and-a-half lagers had steadied his nerves.

"I've still got my pen," Oliver said.

The others laughed: *Parker taking his out too.*

"You heard about the police cover-up?" Parker asked.

"No," said Oliver.

Adams sniffed loudly at the idea.

"What is it?" Oliver asked.

Both Parker and Melissa started to talk, "It's... sorry."

Parker held up his hand as if to say, 'ladies first' and thought the same.

"It's this death in Chedding car park," she said. "Apparently one of the flash rioters was beaten to death, a woman."

"That's nonsense," said Oliver.

"You can't say that."

"I can because I was there," he looked at the others for support. "There was a body, but it was old."

"Old? I heard it was a young woman."

"Young woman, body had been there a while, four or five weeks," Oliver insisted. "I'm investigating the case. Me."

"Pre-Sergeant's Exam?" Parker asked.

"Yes."

Oliver felt immensely proud and was thankful that the pint-and-three-quarters of lager blocked this from the others, so that he could at least act nonchalant.

"Is it going well?" Adams asked.

Oliver waved his hands trying to conjure a good answer. "No. We've nothing to go on."

"It's not the Sergeant's Exam, you can noodle it."

"Really, I'd not tried that one."

"No need for that."

"I know, sorry, but it's frustrating."

"Perhaps you have to rely on skills other than technology?" Melissa said. Oliver realised she was teasing him and that the others were winding him up too.

"Still a dead body though," Oliver said, with more force than he was expecting. "Someone's daughter, someone's follower."

The group's mood turned more sombre.

"And this conspiracy nonsense isn't helping," Oliver added.

"Are you sure there's nothing to it?" Melissa asked.

"I was there."

"But not all the time," she said, putting her hand on his, which struck Oliver as odd, "and these flash riots are started by someone."

Oliver imagined this as a train of thought, not real thought because of the drink, but maybe there was a point. The riot was organised, even if they seemed to spontaneously appear, and with all the police up one end of the city, the Chedding area would have been unpatrolled. Maybe it was a cover for dumping the body. The car may have been stolen and stored, it hadn't necessarily been parked there all this time.

"I don't think so," said Oliver. "You see, we don't patrol that often, so you wouldn't need a diversion."

"Really?" said Adams. "A bit of a jump there surely. I can't follow your train of thought remember."

"Sorry, but I don't think the riot and the murder are connected, other than one caused us to come across the other."

"Murder! I'd like a case like that," Adams said. "It would be good, something to get your teeth into. Wouldn't do my CV any harm."

"They're only good if you can solve them."

"But there was that death in the police station," Melissa said.

"Oh, please, I'm involved in that too, right up to here," Oliver said, holding his hand up to his chin.

So there is a conspiracy, Parker thought.

"No," said Oliver. "We'll solve it."

"I'm sure you will," said Melissa, touching him again. "My round."

The three men watched her walk to the bar admiringly.

"Nice girl," said Adams.

The others agreed.

Melissa glowered back at Parker. Oliver had missed the thought responsible. He could noodle it, of course, but why? You needed three strikes on separate days to even come to the stalker division's attention.

"What are you working on?" Parker asked Adams quickly.

Adams groaned, "The Oscar Peters appeal."

"That was done and dusted, wasn't it?"

"The defence are questioning the rethinking evidence: a case of Chinese Whispers, they say."

"No, seriously?"

"Not in this case... in my opinion only, but apparently 'memetic change in rethinking' has been demonstrated. In America, of course; so, they are trying to establish a precedent here."

"Will they?"

"It's bollocks."

"I'm not sure I agree with you," Oliver said.

"Look," said Adams, "I grant you that whispering in someone's ear can be misheard, and as it goes down the line – it's a children's game, for God's sake – then errors creep in."

Send three and fourpence, thought Parker, *we're going to a dance.*

"Pardon?"

"Send three and four... it's a First World War example: 'send reinforcements, we're going to advance' becomes 'send three–"

"Fair enough – no, good example; however!" Adams raised his finger to emphasise his point. "Rethinking passes the primary thought intact. It's a copy."

"Ah," said Oliver, "but the rethinker can think a further thought that affixes to the primary thought."

"Rubbish."

"It's been demonstrated," Oliver insisted.

"Bollocks, look–"

Parker cut in, "And that's the Oscar Peters defence?"

"Yes, he didn't think a specific element of his thought, but it was inserted by someone else in the chain when they rethought it."

"But you can noodle his original," said Oliver.

"Yes," Adams agreed. "But there's some context nonsense to say he wasn't actually thinking about stealing from the company."

"Really?"

"As a joke, apparently. So," said Parker, "he thought about stealing from the company, but that's, you know, a contextual misconception, and the latter rethinks of the accomplices were identical memetic additions to the original thought?"

"That's the defence!?"

"He's innocent then," said Parker to the assembled company. *I can understand why you're pissed off*, he thought.

"Still twenty grand worth of stuff missing from the safe."

Melissa returned with two lagers.

"Oh," said Parker, and he was on his feet to fetch his drink and Melissa's white wine.

"Drinking at lunchtime, wonderful," said Adams, holding his full glass up to the light.

"You only take a non-Noodle exam once in a blue moon," said Melissa. "What are you irritated by? I caught Matthew's thought on it."

"The Oscar Peters case," said Parker, coming back and indicating Adams with his orange juice. "He's on it."

"Thanks," said Melissa, taking her white wine. "Oh, the Chinese Whispers business? It's interesting and could undermine all sorts of cases."

"Just what I was saying," said Adams.

Parker and Oliver exchanged a glance.

That's what he says now, Parker thought.

"Oh really?" Melissa said, turning on Adams.

"I mean I don't agree... and was going to move on to the ramifications of any ruling in his favour," said Adams. He'd drunk too much for him to reveal if that argument really was his opinion.

"It's one of the techniques that flash rioters use," Melissa said. When they looked at her, she continued, "The organiser stays in the background, thinks the location and instructions, but others pass it on, rethinking... no, not that, er..."

"Thinking again," said Oliver.

"Yes and inserting another thought. If there are enough of them in the chain, it becomes increasingly difficult to track the source, particularly if there's a stooge involved. The thought you are searching for isn't consistent, it changes. Like a virus adapting."

"By memetic engineering," said Parker suddenly.

"Yes, of a sort."

"Memetic engineering? Of a sort?"

"Modification of people's thoughts with other thoughts," said Melissa. "If you receive a thought followed by another, then you may draw a conclusion. The thoughts form a train and there may be a logical–"

"Not necessarily logical," said Parker.

"No... more like... 'obvious' – there may be an obvious next step, so you are taken... oh, led."

"Led down the garden path."

"That's it."

"Or it can be unsubtle," said Parker. "If you are bombarded with spam you might buy, you know, Viagra."

"Exactly."

"Peer pressure," said Oliver. "If everyone riots, then you riot too."

"You can't have original thoughts if you are surrounded by other thoughts that are all on the same theme. Even if you disagree, the sheer weight is persuasive."

"I'd like to think it wouldn't affect me," Oliver said.

"Another round?" Adams said.

"Sure."

"Oh, it's me, isn't it," said Parker standing. "Same again?"

They nodded.

Parker went up to the bar.

As they drank on, the conversation weaving its clumsy way from subject to subject without the fleetness of thought, Oliver felt himself becoming morose. Jürgens' death played on his mind and Unknown 271, his case; even this Zhaodi contact that Inspector Jellicoe had mentioned. Suddenly he realised that everyone was silent.

"Do any of you want a lift?" Parker asked.

"Sure," said Oliver.

"I'm fine," said Adams.

"Me too," Melissa added.

Oliver went with Parker, leaving the other two looking over their glasses at each other. Something had passed between them, unspoken and even unthought.

Parker's car was back at the exam centre's car park, a short walk, and the wind was refreshing. Once they were en route in his green Cheetah Special, Parker asked where Oliver wanted to be dropped off.

"Town's fine," said Oliver.

The area itself was difficult to reach, a pedestrianised zone flanked the south side, so Parker pulled in at a bus stop to let Oliver out.

"Thanks," Oliver said, the alcohol still in his system. He walked towards his flat and found a small shop selling groceries. He noodled the shop and then had to ask for his goods, bread, milk, Hasqueth Finest and a ready meal, aloud and in person to the disapproving gaze of the assistant. He reckoned with his bank, and by the time he'd done this, he was sobering up, glad that it wasn't far.

Shower, he thought, *eat and get some sleep.*

When Oliver came around the corner, he saw a crowd had gathered ahead. Perhaps there was a party or something. There were placards with hashtags, but they were too far away to read.

"Excuse me," he said aloud.

"Who are you?" said the first protester.

"I, er... live here."

The woman switched to thought: *Are you police?*

Oliver was about to answer when he became aware that others were turning towards him. The crowd, now he was across the road, had semi-circled around the entrance to his apartment. It was now gathering around him.

"No," Oliver said.

"I recognise him," said a man, "and..."

The man's expression changed to one of concentration. He was following Oliver, noodling him and scanning back along his thoughts, and would obviously find some reference to his job very quickly.

Hell, the Sergeant's Exam was only a few hours ago.

"What job?" a woman cajoled. Oliver knew her... no, he didn't. He hadn't added all his followings yet. "Do you have something to hide?"

The woman's sign read 'The Police are the Murderers'.

Oh, crap, Oliver thought.

"He's just thought about a Sergeant's Exam!" someone yelled.

This isn't good, Mithering thought.

Oliver took a step backwards, giving ground and revealing too much about himself even to those beyond recognition range. The crowd was turning angry. Oliver noted a hashtag on a placard and followed it only to be bombarded by hate thoughts. It was turning ugly.

"Look," he said, holding up his free hand to placate them. "There's been a mistake."

"Too right," a man said.

Oliver followed a few in recognition range, quickly, to try and build up a gist of what the crowd was thinking.

It's him, it's him, murdering Tepee! Get him...

The people were letting the avalanche of thoughts control them, and so the crowd had become an entity, making decisions much as the weekend's riot had done. No single individual was in control. Any stray thought, something pertinent and explosive, even from someone a continent away, could flip the mob into violence.

Oliver stumbled back, jarring his foot when he stepped off the kerb. The mob loomed over him.

A voice boomed over the noise: "Get in!"

Oliver turned, his groceries spilling out across the pavement.

It was Jellicoe, holding a back door open.

Oliver dropped the rest of his shopping, took two strides and leapt in. He landed on the backseat, half-in, half-out.

"Go!" Jellicoe shouted.

Oliver guessed and added Chen to the list he followed, and only just in time.

Going, thought Chen. The police siren wailed.

Oliver's left foot bounced along the tarmac, smacked up until he managed to pull his legs inside. Just in time, because the car door slammed shut when it connected with a parked car. Alarms sounded from the dashboard. The mob screamed, hammering on the roof, something glass smashed and then the wheels squealed, and the car took off.

Chen must have overridden every safety, because the car was moving fast and had done when the door had been open.

Oliver bounced around in the back seat, pulling himself upright, helped and hindered by Jellicoe.

"Put your seatbelt on," Jellicoe said. The Inspector was gripping his own left arm with his right hand, protectively, as well as wearing a seatbelt.

Oliver did as instructed: his hands jerked around with the metal and material. The clasp went click.

"What the hell was that?" he said.

"Rioters," said Jellicoe.

"It was a fucking lynch mob!"

A lynch mob, he thought, *and if Jellicoe hadn't been there, I'd have been for it.*

You're welcome, Chen thought from the front seat.

A thought popped up from Mithering: *Are you all right?*

I'm still following the bastard was another thought: Martha_556.

"I'm fine," said Oliver, then he realised she was in his head. *I'm fine*, he thought.

Thank goodness, Mithering thought.

The car bounced up over some speed bumps.

Sorry, Chen thought.

And again.

They turned a corner.

"Where are we going?"

"Drink this," said Jellicoe handing him a flask.

"I don't think... OK."

Oliver took a sip, almost choked as it threatened to go the wrong way. It was whiskey, but that hardly mattered. He knocked back the medicine and waited for the familiar prickling sensation.

"Clear?"

"Yes," said Oliver, "so where are we going?"

"I've a spare room," said Jellicoe.

Chen sniggered and lolled.

They drove down the Pelton Road in silence, putting distance between them and the city centre. Finally, after a few turns, Chen dropped them off.

"Thanks," said Oliver. *That new?*

Yea, the old Panther's in the shop.

Oh yes, OK, see you.

And then he was standing on the pavement facing a broken iron gate across a grass patched driveway to a dilapidated garage. Jellicoe's house was in the Pelton district, an old three storey property on a corner. The ferns and bushes threatened to stop them going up the winding path to the old-fashioned porch. Jellicoe fumbled with his keys.

Inside it was dark, the hall had a high ceiling, and a smell that Oliver couldn't place, or even noodle, that increased as they penetrated the interior rooms.

"Drink?" Jellicoe said as he got out two tumblers and a bottle.

"No, thanks."

Jellicoe poured two generous measures.

"Come on."

Oliver took it with a shaking hand and downed it in one. It burnt, tasted peaty and hot.

"Good man," said Jellicoe. "Switches off the little grey cells – just what a detective needs."

"Thanks."

The wall of the lounge was covered in objects hanging from hooks seemingly randomly placed. There were plaques, awards perhaps, and masks: Phantom of the

Opera, that Guy Fawkes mask and Eighteenth Century Masked Ball variants for both men and women. They reminded Oliver of the theatre show he'd seen with Jasmine, and he had the distinct impression they were staring down at him. He shivered: strange to be fine with having people reading your thoughts and yet be disturbed by the gaze of inanimate objects.

"Sit."

Oliver did so, sinking slightly into the large sofa, its springs twanging in complaint. He rested his now empty glass on the arm and it was soon filled up again by Jellicoe.

"Tough day."

"Yes," Oliver agreed.

"Has the whiskey done the trick?"

"Thanks, I feel better."

"Is your brow still quiet?"

Oliver tried to think, couldn't and so said, "Yes."

"All clear then." Jellicoe sat in an arm chair opposite and picked up his own drink. "Hello scotch, glad to meet you," he said.

Oliver took another sip and then waved his glass aloft. "Why?"

"Most criminals are discovered because of their thinking."

"Of course."

"We just go through the motions, mostly to keep the legal vultures happy. I mean, why tell someone they've the right to remain silent–"

"Well, they do."

"When you're reading their thoughts. All fairly pointless, but it's procedure."

"I suppose."

"Occasionally though, we get one that eschews thought."

Oliver grunted; he was coming down from an adrenalin rush and still felt jittery.

"And then we have a proper murderer," Jellicoe announced. "Help yourself."

Oliver shook his head, so Jellicoe heaved himself up and poured a third generous measure into Oliver's glass.

"It's single malt," the old man said.

"Thanks."

"And a pound gets you five, the murderer has tuned into the police hashtags."

"Eh?"

"He's following your thoughts."

Oliver examined the whiskey, seeing the speckled pattern on his thighs, a refraction of the weak light from the bulb above.

"I hadn't thought of that."

"No, but you've thought everything else, every step of the investigation."

"What investigation!?"

"This one."

"We don't know anything we didn't know on the first day of noodling it."

"We know a lot more."

"Oh, really, the name of the woman who owned the car, that it was a series five iBrow, that they left the aircon on, that... nothing of any value."

Oliver went to stand up, but fumbled on the seating and flopped back again.

"I don't have a toothbrush," he said.

"I have spares."

"You live here alone."

"No woman'll have a drunk like me."

"You admit it then."

"Goes with the territory."

"You're sharper than you pretend."

"It's my disguise," and then, when Jellicoe saw where Oliver had glanced, he added, "Presents. I put one up, someone saw it, bought me another, and from then on everyone assumed I was a collector."

"Right."

"You think chummy is a collector of scalps?"

"Could be."

"And the victim?"

"Unknown."

"You'll have to find out."

"How?"

"Look."

"Short of thinking to everyone in turn: are you alive? I can't think what else to do."

"You'd have to see them in person."

"In person!"

"Because whoever she is, the system thinks she's still thinking."

"Or has a damn good reason to assign her death to something else."

Jellicoe lurched forward and stabbed his finger towards Oliver: "That's it! But what?"

Oliver spread his arms, almost spilling his drink as he did so, and breathed in for a few seconds. "I dunno, I can't think how to phrase the question to Noodle."

"You're someone who skips to the back of the textbook first to look at the answers."

"I don't read books," said Oliver. "Who reads books? It's the twenty first century."

"Why are you getting so aggressive?"

"Because I'm drunk."

"Another?"

"Yes."

FRIDAY

Chen thought to Oliver to let him know he was coming to collect them. Jellicoe wouldn't drive in despite having a perfectly good car, something to do with being drunk later. Oliver was still wearing yesterday's clothes and his charge was around 65%.

I'll have to get some stuff from my apartment, he thought.

We'll be waiting.

Shit.

Ha ha.

Why hasn't Martha_556 been arrested?

Too clever.

Lots of her followers liked that.

Breakfast in the kitchen was tense, Jellicoe was unaccustomedly sober. The older man had been taking his tablets and was not pleased when Oliver barged in.

"Don't you bloody dare," Jellicoe said.

Oliver had in fact been about to follow him, a reflex reaction when seeing someone not on his list.

OK, OK, Oliver thought.

"OK?"

"OK."

Jellicoe took a plate and knife from the drainer. Thick pieces of toast gave off smoke under the grill and came out both black and white. He had butter and marmalade.

"Help yourself."

"Where are the plates?"

Jellicoe waved, and Oliver realised that the man didn't know himself, so he began a search, pleased that the banging of the cupboard door clearly irritated the Inspector. Oliver found a plate and eventually a knife. There didn't appear to be any coffee worth talking about, no Hasqueth's Finest certainly in Jellicoe's cupboards, so Oliver had to make do with an own brand. He too had toast, although Jellicoe had finished his by the time Oliver's was ready. Oliver sat down opposite Jellicoe just as the old man got up, washed his single plate and knife before returning it to the drainer. Oliver's seat was too close to the fridge, so he had to shift to let the man through.

"Chen's here," said Jellicoe.

"Ur... um..." but Oliver's mouth was full. *Chen, stall him so I can finish breakfast.*

No chance, Chen thought.

Jellicoe chuckled.

Oliver was still trying to put on his tie, and eat his toast, as he came out to join Jellicoe.

"And you want to be a sergeant," said Jellicoe.

Chen sniggered in reply.

They're a positive double act, Oliver thought.

"The three stooges," said Jellicoe.

Oliver settled down to staring out of the window and digest his meal in peace, but Jellicoe had other ideas.

"Let's consider the Chedding case."

OK, Oliver thought.

"Motive, opportunity and method," the Inspector said, counting the items on his fingers. "We rely far too much on the first: motive. A man wants to commit murder, or does, he always thinks about why. We noodle it, Bob's your Uncle."

"And then we check his thinking for the opportunity and the method."

"Exactly."

"With the body in the car," Oliver said, "we've method... and I suppose given the time frame pretty much everybody had the opportunity, but we've no motive."

Jellicoe saluted with his index finger.

"If we had a list of suspects," Oliver said, "then we'd go through their thoughts and we'd have our criminal."

"But that's not detection."

You're saying you had better detectives in your day?

"We had to be," said Jellicoe, without any victory in his voice, "there was no other choice and no technology to make us lazy. We dealt with facts."

We catch more criminals.

"True, but there's a flaw in the system and if others learn of this flaw, and exploit it..."

Jellicoe let the idea settle.

Thought was a panacea, like antibiotics, and perhaps they were seeing the first Noodle resistant criminals.

At the station, Freya was there in person to meet him. He'd not twigged that one, and then he realised that he hadn't got around to adding her to his list of those he followed. He did quickly and scanned back. She'd already thought at him.

How did the exam go?

"Fine," Oliver said.

I knew it, she thought in reply, and then she tilted her head as she realised that he had spoken aloud. "Has 'no thought' become your thing?" she asked.

She had a nice voice, Oliver realised, almost tuneful.

Thank you, Freya thought with a smile, *and people who talk too much, don't think.*

"Yes, I mean..." *No, I've been staying with you know who. You know who?*

On account... "on account of the rioters. They protested outside my apartment."

"Oh yes," said Freya, picking up on the need to talk, and more importantly not think, on this subject. "I'll keep you two assigned together until it blows over."

"Thanks..." *...although*, thought Oliver, *I don't want to be lumbered with him all day and all night.*

"Beggars can't be choosers," said Freya.

"Ha!"

The Chief Superintendent mimed a drinking action.

Don't I know it... not that I've, you know.

His group have special dispensations.

Is that what it's called?

Anyway, well done with the exam, she thought, moving on towards the stairs. She nodded to the Desk Sergeant, which must have been a routine, because there was no thought associated before or after.

Thank you, Oliver thought.

Anything you need, let me know, Freya added as an afterthought. She disappeared through the big double doors.

Will do. I'm going upstairs to do some investigation work.

Oh, nearly forgot, you'll need to think with Inspector Dartford, Freya added, *he's pissed that you weren't around yesterday for questioning.*

I was taking my exam.

Yes, but all afternoon without being able to think with you.

Oliver followed Inspector Dartford.

There were questions backed up, so while he climbed the stairs to his office, he noodled them together and made a questionnaire. They were all things that he'd gone over before and he was tempted to add pointers to his previous thoughts, but he didn't. Instead, he did it properly and so described again finding Jürgens' body and so forth. It took him until he'd reached his desk.

One of the questions asked him about the scalping aspect of his own murder case. Clearly the man was interested in the salacious side. However, it was one area of the murder that he hadn't explored himself. His focus had been on identifying the body, so that the victim's thoughts would give him the answers he needed. That hadn't worked, examining the scene hadn't worked, but perhaps some other searches might turn up a lead.

Facts, he thought.

He was up on his feet and going downstairs before he realised what he was doing. Do it the old-fashioned way, Jellicoe had said. *Check out the scene of the crime.*

No-one had thought the cell door open, so it was a locked door mystery, but the thing had a code, for God's sake. You go up to the door and into recognition range, and you thought to open it, it knew who you were, and if you were on its list, it opened.

A simple noodle revealed all the people who had thought to open this particular door, whether they succeeded or not. There was no way that a euphemism could get around this, because the door had a code. Anyone could find out the code, of course; it only existed to identify this particular door from the billions of other doors: it was the person's ID that flicked the switch. You had to be on its list, which gave them a very convenient and finite set of suspects: themselves.

Drink is Jellicoe's system to stop being followed, Oliver thought. *What else might work?*

You could be asleep, Mithering thought.

No, even if you sleep walked to the cell, you wouldn't be able to think and therefore open the door.

Drink or drugs prevented thought and so that was a non-starter.

Sergeant Draith was on duty, looking far more alert and on edge than normal. Mox was on guard, again he was at his imposing best. Indeed, such was the disaster that the whole station was nervous and fired up.

I'm checking the cell, Oliver thought.

Why? I'm not sure you should, Draith thought, getting out of his seat.

Got to do something.

Draith nodded.

Oliver went down the corridor to Cell 15. There was crime scene tape across the door, which seemed a strange and surreal sight inside a police station.

Oliver thought at the door: it clicked although the heavy metal itself didn't move. He pushed it open and looked inside, half expecting to see Jürgens, his contorted face staring up at him accusingly. Oliver ducked under the tape.

How?

We don't know, Mox thought.

Oliver was half-in and half-out of the cell.

It was a cell: a simple shelf for bedding, a steel toilet, white tiles, a high window with bars, the thick metal door he was holding open with its sliding hatch, and high up some LED lights in the ceiling. Concrete floor, walls, ceiling.

And then he realised: *The murderer fired the Taser through the hatch!*

It's got security glass, Draith thought. *Everyone's come up with that one.*

Oliver looked: he felt foolish. The window in the hatch was slightly smeared and had a grid of wire reinforcement set in the glass.

Oliver ran his thumb up and down the heavy door: it was impossible. He felt the sharp steel of the lock, the recessed bumps of the screws holding it together.

Fired through the keyhole.

Electronic thought lock, Draith thought. *Most people came up with that one. You'll have to do better.*

I saw an old movie where the first person to find the body had fired a gun as everyone rushed to the scene, Mithering thought.

Except I was the first person to find the body. Oliver didn't remember firing a Taser. Noodle confirmed that. *Unless my thoughts have been manipulated? That was stupid. God, he needed a coffee. Or a beer.*

132

He'd know if he'd handled a Taser, the things always made him nervous as did electricity in general. No-one wanted to short-out their brow, the shock could kill you. It had killed Jürgens.

Oliver felt something catch, a slight stickiness on the door edge. He'd been moving his thumb up and down, idly, but now he squatted down and took a good look.

There was... something white above and below the bolt.

He pushed his finger against it and thought the door locked.

The metal jumped, detected the slight pressure of his finger and stayed put.

The door was locked, but not locked.

To all intents and purposes, to anyone walking past, the door would noodle as locked. It had been locked, it was just that the bolt hadn't engaged. So, this stickiness might have been left by a piece of tape. Any number of officers could come and go, lock and unlock the door, and the heavy steel would stay shut and lie that it was locked.

But Jürgens would have just been able to walk out.

"Dead end," Oliver whispered to himself.

But why would he?

Why would he what, Draith asked.

Nothing, Oliver thought. *If the door was closed, you'd simply assume it was locked. And* – Oliver checked – *there was no handle on the inside.*

"It wasn't a locked door mystery," Oliver whispered to himself. "It was open all the time." *Someone had done something really quite complicated and premeditated without thinking about it. But how?*

One impossibility replaced by another impossibility, Mithering thought.

A drunk person, Draith suggested.

No, Oliver thought back, *they'd have to think to the Desk Sergeant and that was you.*

Not me, Draith thought, *you can check my thoughts. Perhaps someone else on duty?*

No, because there's someone here all the time: Mox, Chen, whoever, on duty and he's not allowed to leave the desk.

Dead end then, Draith thought.

Oliver noodled Draith's thoughts anyway, but they fitted the analysis. Of course, they did. The analysis was based on his, and everyone else's, thoughts. The man was nervous now, worried that Oliver suspected him. Oliver did the same with Mox, who was still thinking about his cerebral even if he wasn't playing it, and then Chen, Mike, Maxine, Zack, Bob and finally, feeling guilty and disloyal, Freya. He noodled the morning's Duty Roster: Nancy, who he'd not met, Tim Too, Rose and Tim.

No thought seemed to involve tape, locks, doors, Tasers or any euphemism that might relate to them.

It just doesn't work, Oliver thought.

That's the worry, Draith thought.

On his way back to his desk, Oliver noodled about scalping, his other potential line of enquiry, and remembered that it had been used by the Ancient Scythians to create war trophies that they then used as napkins. Shame Noodle didn't have a forget function. These were all references to the removal of the hair and skin, not the forehead as the word meant now. Oliver skipped ahead to the modern entries. Scalping, the removal of brow technology was an activity briefly ascribed to anti-cyborg groups. Oliver thought it made the plot of the last ever movie, but a noodle reminded him that it wasn't. *Cyborg Serial Killer* gained one star on the movie summary according to Noodle and it was about a cyborg who killed three or more people rather than someone who killed cyborgs.

Ollie, Mithering thought, *why are you thinking about the last movie?*

Just trying to figure out why the victim was scalped.

Surely to hide their identity.

It could be as a trophy or a protest though.

I suppose.

Though surely if you wanted to stop people implanting brows, then half a dozen deaths isn't going to make much difference.

And pointless if you hide the fact.

Oliver hadn't realised that before.

You're welcome, Mithering thought back.

You're not hunting a cyborg killer, Chen thought, *are you?*

Might be.

Did you have the glowing dagger?

What?

The glowing dagger, Chen thought, *it was part of the merchandising for the film.*

This took Oliver by surprise: *Why are you noodling the film?*

I'm not, I had one as a kid.

Was it good?

I broke it.

I had a pair of Heads-up glasses, Oliver admitted.

No way.

Yes, it used to show text boxes in front of you to tell you what you were looking at.

And you had to read these?

Yes.

Oliver remembered the text balloons floating in front of him as the various hints appeared depending on his view. He wondered what happened to the device. It was probably in the loft at his parents' house.

I've just found a glowing dagger for sale, Chen thought.

Oliver followed the link and felt a sudden wave of nostalgia. Other people had bought the magic orb, the pyjamas and the electronic gun. Oliver shuddered, although a gun that lights up and makes strange noises was not the same as a Taser, the similarity was disturbing.

Mithering's thought interrupted them: *Perhaps we should focus?*

Good point, Oliver thought as he remembered that Heads-up glasses could be bought in presentation boxes for £59.99 from Vintage Tech. Others who bought it went on to purchase tie-in t-shirts and the director's cut on download. It had 4.5 stars from 158 reviews.

Focus!

Sorry Mithering.

Chen thought: *Who's Mithering?*

Someone following the case, Oliver thought back. *Now, let's review.*

Oliver noodled the case notes.

It's a puzzle all right, Mithering thought.

"A Chinese Puzzle," said Oliver to himself: *Chinese Puzzle, Jellicoe had said that outside Westbourne's house.* He'd heard it before, of course. *No, Carl Jürgens, that stalker, had said Chinese... something.* Oliver noodled through Jürgens last two days of thinking for anything Chinese. Maybe by focusing on rooms, boxes and whispering, he'd missed something.

Jürgens had had a Chinese takeaway, another Chinese takeaway, more takeaway, and then he remembered that he'd threatened Maxine in the cell with the Chinese Room. Luckily, this was in his thought stream in the Thinkersphere and not in one of the numerous gaps caused by all the talking and shouting.

Chinese Puzzle. Chinese Room. Chinese Box... There weren't any Chinese associated with this – were there?

What about Chen, Mithering thought.

Chen's from Slough.

I am, Chen thought, *so what?*

There was a Chinese quarter in town, nowhere near Chedding, that was called Chinatown. There were a few intersecting streets that had the right architecture and design to give it an exotic flavour. There were restaurants and shops, so if you wanted a Chinese Puzzle or a Chinese Box, then that would be a good place to go to find something authentic. There would be Chinese Rooms aplenty too.

Or it was code, a mechanism to obscure your thinking.

In which case, Mithering thought, *the Chinese Room could be anywhere and not even a room.*

That doesn't really make sense: the Chinese Box was a Chinese Box, lacquered and red with traditional scrawls on the lid.

Oliver fished it out from his drawer and put it down in front of him.

It was beautiful and, when he examined it, he was impressed by the craftsmanship. The catch opened easily and... nothing. It was painted black inside, a gloss finish that caught the light.

Chinese Puzzle, Jellicoe had said.

A man has died to hide this, so it has to mean something.

There was a maker's mark on the base, so Oliver noodled it and remembered that it was a Chinese Box, on special offer via Amazon, that they came in three sizes and they were eligible for free delivery. Others who thought about it also thought about Chinese Lanterns, Chinese Firecrackers and Chinese Fortune Cookies. So the box itself really wasn't worth killing over. It wasn't an antique or a collector's item. You could get them on a three-for-two offer.

"Maybe... hmm...."

Oliver turned it over and examined every surface. He touched the inside and outside, felt the distance and eventually came to the conclusion that it hadn't been altered. There were no hidden compartments or false bottoms.

Perhaps the box itself was the puzzle?

A box was a kind of small space, so a Chinese Box might represent the Chinese Room. It could be, say, a particular room with red on the outside and black on the inside. *But why not just think the address?*

What address?

It was empty: was that the clue?

What's the clue?

The box is empty, Oliver thought conscious that Mithering was still following him.

Was there something in it?

No.

Maybe a direct approach.

Jellicoe had mentioned something about... Oliver had to noodle it: Zhaodi and the Peking Duck.

Chen, Oliver thought at Chen, *can you take me to Chinatown?*

Only too happy, Chen thought, *get me away from the station.*

As they drove along, Chen asked him about the case.

No progress really, just trying one of Jellicoe's mad schemes.

Chen thought: *And the latest game is?*

Some contact in Chinatown of all places.

It comes out when?

Sorry?

Hang on, Mox, Chen thought, *Oliver, I was asking Mox about the latest cerebral.*

Sorry.

Oliver stared out of the window, soon letting Chen and Mox's conversation skip past. Other thoughts intruded.

If he was thinking about eating Chinese, perhaps he should consider the Palatine's new menu.

Hasqueth's Finest for that special taste, so good.

Don't you deserve a special thought this weekend?

Hash Charlie and hash Foxtrot, beer and skittles, now 7:30 today — that's today!

There was a crowd of people across the street when they reached Chinatown and the car slowed right down. People bumping and knocking the car as Chen inched it along. The dashboard warned about pedestrian proximity.

As if I didn't know, Chen thought. *This is ridiculous.*

I'll get out here, Oliver thought.

OK.

Chen thought at the car and the lock clunked. Oliver eased the door open and slipped out into the throng. His going was much easier on foot as he simply let the crowd move him along.

A banging noise started up, drums and cymbals, a clattering noise and then a smattering of distant gunfire.

Panicked, Oliver went around the corner and met an extraordinary spectacle. A huge, angry dragon weaved through the crowd, its majestic face picked out in gold and its long fabric body rippled sinuously above a multitude of feet. The crowd held lanterns above them, and musical instruments competed and added to the cacophony. Another batch of firecrackers went off, showering sparks and causing those nearby to jump, squeal and giggle.

The parade made progress impossible, so Oliver just stopped and enjoyed it, letting the colours and vibrancy wash over him. Once the main feature had turned the corner, the crowd began to move on. Cordite drifted on the breeze, but it was soon replaced by the smells of Chinese cooking.

The Peking Duck was constructed in wood and looked authentic to Oliver's untutored eyes. He climbed a few wooden steps and went inside. It was dark, but there was enough light from the flickering flames for him to see the clientele. They were oriental, which he believed was always a sign of a good Chinese restaurant, and he recognised nothing but Chinese names. They were hunkered down with small bowls and chopsticks, clicking away as they ate.

A waitress, dressed in traditional garb, took a flurry of small steps to approach. "Table for one?"

He recognised Jade as she showed him the restaurant's hashtag on a wooden plaque fixed to the wall. Oliver linked in.

"I'm joining someone," he said. "Er... Za-odi."

"Zhaodi!"

"Zha..."

The knowledge was so clear in his memory, but he realised that he'd never said it aloud.

Zhaodi, he thought at her.

Are you expected?

No.

Please to wait.

She bowed and shuffled off.

So, you get to commit crimes for points, Chen thought.

Thoughts had been chuntering in the background, but it jumped out to Oliver. Oliver tried to ignore it, it was like they were spamming. He flicked through his own collected thoughts: Jasmine's friend was having a party on Saturday, Dartford wanted to know why he'd gone to see Jürgens, the Beer and Skittles was tonight – *it's Friday today!*

Oliver thought at Dartford: *I considered it might be pertinent to the Chedding murder case.*

Dartford's response came straight back: *Why?*

There were thoughts about a Chinese Box.

Did it come to anything?

Oliver glanced around the Peking Duck.

Not yet, he thought.

Let me know if it does.

Jade, the waitress, returned: *Please to follow,* she thought with a bow.

Oliver bowed and accompanied her, trying to modify his longer stride to avoid bumping into her. She took him through the steaming kitchens, full of smells and noise, and then into another eating area. This one had no tables and chairs, and the patrons looked up from the floor suspiciously.

Please to remove shoes, the waitress thought.

Oliver did so, placing them on a rack provided. He felt foolish walking across in his socks with a jacket and tie on.

The waitress took him to the far end where there was an area set aside, raised and demarcated with fancy lattice screens. Oliver was surprised to see an old woman sitting in the alcove on a bench behind a table. Shockingly, despite the obvious close proximity, he didn't recognise her.

"DC Braddon," Oliver said aloud showing her his card. He held it waiting for an acknowledgement thought, but instead the imperious woman waved it away.

"I know who you are," she said. "Sit! Sit!"

"Thank you."

Oliver sat on the bench in front of the table. He still felt tall.

Oliver jumped: the woman had clapped her hands twice, loudly. She was surprisingly quick for such an old person.

"Tea," she said.

Oliver turned round to ask for a coffee, or perhaps a beer if there was no Hasqueth, but the waitress was already hastening away.

I'm drinking tea then, he thought.

When he turned back, he saw that the woman was scrutinising him, tilting her head to one side and frowning as she did so. Oliver noticed with a horror that her forehead didn't crease properly, the familiar faint outline of the iBrow didn't appear. She was one of the thoughtless. This was why he hadn't recognised her. He felt slightly nauseous as if he'd met someone with body odour.

This woman, he thought, *can't know anything about the world, not truly.* Her horizons were limited to what she saw and heard and, maybe, read, but printed matter or ebooks were, by their very nature, out of date. She was living in the past in a very real way. At this moment, she knew only what was in this oriental room and nothing else. She was like someone truly locked up. He felt pity, but he was simultaneously repelled, like seeing someone with a severe disability, and he felt guilty about this.

The tea arrived in a pot on a tray. Also present were two small bowls and a variety of strange implements. The woman took hold of these in a perfunctory way and moved the items around like chess pieces until she was satisfied with the arrangement.

Finally, she poured the tea.

When she nodded at him, Oliver took a sip. It was scalding.

"Madam er... Za-odi–"

"Zhaodi, yes?"

"Inspector Jellicoe sends his regards."

"Does he? He is a friend of yours?"

"Yes."

"In that case, please to tell to him, if I see him again, I shall cut his tongue out and have it fried in sauce."

"…right."

"And as you are his friend, then I shall do what I can for you, but him–"

She motioned with a long nail across her crinkled neck.

Oliver couldn't come up with anything to think, let alone say.

"Your question?"

"Question?"

"Policemen love questions: what happened to this man's watch, what happened to this lady's purse, what was in those bags you flushed down the toilet? And always, always, when they cannot read your mind: what have you got to hide?"

"What have you got to hide?"

"See, I was right, jerk of the knee reaction, prejudice... your question please."

"I'm seeking the Chinese Room."

The woman laughed, "I am also seeking – Zhaodi."

"I'm sorry."

"My name, 'Zhaodi', it means 'seeking little brother'," she said. "It is the sexism, Chinese family always prefer male offspring."

"Ah, the one child policy."

"China was the first nation."

"Yes."

"But even before, men have always preferred male children. Your Spartans exposed their infants on hillside."

"I'm not really a Spartan."

"Women have always been locked away, kept from light. You know this?"

"Yes," said Oliver, without noodling. He'd revised it for his exam. "Sexism, completely wrong."

"Pah," she waved the whole idea away. Oliver saw that her hands were like claws, bent and twisted.

The waitress, Jade, returned, placing a bowl in front of each of them and a woven basket with a lid in the middle of the table. She bowed to the old woman and retreated.

"Help yourself," the woman said.

Oliver opened the basket and saw a variety of strange morsels on a bed of steaming string.

"What's this?" he asked.

The woman laughed, more a cackle, and pointed to her forehead: "Noodle, noodle."

"Oh, I see."

Oliver struggled, but managed to extract some noodles and various pieces of meat and vegetable. As he did so, he noodled the restaurant's menu and was relieved to remember that everything seemed to be made of conventional animals.

The woman took her own chopsticks and quickly filled her bowl. She ate without slurping, something Oliver's experiment didn't achieve. He'd been to Chinese restaurants before and he'd used chopsticks, even considered himself an expert, but this woman made him feel naïve and clumsy.

"Why should I help you?"

"It's your duty."

"You are policeman. You affect business."

"I'm not on the drugs squad."

"Drugs, we no do drugs."

"Of course," said Oliver. *Likely story*, he thought.

"Counterfeit goods. Good quality. No rubbish. You want. I give you sample."

"Er... no, best not. It would be corrupt."

"Suit yourself."

"So, will you?"

The woman considered, again her forehead betraying her. Oliver tried to smile and somehow convey trustworthiness, but he felt his face was letting him down. Without thought, he was as inept as he was without a knife and fork.

"I help you because they take our business: racketeering."

"Who are they?"

"We don't know. Maybe Westbourne, maybe Westbourne's son, maybe another."

"How can they operate without their thoughts giving them away?"

"We know not. Perhaps they have brainless wonders too." She tapped her own forehead. "How would I know? I am not cyborg."

"Your business is smuggling using thoughtless... I mean, disconnected people."

"Yes, humans come to docks, humans move to market, humans sell to cyborgs, police arrest, make line-up parade, cyborgs think we all look alike."

Oliver smiled: she was right, and, of course, it just wasn't worth the effort to investigate a few copyright infringements once you reached the end of the thought trail. There were budgetary considerations too. These 'humans', as she called them, were always treated with suspicion. Why be disconnected unless you had something to hide? The police were always accused of being unfair when they arrested the thoughtless, but statistically those without brows were always criminal. Pretty much.

And they did all look alike: without the recognition between brows, how could you know who someone was? Facial features were notoriously difficult to fathom.

"These people, maybe Westbourne as you say," Oliver said. "They're involved in white collar crime."

"Someone found a way around Thought Police?"

"We're not... possibly."

"You think it us?"

"Yes, there's a Chinese connection."

"This room?"

"Where they meet, we assume," Oliver said, nodding. "Probably a way of shielding their thoughts."

That doesn't make sense, Oliver thought. There were a few black spots here and there, like the morgue, but they'd still think about their plans once they were in the open and connected. A Faraday cage wouldn't be a permanent solution and there must be some risk building something that illegal.

And Chinese Whispers, he thought; *if they were protected why would talking quietly make any difference? Perhaps they feared old fashioned surveillance bugs. Did they even have any of those in the police station's storeroom anymore?*

"I have heard of this room," she said. "A whisper here, a whisper there."

"Chinese Whispers?"

She laughed, a grating sound.

"This Chinese Room," she said. "Not here."

"But where in Chinatown?"

"Not in Chinatown," she said. "Not here."

"I'm sorry?"

"It's not in Chinatown. I know all that goes on in whole district. Room not here."

"Where then?"

She shrugged, throwing her hands wide as if she was preparing to pounce. "Who can say?"

"You can't then?"

"It is new."

"New?"

"As in 'not old'."

Not an old room, a new room, he thought.

"You think that to remember it."

"Sorry?"

"Your eyes, they look far away," she said. "You have so many thoughts, I wonder if you lost in them."

"I am my thoughts."

"Then you are not you."

"That sounds like a saying."

"Do you know Chinese proverb?"

Oliver noodled: he remembered many, many Chinese proverbs.

"Which one?"

"He who eats Chinese food wants Chinese food in half an hour, but he who owns Chinese restaurant always eats Chinese food."

"I'd not heard that," Oliver said politely. He knew he'd got all he was going to get and thought it best to leave. He just wasn't sure how to excuse himself.

The woman, Zhaodi, cackled, "I thought cyborgs know everything."

Jade, the waitress, appeared at his shoulder, bowing. She held out his shoes for him to take. "It is best," she said.

Oliver was thrown by her comment.

The waitress smiled patiently: "You thought it best."

She'd been following him. Oliver scanned back through his own thoughts and realised that he had thought it best to leave.

Oliver stood and bowed awkwardly to the old lady: "Thank you."

The waitress showed him out, pausing only for him to bend and clumsily put on his shoes.

Outside it was the usual bustle of this quarter, the celebration long gone.

"Now what?" he said, loudly. *I need a drink*, he thought.

He set off randomly with a nagging sense that he was being followed. *What a stupid thing to think*, he thought, *of course I'm being followed.* There were any number of followers tuned into his thoughts.

I am, thought Mithering.

There you go.

He found a bar and ordered a lager.

People who bought this lager also bought peanuts.

Write it down, Jellicoe had said.

Mithering questioned this: *Write what down?*

Anything, Oliver thought, *clues.*

Good idea, Mithering thought, *go through the facts.*

The lager arrived. *Hello lager, glad to meet you.* The first sip was refreshing.

"Paper?" he asked the barmaid as she passed.

Paper?

"Please."

She wrinkled her nose at the idea and then ambled off looking up and down. When she returned with a pad of A5, Oliver's pint was finished.

This do?

"That's fine," said Oliver, "and another please."

Oliver leant towards the till and waited for the buzz before reckoning with his bank.

"Is there somewhere quiet?" he asked.

You could try round the back.

Round the back consisted of a cluster of awkward spaces with tables and chairs. Oliver picked the most private and settled down. He put the pad down. He actually rubbed the paper with his index finger before he realised.

Back at the bar: "Pen please?"

Pen?

"Please."

The barmaid went off, looking up and down again, and she came back with a shrug.

What a waste of time, he thought, *and the second time I've forgotten a pen. Wait!*

He'd kept the pen from his Sergeant's Exam. Yes, still tucked in his jacket pocket.

"It's all right," he said.

Back at his table, he did a few swirls to check that the pen still worked. The second pint arrived and a gulp later his iBrow closed down. Thank goodness for the safety:

you wouldn't want to irritate everyone with your alcoholic ramblings.

Write it down, Jellicoe had said.

Go through the facts, Mithering had thought.

There didn't seem to be that many: body, scalped, not on the missing list... and that was it. There were facts and 'information', the latter being 'facts with meaning', which was, in other words, motive. Oliver doodled on the page trying to rearrange... but it was written in biro: permanent, set, unchanging. How you were supposed to reorganise these written imitations of thoughts, he wondered. There was the classic triumvirate of detection: motive, opportunity and method. He wrote the words down. Method and opportunity always seemed linked, part of the same action, which left motive as the most promising option. He underlined it, and then twice more.

Why?

Usually the police just noodled for a thought associated with an event and that was the motive, and then, having caught the suspect, they asked when and how.

There were other questions too: he noodled and remembered Rudyard Kipling's six honest serving men: what, why, when, how, where and who. He made a new list and then next to each wrote: murder, unknown, one month ago, violently, Chedding car park or elsewhere and, finally, unknown. After a moment he added '271'. After a moment's consideration, he changed 'who' to 'whom' and added 'who'. He tapped his pen there, stabbing the place where the name of the murderer should be.

This was 'thinking without thinking' with the actual cognition being on the page, or rather in his head and on the page. But somehow it bypassed the iBrow. The words were no longer words, something that the technology could grab and transmit, but were pictorial enough to pass back to the hind brain. It enabled his unconscious mind to reveal itself to be... completely stumped.

What did he know about murderers in general?

He started a list.

They always asked for their lawyers. They tended to act on impulse in the heat of the moment. A large number of them had body odour. Their thoughts were full of self-justification. They had drinking problems. He was getting a drinking problem.

He took a sip.

Pre-meditated murders were unknown.

Hot-blooded killers' thoughts were always full of swear words afterwards.

Murderers always returned to the scene of the crime.

Oliver noodled those who had been to Chedding car park. Top of the list was Detective Constable Oliver Braddon, then various police, crime scene investigators and the mechanics who'd towed the car away.

But the murder had been elsewhere: where? The Chinese Room, somewhere new? This murder, the method, was new.

Did he murder her as the conspiracy theorists kept suggesting?

He had been at the second murder in the police station.

Was he part of a conspiracy?

His hand felt cramped, just as it had in the exam, but he ignored it.

Could a policeman really have killed Jürgens?

Oliver started to list suspects: Draith, Chen, Mox, Freya, Oliver... Mike, Zack, Nancy, Rose, Tim, Tim Too; but he stopped.

None of them could have done it, because the murder was impossible. And yet it had been done.

Someone else perhaps?

Who else has showed an interest?

Go through the facts, Mithering had thought.

Mithering.

She had shown an interest.

Oliver wrote 'Mithering' down.

Jellicoe used paper: was he turning into Jellicoe? Oliver dismissed the idea; after all, they had nothing in common.

Oliver finished his drink and then set off to find transport back to Jellicoe's. He noodled the area of his apartment, but the advice was still to keep away. There were protests at the police station too now. He was going to become a pariah unable to go to his place of work, unable to see family and friends, and under suspicion of murder.

At least he got to drink a lot to avoid giving away his location. Perhaps he could claim it as a justifiable expense?

Back to Jellicoe's then.

He couldn't think for a cab.

On the way home, Oliver bought a charger for his iBrow, and in the busier part of town hailed a cab that was dropping someone off. He was back at Jellicoe's, wondering how to get in, when the Inspector himself arrived.

Chen waved from the car as he pulled away.

Jellicoe opened the door. "I can smell drink on your breath."

"Chinatown."

"What did you learn?" Jellicoe asked. "No, let me guess. Nothing, because you couldn't think."

Oliver handed over his notes.

"I'm impressed," said Jellicoe, he glanced down them as he dropped his keys in a bowl. "Lots of questions, few answers."

"It's a start."

"Indeed it is – we'll make a detective of you yet."

"We need some more data," said Oliver.

"Take-away?"

"All right."

"Chinese?"

"Indian."

"One of us will have to sober up."

"Half an hour," said Oliver, guessing. He noodled: two pints, five units, *when had I stopped drinking? Ah!*

"What would you like?"

"Chicken tikka masala, plain naan, those crisps."

Oliver noodled an Indian take-away and ordered for both of them, reckoning with his bank. They were eligible for a free starter, so he added onion bhajis. There was a hashtag to follow.

"It's not data you want, it's knowledge," Jellicoe said. "Everyone has infinite data, or it may as well be, but knowledge? Lager with Indian, I think. It's the difference between knowing and understanding, between being a cop and a detective. You're only as smart as your own brain."

It's knowing what to noodle, Oliver thought.

"I'm not sure you're following me."

You told me not to follow you.

"Very funny."

"Look," Oliver said, "we know everything there is to know, instantly. That's progress." *I'm too tired for this.*

"Human progress stopped when the like-button appeared on peer reviewed papers."

Ha!

The take-away chef intruded: *Would you like extra onions?*

Yes.

"Drink?"

"Lager."

And coriander?

Yes.

Cooking now... pass me the other oil.

"I've got beer."

"Fine."

They both got in each other's way in the kitchen and set the table for the forthcoming feast. They took their time, Oliver followed the progress via Noodle as the meals were cooked, packed, and Sanjeev was told that, yes, he had to go out again straight away, and finally it was at the door.

They sat and ate in silence for a while.

Is the meal to your satisfaction?

Yes, thanks.

Oliver liked the Indian take-away and then stopped following it.

The beer was light, hoppy, and the food was delicious.

"It's a long time since I've had a meal with someone," Jellicoe said.

"It's not a date."

"I remember before thought."

"Really?"

"We had this... dream that women thought about us all the time. After all, we thought about women every fifteen seconds."

"Sex every fifteen seconds."

"And then thought came along and lo! Imagine discovering that your fiancée spent the whole day thinking about Nietzsche and not about you. Nietzsche, I mean, honestly."

"What doesn't kill you makes you stronger."

"But women," Jellicoe pointed with a piece of poppadum in his hand, "they shouldn't think about that unpleasant nonsense."

"That's not very politically correct."

"Nowadays they only think about shoes and fashion and the latest celebrity gossip."

"That's what everyone thinks about nowadays."

Jellicoe looked at him and frowned, his iBrow visible for a moment, and then he took a long swig of his beer.

"Do you drink to forget?" Oliver asked.

"I drink to not think in the first place."

"Hmm."

Oliver drank too.

"Do you think it's progress?"

"Of course," Oliver said. "Less fingers."

"Eh?"

"We used to have keyboards, ten fingers—"

"Two fingers."

"Two fingers, then phones with two thumbs."

"Social media," said Jellicoe and he made a thumbs-up sign.

"Exactly, one thumb," Oliver acknowledged. "And finally, we 'think', which is a hands-off experience."

"We used to invent things too."

"We don't need things."

"You mean 'it's all in the head'."

"We do invent things: thought allowed much more effective crowd sourcing."

"Like what?"

"The iBrow series 6."

Jellicoe snorted.

"There are thapps for all sorts of things."

"We've not gone to the stars or solved climate change or cured cancer," said Jellicoe, and then he went quiet.

They finished their meal and their beer.

Oliver dropped out of thinking and then back in again.

"I must go," said Jellicoe. He picked up his coat and scooped his keys from a bowl in the hallway.

"You're in no fit state to drive," Oliver said.

Jellicoe dangled the keys: "Old car, doesn't need thought."

"I mean... give it here, I'll drive you."

Jellicoe pondered this, and Oliver thought he was going to say 'no'.

No to what, Mithering thought.

Never you mind.

But Jellicoe nodded and flung the keys over to him. Oliver caught them in one hand and out they went into the cold drizzle of the night. It was an old car, hidden in a garage that Jellicoe opened manually, and Oliver had to adjust the seat.

"Not too much," said Jellicoe. "Pain to put back."

The dashboard was confusing with displays in strange places. There was even an inbuilt sat nav, which proved it was a genuine classic, and it wasn't just electric, but an electric-petrol hybrid. *What'll he do when the tank's dry?* Oliver shunted the car out and Jellicoe closed the garage behind them. Once he was settled, Oliver put it into drive again and lurched forward.

"Careful!"

"Where to?"

"Right."

As they drove though the dark streets, Jellicoe became morose, his occasional 'left', 'right' and 'straight on' more and more terse. Finally, they pulled into the driveway of a Rest Home.

"This it?"

"Visitors park there," Jellicoe said, pointing. "I won't be long."

Jellicoe slammed the door, turned up his collar and ambled across the pavement and into the main entrance. Oliver could see him greeting a friendly looking nurse at the reception desk, a tiny illuminated scene in all the darkness, and then the two of figures went as if off-stage.

Oliver went through some recent thoughts, reviewing comments from Chen, Jasmine and Mithering in particular, but his heart wasn't in it. It was cold, and he realised he had the keys. It wouldn't do any harm to wait indoors.

The drizzle was something of a shock as he got out and fumbled to lock the door. He ran over and found the main entrance closed. He searched for a buzzer and saw a woman waving at him. She was gesticulating downwards, and Oliver saw the intercom.

"Hello... I'm with Jellicoe," he said.

The door buzzed.

He went in, gratefully and shook some of the rain off.

"Mister Oliver Jellicoe," said the woman. Oliver recognised her as Sharon.

"No, I'm... police," said Oliver.

"Sorry, Inspector Jellicoe."

"No."

"This way."

Although he was in range and she must have recognised him, she wasn't following him properly. He realised that he hadn't followed her either, not wanting to clutter his mind up with irrelevant people. He felt guilty about that. The woman, Sharon, led the way, her hips swinging as she went, and Oliver had little choice but to follow her. They padded along a rich carpet, turning abruptly at various intersections, until they reached a door. Probably in a rest home, she had to deal with a lot of Unbrows or people with Series 3s.

"She's in here," Sharon said. She turned and walked past him back the way they had come. The door just had a number on it, '21', and no hint of its purpose.

Oliver, not knowing what else to do, went in.

Jellicoe's face jumped into his view, almost hitting him. The man practically spat in Oliver's face: "Get out!"

Oliver held up his arms. "Sharon... the woman said... I... sorry."

Oliver turned and made his way down the corridor, certain he was going the wrong way, but he wasn't going to turn round, except–

"Oi!"

"Yes."

"You better come in."

Jellicoe held the door open and despite himself, Oliver went back and inside.

It was dark, strangely lit with a child's night-light plugged into the wall just above the skirting board, and in the middle was a large bed, the focus of a bewildering array of medical equipment. A large bellows huffed and then hissed, and lights blinked to say all was well. With a shock, Oliver realised that there was someone in the bed, a woman, thin and emaciated, dwarfed by the paraphernalia around her.

"Er..."

"My wife, Pamela."

Oliver nodded.

Pamela breathed again with a loud huff and a gradual, mechanical hiss.

Jellicoe moved past him and stood by the bed, looking down tenderly.

Oliver wasn't sure what to do or say. His arms seemed suddenly superfluous; he went to fold them in front, but then he put them behind him.

"Do we talk to her?" Oliver asked, painfully aware that he had directed this to Jellicoe and had ignored his wife.

"No," said Jellicoe. "We know she can't hear us."

"Oh."

The machine huffed again on its next cycle.

"I can hear her thoughts," said Jellicoe. He put his hand on her forehead as if he was taking her temperature. "Back in the day, they'd have declared her in a vegetative state and switched off the machine. These days, we're more... enlightened."

The breathing machine huffed, its beat as regular as digital clockwork.

"Perhaps she knows your thoughts?"

"No," said Jellicoe, "and I wouldn't want her to know my thoughts."

Oliver stepped forward, around life support equipment, and recognised Pammie. It was a shock, she was suddenly there as the brow-to-brow signal was no longer screened by the machinery's EM shielding. With a creeping horror, he couldn't resist and followed her.

House, thought Pammie, *house, house... Ollie... have we met... hello... house.*

Oliver stepped back: *Jeez!*

Jeez... gee... gee... two lines, thirty-five.

Oliver unfollowed, revolted that his own thoughts were still flowing into her and affecting her, but unable to stop it. Clearly her brow was set to follow anyone it recognised, and she was too far gone to change that. He could step back, hide behind the machine, but he didn't want Jellicoe to know he'd been in her head. It was an invasion. So, trapped, he stood for a long time, the huff and hiss puncturing any peace. The room was claustrophobic. Here was a woman, whose mind had gone, and yet her body breathed and her thoughts drifted into the heads of those nearby.

"I'll..." Oliver suggested.

"Thank you."

Oliver waited a few paces down the corridor, glad to be out of the antiseptic smell, but most of all away from Pammie. He felt tired, unable to form his own thoughts properly and afraid that everyone who followed him would know, but there was nothing he could do about that.

Presently, Jellicoe came out.

"Let's go," he said, and they moved off down the corridor, soon in step like soldiers. At reception, Oliver held back while Jellicoe talked to the nurse.

The rain was worse, and they dashed across to the car.

Once they were safely inside, steaming slightly, Oliver started the vehicle. The windscreen wipers thwacked across the screen – swish-swash – and for a moment Oliver was reminded of the breathing machine.

"She's asleep," he said, "not suffering, I mean. That must be a comfort."

"If she was asleep, she wouldn't think," Jellicoe said, his voice flat. "It's not a coma, it's Calton's Disease, a type of locked-in syndrome."

"What does she think about?" he asked, regretting it immediately.

"Bingo."

"I... what?"

"It's what she followed," Jellicoe said, matter-of-factly, "and now she doesn't have the mental faculties to turn it off. Her thoughts are all numbers."

Oliver felt physically ill: the swish-swash now bringing up the image of Doctor Ridge mopping the floor in the morgue.

"I could do with a drink," Oliver said.

"There's a pub on the corner of the road."

Oliver knew the way back to Pelton, so the return journey seemed much quicker, and they soon pulled into Jellicoe's driveway. The headlights illuminated the garage door and its combination lock.

"Just leave it here," said Jellicoe. "It needs a wash."

They walked together in the rain, somehow content to have it wash them too. They were quite soaked when they reached the Oak: its interior such a relief. There were plenty of people there, but of course it was completely quiet as everyone sat rapt in the thoughts of others; except for the regulars, who had to talk, but had no-one to talk to.

Oliver looked for the hashtag.

"Two pints," said Jellicoe, loudly.

As the landlord poured, Jellicoe stared at the till machine as if he was hypnotising it as well as reckoning with his bank. When they reached the bar, there was the usual flash of recognition, but somehow it passed Oliver by.

The beer was frothy, dark, warm and very welcome, much like the surroundings. They found somewhere to sit. Oliver could feel the rainwater seeping from his clothing and soaking into the padded seat.

"I'm sorry," he said eventually.

"Thank you."

"Has she... long?"

"Three years, two months... I could noodle the days."

"And–"

"I'd rather not talk about it."

They drank for a while and once it was clear that they'd be needing another soon, Oliver caught the landlord's eye. He held up two fingers and the man nodded.

"I guess this explains your devotion to duty and the drinking."

"I'd rather not talk about it."

Two more pints arrived. Oliver eased himself out to go and pay, but the landlord shook his head. "When you are ready," he said.

"Thanks," said Oliver. "I'll think to you when we're done."

"You're already too pissed to do that," said the Landlord, but in a friendly, jovial manner.

They drank until they could pour the dregs into the settled head of the new pint.

"I don't."

Oliver was surprised: "Sorry?"

"I don't drink to forget or any such nonsense."

"No, of course not," said Oliver automatically.

"It's to stop eavesdroppers."

"Your thoughts are your own."

"I'm no activist in the anti-cyber league."

"No."

"But it would be good to have an off button."

"We do. Don't we?" Oliver noodled. "We do."

"Do you use it?"

"No."

"Can you use it?" Jellicoe asked.

There had been a moment in the morgue with Doctor Ridge, when Oliver had discovered, or perhaps 'rediscovered' because it must have been covered in his initial induction, how to edit and delete his thoughts. It had not been, however, natural. It was normal to be part of the crowd, to belong: humans were social networking animals after all. To be alone was a status no one wanted. Here, and for the last few days, Oliver seemed to be occupying a twilight zone. But to switch it off, to actually deliberately disconnect, would be like rejecting all his friends, and deciding to be Unbrow would make him 'not human', despite what Zhaodi had said about her sort. Just as early hominids hadn't consciousness, so those a scant two generations ago were thoughtless.

"No," Oliver admitted finally. "Just unfollowing all my friends for the Sergeant's Exam was hard enough. That was what, an hour... less."

"Some have tried," said Jellicoe. "Some even managed twenty-four hours, but they go twitchy and turn it back on. I remember... one drug addict didn't want his rehab buddy finding out he'd taken amphetamines. He was a screaming wreck when they brought him into the station. Couldn't think at all. It took four officers to subdue him and he was tranquillised before they carted him off to the funny farm."

"Really?"

"Thought he'd been turned into a zombie."

Oliver lolled.

Jellicoe didn't: "In a way, he had."

"Not being able to think must be like going blind or deaf."

"Worse."

"You disagree with the technology."

"Do you?"

"Of course not," Oliver replied. "It was a big change, but we adapted. And we'll adapt to whatever the next change is."

"You think?"

"Of course: industrial revolution, global village, brow technology; it's all part of a trend."

Oliver was certain that nine tenths of what he was saying was the drink talking, but it was what he believed.

"There used to be lots of changes," said Jellicoe. "The latest this, the brand new that, the next big thing – not now."

"It's settled down. We've reached a plateau, that's all. Bound to happen. Technology can't advance indefinitely."

"Everyone spends all their time rethinking others' thoughts." Jellicoe stabbed his finger onto the table top.

"No-one has original thoughts. It's all 'share my cuddly thoughts about my cat' or 'here's a funny thought' or—"

"There are important thoughts too."

"And if that's not enough you can join a cerebral and have 'special' thoughts and be famous. And even own a celebrity cat."

"Oh come on."

"So much time is spent socialising that no-one does anything anymore."

"That's not true."

"No?"

"No."

Jellicoe squeaked his finger around and then supped his beer. "We're the only two people here who are actually communicating with each other."

Oliver looked around: no-one was alone, every table had groups of two, three or more, but everyone had that vacant look, their faces aglow with that apparent inattention that came with scanning the Thinkersphere. So many people were clambering into his own head, despite the cull due to the non-Noodle exam, that he found his attention wavering from the here-and-now: Freya was arguing with her husband, Parker complaining about orange juice again, Adams and Melissa making love, etc., etc., etc.

But it wasn't all mindless, surely?

He didn't deliberately think about, say, his breakfast.

"I have original thoughts," Oliver insisted.

"Do you?"

"Yes."

"And you know a lot."

"Yes."

He did too, of course he did.

Oliver thought, and he received a sharp pain as his iBrow reminded him that he'd had too much. He was drunk. Again.

But it was a brave new world, certainly; there were now so many thoughts, the sum of human knowledge was vast, beyond even the previous generation's wildest imagining, and available straight to your frontal lobe. Noodle and there it was. Anything. Everything. Information that enabled you to do whatever you wanted. Someone having an idea in Australia, there it was in your memory before you even knew you wanted it. The latest musing of the philosophers in Italy, summed up and presented in your own language. A happening in the States, you could be there in mind. The latest offers from Brazil. A flash event in your own neighbourhood. All without any effort. It was all as wonderful as, say, Hasqueth's Finest. So good. And, yes, thoughts about cats. So much, and much more, more than anyone could need in a lifetime.

"It is kind of true," Jellicoe said.

Oliver could only nod in agreement.

SATURDAY

Jellicoe wore the same clothing despite it being the weekend. They were both technically off-shift, but the day started in exactly the same way. Oliver had wanted to lie-in, but he'd woken at his usual time, despite the lack of alarm thought. He'd tried closing his eyes, but the curtains in the spare room of Jellicoe's house were thin and old, so the light streamed through. He got up, showered and went downstairs.

Jellicoe had made him a coffee: it was far too strong. He wanted a Hasqueth Finest – so good – and they also did it with cinnamon and there was a deep roasted special. Seventeen of his friends liked it, which reminded him to increase the number of people he followed. It was still reclusively low.

"Is it hot or cold?" Jellicoe asked.

It's warm enough.

"The murder – hot or cold blood?"

I don't know.

"Come on, talk."

"I don't know." *And I don't care.*

Despite it being own brand and bargain basement, the coffee started to bring him round.

"Most modern murders are hot blooded," Jellicoe said, shuffling to the toaster. "Someone loses it, emotions run away with them. Easy to read, murderous emotions – the ones that end in three exclamation marks. You know how we perceive emotions?"

"Hashtags, emoticons."

"Come on!"

"You just feel it."

"In others?"

"The... you know, emotions, that part of the thought message that transmits emotions. And I suppose there's technically facial expression, body language, emoticons, tone of voice..."

"Emoticons are the thought-based method, they're the punctuation and codes that represent things."

"I went to school."

"Well, do you perceive smiling as I do? Bear with me, you have a thought and it becomes whatever the code is – right? But, although your code and mine may be the same, and we describe the feeling in the same way – is it? Is your 'happiness', just my 'contentment'?"

I can't imagine you being happy.

"Answer the question."

It's obviously–

"Aloud."

I'm trying to drink my coffee here... "It's obviously, er... clearer than when we only had spoken language," said Oliver, aware that he was trying to drink and talk at the same time. "We don't have telepathy, but it's as good as."

"What about emotions that don't have words, but do have codes."

"Eh?"

"There are some codes, weird punctuation, that are common to an awful lot of people. They are part of the zeitgeist – awful word – and no-one knows what they mean."

"Surely–"

"They aren't part of the original brow specification."

"Surely," Oliver insisted, "they are simply developments like the invention of new words, street slang, that sort of thing."

"Yes, but they aren't written down."

"This isn't another of those virus junk thought theories, is it?"

"Could be, could be."

"It's nonsense, 'thoughts going from head-to-head without meaning anything', just nonsense. Anyway, it's never been proved."

"There are thoughts that they've extracted and read," said Jellicoe, "and they've codes that make no sense."

"No sense written down, but read by an iBrow and transferred to your brain, then it is... er... what's the word?"

"Interpreted."

"Exactly. And communication has been made."

"But what if one thought is cross-wired with another: someone has a murderous emotion, but their iBrow interprets it as... wanting toast."

Oliver needed more stimulant and busied himself making another coffee. Jellicoe put some toast on a plate and plonked it in the middle of the table. Oliver took a slice and spread some margarine on it. There was a choice of marmalade and what looked like home-made jam. He tried the marmalade and it tasted all right.

"Well?" said Jellicoe.

Oliver mumbled until he'd swallowed: *Why did he always want to use spoken language?*

"Because?"

"Such a person wouldn't be able to function, they'd be locked up."

"There are plenty of people with psychological problems," said Jellicoe.

"You've only got to look round the station to see sociopaths and borderline psychotics," said Oliver. *And maybe worse.*

"And there's the police as well," said Jellicoe.

"I meant the police." *Do I? Was Jürgens killed by one of us?*

"There are miscommunications in thought."

"Hardly... some," Oliver considered for a moment. "There are always glitches, emergent behaviour... so what?"

"And the unintended consequences?"

"Brow technology has been around for–" Oliver had to noodle, "fifty years, stable and error free–"

"Error free?"

"Electrical damage, physical shocks, brain tumours, some chemicals... scar tissue build up in the frontal lobe, but they are all external forces."

"A brain tumour isn't external."

"You know what I mean, external to the... er... not part of the technology."

Jellicoe sat down. "Too many iBrow issues and the person can't function..."

"Funny farm and a refit."

"Or minor glitches–"

"As we all have, but you couldn't murder someone without something leaking out, thinking about..." Oliver waved his toast to illustrate the point, "say, 'toast' instead or not."

"Yes, it was a theory."

Oliver relented: "Best one so far."

"Cold blooded then."

"How the hell would anyone walk around, bump into people, be recognised, without their whole plan leaking?"

"Unless you were thoughtless," said Jellicoe. "The one-eyed man in the valley of the blind."

"And thus monitored and watched with suspicion by everyone who passes them on the street. Anyone in a suit worried about work, we ignore; but, boy, do we remember

– witness – the tramps and the rare unthinking. Why do you think they're all living in ghettos?"

"So, it's not the one-eyed man, but the blind person in the valley of the overburdened with eyes," said Jellicoe. "I'm just trying to find a hawk."

"A hawk?"

"The one-eyed man in the valley is a hawk," Jellicoe explained. "He preys upon the blind. The hawks and the doves is a metaphor for competition and co-operation."

Oliver noodled and then said, "Ah, yes, lots of hawks too much fighting, so they all starve. Lots of doves, lots of co-operation, everyone does the best, but a single hawk amongst doves does better and so prospers. We're a social species, we work together, the dove strategy, but there's always a hawk popping up."

"Hence the police," said Jellicoe. "We enforce dove behaviour."

"Hmmm..."

"With iBrows to let us look into people's minds."

"Social networking came first."

"Yes," Jellicoe agreed. "All those people posting... no, boasting about their crimes. With pictures too. It was a golden age for detection and the start of the trend to give away all our rights to privacy."

"We have rights to privacy," Oliver countered. "Legal rights."

"They aren't enforceable. The right to silence, for example, is useless when you are haemorrhaging information with your thoughts. If you couldn't read and write, you couldn't send letters; no phone means no phone business, no email, no fax, no... you know, all that stuff you studied in school. If you can't think in this society, then you can't bank, hail a cab, order a take-away delivery, do the lottery, so you become an unperson."

"A zombie... sub-human."

"Traditionally we humans haven't treated those we consider sub-human very well. Wait..."

Jellicoe paused, clearly receiving some thoughts from someone and then he tilted his head.

So he does use Noodle, Oliver realised.

Finally, Jellicoe spoke, "They've found another body."

Oliver had time to check he had everything and flip his iBrow settings to a weekday, so that he was following the Desk Sergeant and the police hashtags. Chen arrived in the car and quickly whisked them back towards the city.

Ollie, where were you last night?

Oliver thought back: *Last night?*

Beer and skittles.

That was last night?

Yes.

Shit, sorry.

They arrived at the police station and checked in: Sergeant Draith looked at Oliver suspiciously as they made their way to the morgue. Oliver glanced along Draith's recent thoughts: he really resented Inspector Dartford's investigations. No-one liked the idea that the any of them had killed Jürgens. And why? It had been a good collar.

Jellicoe hadn't explained anything and didn't even talk until the cold clammy atmosphere had enveloped Oliver again. The world drifting away until there was only Oliver, Jellicoe and Doctor Ridge.

Oliver felt like he was about to take another exam.

"Ridge," said Jellicoe.

"Inspector."

This was going to be so thrilling if they speak one word at a time... oh...

Oliver started going through the poke-and-delete routine, and then gave up.

"This is a cold place," said Jellicoe.

"Lacks the warmth of human contact," said Doctor Ridge.

You two are playing some damn silly game, but via recognition only. *Oh... ow!*

"Number twenty," said Doctor Ridge, going to the drawers. He pulled one out to reveal a body shape hidden under a shroud. "Scalped."

"Can we take your word for it?" Oliver asked.

"Of course." *Oh, it's newbie. One of yours, Jelly?*

"Yes," said Jellicoe. He lifted the corner of the sheet to look at the body.

"Scalped, like Unknown 271, you're going to get copycat killings."

"Cyborg Serial Killer," said Oliver.

I remember that; saw it as a kid, Ridge thought, brow-to-brow, *dreadful.*

"Any identification?"

Ridge shook his head.

"Series 5?"

"Yes... this bloke, Unknown 271 and about three billion other people."

Three billion was a vague total, but then Noodle didn't reach into the morgue.

"This one won't be thinking again," said Jellicoe. He didn't seem bothered by the corpse's appearance.

"He still has his frontal lobe, parietal lobe, occipital lobe and so forth," Doctor Ridge replied. "It's only the brow that's gone."

"No, I mean, he's dead."

"Ah. That."

"I'd have thought a Doctor of your reputation would have noticed that."

"Is it one of those other lobes that's responsible for the unconscious?" Oliver asked.

"The reptile brain," said Jellicoe. "It's what gives a detective their intuition, we think with our gut."

"Anatomy's not your strong point, is it?" said Doctor Ridge. "The Inspector is right though, the cerebellum evolved by adding functionality to the front, layers if you like from the first node at the top of the spine and on forwards." Doctor Ridge moved his hand in jerks from the back of his head to the front. "The frontal lobe being the seat of consciousness."

"And then the clever dicks added another layer at the front," said Jellicoe. "Only this one was cybernetic."

Oliver realised where this was going: "The iBrow."

"That's the devil," said Jellicoe.

"Brow technology is a force for good: we're a social animal and social networking means we can be in touch with anyone, anywhere, anytime."

Jellicoe snorted in derision.

"And police work," said Oliver, "once thoughts were admissible in court, then crime dropped to its present low level and premeditated crime became a thing of the past."

"Not in this case."

"One exception then."

"Two," said Jellicoe.

"Three," said Doctor Ridge. They looked at him. "Three exceptions," he repeated.

Oliver went over to the drawers.

"It's not here," said Ridge. "There was another body found that had been scalped, six months ago, and never identified."

"What happened?" Oliver asked. If only he could noodle down here.

"Cremated," said Ridge.

"Cremated!? But it was evidence."

"It wasn't considered a crime."

"What?"

"No victim, no crime."

"No victim..." *Oh, come on.*

"That's the way the bean counters had it."

"The perfect crime," Jellicoe said. "No-one's missing, so no missing person's case; a corpse, but no identification, therefore no official victim."

Oliver was shocked: *Someone's murdered three people and got away with it.*

"Three here," said Doctor Ridge. "There are other morgues."

"Jeez." *This is supposed to be impossible.*

"Because thought gives people away," said Ridge.

"Social media allows everyone to keep tabs on everyone else, so..." *Oh, you know.*

"Like the whites of the eyes," said Doctor Ridge.

"Eyes?"

"All animals have black eyes," Ridge explained. "The sclera, the white of the eye, exists only in humans. It's not even in other primates. We're the only creatures that give away where we're looking. There's an evolutionary advantage to know what your fellow tribesmen are thinking."

"And all the ticks and jerks and furtive looks when people are lying," Jellicoe added. "Dove behaviour."

Oliver realised that Jellicoe had mentioned this before, but verbally, so Oliver couldn't track back to remind himself of what had been said.

"Exactly..." Ridge agreed, and then he saw Oliver's confused expression. "Before thought, you could tell if someone was lying by their body language."

"Wouldn't it be easier just to noodle their thoughts... ah, before thought, sorry."

"We've finally achieved the perfect transparent society," said Ridge.

"The land of the doves," Jellicoe added. "There have always been hawks and doves. We catch hawks for the doves. We weed out those who aren't right in the head and ensure that the country is nothing but doves."

"Or thoughtless immigrants."

"They stay put."

Oliver thought about Carl Jürgens, a man who hadn't 'done' anything. Not that many decades ago, he realised, they wouldn't have even considered him guilty of a crime. Stalking had been against the law, but what was the iBrow if it wasn't a stalking machine.

"So..." said Oliver, figuring it out, "these deaths are examples of hawk behaviour, someone's figured out how to hunt in dove land."

"Yes, and some hawk has been very busy here," said Jellicoe, pointing to the bodies.

"Jürgens was killed... differently," Oliver said. "He's... dead. I mean, registered as not thinking, whereas this man and Unknown 271 aren't missing."

"Well, that's your department," said Doctor Ridge and he pushed the drawer shut with a loud clang. "Check your iBrow buffers before you leave."

Oliver spent time deleting thoughts, and then had to delete a thought about deleting.

He nodded to Jellicoe and they walked down the corridor into the hustle and bustle of the thinking world. In amongst the mess was a directive to think at Freya.

At the Sergeant's desk there was a kerfuffle. Draith was trying to process a suspect brought in by Mox. She was struggling.

Fascists, fascists, fucking thought police, she was thinking.

Oliver recognized her as Martha_556. *Thank goodness we've finally got her.*

You! Yes, you – Oliver Braddon, you're the Tepee bastard who murdered that woman in Chedding car park.

Oh please, Oliver thought back.

See, see, it's all a conspiracy.

Oliver ignored her: *I'm not... you're mad. Where's your foil hat?*

We'll get you, we'll get you.

Others liked this idea.

Oliver went around the corner with Jellicoe, trying to distance himself from the woman, which was of course, impossible. He had other things to worry about.

At Ollie.

That's ominous. Oliver thought back to the Chief Superintendent: *At Freya?*

I'm afraid I have some bad news, Freya thought, *I'm going to have to suspend you.*

What!

It's just a suspension, nothing to worry about, but I have to be seen to be following procedure.

But—

You were involved with the Jürgens murder, you found the body; you found the Chedding victim.

Doing my job, Ma'am!

Murderer.

I'm not a murderer.

No-one thinks you are, Detective Constable.

Sorry, Freya... Chief Superintendent, it was someone else thinking.

I see. And there's also the accusation of Police brutality at last week's Flash Riot.

That's absolute nonsense!!!

Oliver could almost sense his emotions scrambling into punctuation – an exclamation mark, two exclamations!! His hands felt clammy. *You can't believe this nonsense, surely?*

I don't, Freya thought, *but it would be best to distance you from it until everything sorts itself out. You know how these things can escalate.*

Yes.

Once it's stopped being rethought all over the Thinkersphere and we've had the enquiry, you'll be reinstated.

Thanks.

Providing there's no grounds otherwise—

But—

"No smoke without fire," said Jellicoe.

Oliver gritted his teeth.

"No smoke without fire," Jellicoe repeated. "Say it!"

"No smoke without fire."

"Calm down."

"I am..."

"Now think it."

I understand, Chief Superintendent. Ma'am.

Good man, Freya thought, and then, *Detective Constable Oliver Braddon suspended at... 11:15am.*

"Being suspended is like your Sergeant's Exam," Jellicoe said. "Something we all have to get through to climb the rickety ladder."

Oliver couldn't even bring himself to loll at this gem.

"Do you want to get some things from your place or move back there?" Jellicoe asked.

"Will it be safe now I'm not a policeman? Which would you prefer?"

"I don't mind."

Oliver couldn't judge the man's tone of voice, it was unreadable. If only he could see where the whites of the man's inner eye were looking or interpret the emoticons of his thoughts.

"You better change your status," Jellicoe said.

Oliver felt a sudden rush of anger, fury that he was being treated like this by the force that he had dedicated his life to... and then he was laughing, tears rolling down his cheeks: he had no idea why.

"That's the spirit," Jellicoe.

So Oliver changed his status to 'suspended'.

Murderer.

Are you all right, Mithering thought, *you've been suspended?*

"I could do with a drink," Oliver said.

"You don't need it to hide your thoughts on the investigation," said Jellicoe.

"I don't need it for that and I'm no longer on duty."

They were entering the Lamp, when a thought from Jasmine arrived at Oliver.

Oh, er...

"I'll get the drinks," the Inspector said.

Oliver hovered, trying to stand in the largest open area.

Jasmine, hi.

Your status is 'suspended'.

Murderer.

It is. I have been. Jasmine, it's only procedure.

Mine's 'in a relationship with Ollie'.
Oh.
Oh? Just oh?
I'm in public, Oliver thought, embarrassed at the looks he was receiving from the other detectives.
We're always in public!
Jasmine—
I'm changing my status: single.
Look—
Bye Oliver.
Jasmine, it's not like that, but he knew, down in his reptile brain, that he was thinking to the whole world, except one.

Jellicoe put a pint down on the table. "Get that down you," he said.

"Drown my sorrows?"

"Something like that."

As he drank, he wondered: *Am I being diminished? It's not what you know, it's who you know. With Noodle you know everything and with thought you could know everyone. And they could know you.*

He felt the familiar prickle across his forehead: his brow shutting down, and the alcohol would slowly work its magic back through his head: iBrow, frontal lobe, parietal lobe, occipital lobe and so forth gradually undoing millions of years of evolution. There were creatures that didn't have this desperate primate need for company.

They must be leaving him now, unfriending him. Would they miss him? Would he miss them? Would he even notice?

How many friends had he lost now?

Where they ever his friends or just a circle in Jasmine's followings?

If you don't meet a friend for a while, you don't notice. A while longer and, well, there are lots more fish in the sea and your old friends' thoughts are present until you stop following them. These ignored thoughts were like... Christmas cards in history.

"Do you remember that kids' game we used to play in the playground?" Jellicoe asked. He was sitting opposite in the usual booth. Oliver hadn't really noticed joining him.

"Which one?"

"The staring game: you face each other, staring into each other's eyes and the first one who thinks, loses."

"Yes."

"Were you any good?"

"I was OK."

"Penny for your thoughts?"

Oliver felt cross: "You could just follow them."

"You're drunk."

"I'm suspended and Jasmine, my girlfriend, dumped me."

"I got one side of that."

"So you do follow me."

"And you're worried you won't have any friends."

"Yes. It's an acceptable medical condition."

"Have you noticed that all friends are the same?"

"No."

"There used to be words like 'friend', 'mate', 'buddy', 'acquaintance' and 'colleague'."

"I do believe Noodle has a thesaurus."

"My point is that all these subtle differences, these shades of friendship, have all been replaced by 'follower'. There are no real friends now."

"It's been like that since before I was born and for me personally since I was eleven."

"We're sheep."

"No," Oliver said. "People follow us, so we're shepherds or sheep dogs."

"But we follow others, many, many others."

"True."

"We're a herd of sheep, bleating away as we lead everyone round and round, everyone full of speculation that we're going somewhere."

"Very deep."

"What does Jasmine look like?"

Oliver frowned and–

"Without Noodle."

"Is this an exam?"

"Yes."

"She's long dark hair and–"

"Who's her best friend?"

"This is a little personal."

"I could noodle it," Jellicoe reminded him.

"Go on then."

"Cheryl," said Jellicoe, clearly quite capable of using Noodle. "What does she look like?"

"She... I don't know."

"Jürgens, what did he look like?"

"Well, er..."

"If I got a photofit artist–"

"A what?"

"A photofit artist. They used to make up a suspect's face using bits of other people: these eyes, that nose, those ears and... never mind. A police artist, say, to draw a picture based on your description, except that you can't describe the suspect."

"I don't need to. There's a photograph on Noodle, thousands of photographs and when you are within recognition range, you'd recognise them."

"And Cheryl?"

"Yes."

"And how long before you forget what Jasmine looks like?"

"I won't forget Jasmine."

"What do I look like?"

Murderer.

Oliver looked at the Inspector. The man's face was only a metre away; he knew him because he was in recognition range as someone he could follow, but his appearance was obscured. It wasn't by anything physical or virtual, but because Oliver's brain was completely satisfied by the information from his brow.

"What about your colleagues?" Jellicoe continued. "How many are black, white, Asian? Are they aware of your colour?"

"Of course."

"Without Noodle?"

"I don't know," Oliver snapped. "You can't tell from thought."

Oliver's recognition of Jellicoe consisted of a name and a link to follow. It was sparse, lacking any status other than 'Inspector', which was a strange choice. 'Suspended' was perhaps stranger. It was a kind of mask.

"Jellicoe, do you know what I look like?"

"You look like shit," the Inspector said. "Your round."

Murderer.

"Yes," said Oliver. "I could murder another round."

Murderer.

Oliver went up to the bar: Babs Lamp was there, and Skittle, Smith, Terry – he recognised a lot of the people now, he'd read their identifications before. He knew their names, but not, as he now realised, their faces. He could follow them, make up for the loss of Jasmine's friends.

Or he could just unfollow them all.

Murderer.

Was he a murderer of a sort when he unfriended people? Wasn't that diminishing them? If you weren't in people's thoughts, did you exist?

Murderer.

Yes, Oliver thought... *oh, what was that?*

Murderer.

That was getting to be a bother.

Murderer!

He could block it, but it kept coming at him from different sources.

Oliver held up a couple of fingers to Babs Lamp and then pointed to himself and to the third booth where Jellicoe sat.

The thought came again, *murderer*, and again: *Murderer! Murderer!*

Oliver stumbled.

Murder! Murderer! Murderer!

Something whipped past his attention about... no, he'd missed it. Chen had- *Murderer!* But Mithering wanted him, but it was all lost in vitriol, too fast now to follow except for a subliminal flash and a growing averaging. *Murderer.* He tried to backtrack, but the thoughts now were arriving faster than he could process them.

MurderMurderMurMuMMMM...

His head flared with pain and he stumbled, going down onto his hands and knees.

"You've had enough," said Babs Lamp. *More than enough.*

"Denial of service," he said, aloud to force himself to concentrate. He knew this trick, and he knew the techniques to cope as he'd been taught them at Police College. They all – *God, it hurt* – gathered in a circle and thought at each other to much hilarity, but that was a class of thirty and this was... thousands, millions... who knew? What was it? He didn't know and noodled it.

He climbed to his feet and staggered to a chair.

Faces, unknown and unmemorable, looked shocked. There was fear across their features. In the corner of his eye, he saw someone running towards him.

There had been a lesson, but it was all fractured, interspersed with the trolling: conspiracy nonsense and abuse.

He put his fists to his temples.

His vision was fine, he could see, he could imagine options, but his consciousness had been hijacked making it impossible to make a decision. He needed... *drink – murderer – wouldn't stop the onrush – fascist – only – killer –*

something like – Tepee pig – you murdered the woman in the car park – but he didn't know.

"Jellicoe!"

He was there: "Look into my eyes, son, look into my eyes, concentrate."

Jellicoe's eyes were bloodshot, the whites stained and, although his concerned face was inches away, the man's recognition was jostled away by the incoming hail until the Inspector was no longer really there.

"Paramedics are on their way," Jellicoe said.

"Mithering," Oliver pleaded, but the inflow of thought – *murderer* – meant that he could no longer think. She wouldn't know, no-one would know that he was a monster, a murderer, a killer, a...

"Can you hear me? Can you hear me? Hold on, son."

He had to hold on.

To something.

Anything.

Even something as fleeting as a memory.

The sense of smell.

Evocative: always conjuring up memories.

The smell the coffee.

So good.

The smell of Jasmine's long black hair.

Lovely.

The smell of whiskey flavoured blood.

The woman on the back seat in the car park.

Oh God, he thought, *I killed her!*

He admits it – over and over, coming back a thousand times until he knew he had confessed and then, amongst all the explanations, of course he had. He must have. How could all this be wrong? It was enlightening, and even in the pain it was a relief to stop fighting it and let it all engulf him.

He was vaguely aware of Chen and Mox, a car, sirens, but that was outside his skull and therefore far away. Inside it was screaming, howling, noise and bedlam.

At Elenor3941...

The stream of thoughts flaring over each other, the next arriving before the impression of the others had passed thought. It was like letters on an old fashioned digital clock speeding up, the bars flickering so quickly that it became '88:88' – the Chinese lucky number – repeated. Or the talking of a crowd becoming meaningless babble. He scratched at his forehead, knowing that he couldn't rip the device out, couldn't, shouldn't and wouldn't want to, but needing some respite, but the itch was centimetres under his scalp locked behind hair, skin and bone. He stumbled, falling towards the light that burned inside. He struck the ground, rolled, stared up and saw the sun. It became square and flew repeatedly overhead as the days rushed by. Someone was talking to him?

"What's your password?"

The person was concerned, dressed in regulation hospital fatigues.

"Talk," they said. "Talk... repeat after me: one, two... ONE! TWO!"

"One, two," said Oliver.

"Three?"

"Three, four... five..."

He was in hospital on a trolley being wheeled rapidly down a corridor. The lights moved overhead in a steady rhythm. How had he got there? They swung round into an office full of... computers.

There were shadows, people talking aloud, "Thank you officer, we'll take it from here. Now, Oliver, six? Come on, say 'six'."

"Six..." Oliver repeated. "Pick-up sticks. Seven, eight, big fat, denial of service, attack, nine, ten... ten..."

"The authorities have released your pin code, Oliver, so just give us your password?"

"Every good boy deserves chocolate."

"Every good... got it... Nurse! Connect: send!"

Oliver was floating, his mind freewheeling, and everything seemed hyper-real, the colours brighter and the stains on the medic's coat sharper and distinct. He moved his hand, which floated gently as everyone around him moved even slower.

A face loomed into view, huge and pock marked. He recognised Doctor Trantor with an incredible clarity.

"You've been disconnected from the network," he said, his mouth moving slowly and the words reaching him as elongated whale song.

With no one else's thoughts to contend with, his brain worked so much faster.

"I'm feeling..." he began, but he didn't know how he was feeling, so he noodled it and threw up, vomiting over the medic and the floor. He lurched off the trolley to try to control it, but the movement made it worse. Someone found a bin and he disgorged over tissues and water bottles. His eyes filled with tears and he cried, "Oh God."

"It's OK, you're going to be OK."

"Where am I?"

"Sanderson Medical."

Sanderson... what was that? The thought went nowhere, free floating away vertiginously. Medical... that was something to do with hospitals. *Was he ill? Oh God, yes, he was ill, really ill.* In fact, he was dying. He felt he was dying. He thought... *oh, shit... catch me, catch me.*

Oliver flailed about trying to grab hold of something and keep himself steady, but he was secure, held down by two orderlies, but even so he felt like he was falling.

A wasp stung him in the arm... no, a... *what was the word* – pointy sharp needle thing that... made... him... and anyway... his forehead prickled like it did when he drank as the human and reptile parts of his brain switched off.

WEEK TWO

SUNDAY

Oliver was walking through an underground labyrinth of concrete corridors, past pillars, to a car. Jasmine was in the back seat. She took off her face to show him the mask that it had been all along. Underneath was nothing. She'd changed her status to 'unknown': 271 people liked this. Outside there were discarded masks parked in neat rows.

He didn't know when he was dreaming and when he was awake. Consciousness had that same empty feeling of drifting that sleep possessed, except that his eyes were open and he was doing things. His hands shook. He wanted a drink, but what he really needed were thoughts. Other people seemed unreal, their thoughts kept beyond recognition range, as if all the passers-by had put on disguises and whispered behind cupped hands.

A nurse walked down the corridor looking like a robot.

She kept out of recognition range in case the slightest human contact broke his quarantine. There was black and yellow tape across the floor and a plastic pod attached to the wall to warn people. When he got up to go to the bathroom, he heard its thoughts in his head reminding him to keep away.

When he had an operational brow, he didn't follow everyone's thoughts. He wouldn't have been following that particular nurse's, for example, but the lack of any thoughts at all, tarred everyone he saw with the same brush. Flat video looked fake next to 3D, and black-and-white television was simply unreal – he'd seen them together once in a museum – and this was horribly close to that. They seemed dead like zombies.

It was a stray thought, like you get just on the limit of recognition range, and it nudged and inveigled itself into Oliver's mind. He tilted his head first one way and then another as if that would make a difference.

What are you in here for?

Not his imagination then: *I'd rather not think about that, thank you.*

Ah, that'll be because you're a murderer.

What!?

Don't worry, we're all in here for something.

What are you in here for?

Schizophrenia. I hear voices.

God, I'm in the loony bin.

You must be a looney then, you hear voices too.

I do not.

You hear mine.

That's different.

In what way is it different?

My voices are real.

Laugh out loud, an ongoing chuckle that couldn't be contained: *Do you hear that, do you hear that, his voices are real.*

I'm not part of the tin hat brigade.

Really? Do you hear that?

Listen... "Listen!"

Oliver looked up, around, but there was no-one there. There were cream walls, a window with a view of the dark sky, the door to the empty corridor, an old bracket that used to hold a television set, the curtains and a bedside cabinet.

"I don't hear voices," he said aloud.

No, of course not.

Oliver got up, felt the cold floor on the soles of his feet and he shuffled over to the en suite. He washed his face, splashing the cold water onto what felt like weary skin drawn across his skull. As he rubbed, he felt a two day growth of stubble and the hard brow beneath the flesh of his forehead.

When he straightened up, he saw himself in the mirror.

Jellicoe had talking about everyone's lack of ability to remember faces. This was a face he ought to know because the iBrow didn't recognise itself, of course; and there was no-one really there. It was just his image in the mirror, but, by the same token, the face seemed blank. This other person, this reflection living in the reversed bathroom, was an enigma, an unknown, as if it was wearing an Oliver Braddon mask, and his unfollowable thoughts were his own.

How did he rate this person – objectively?

He couldn't.

The eyes weren't cunning, the chin wasn't heroic, the smile wasn't welcoming: all the constituents were anonymous. The whole was a photofit from the boring box. He didn't judge people on their appearance. He never had, because he had never needed to. Everything about someone was either in the recognition, or their status or gained by a deep noodle of their thoughts. Maybe when he was ten before the brow fitting, but he couldn't remember that, not properly, because those childish thoughts hadn't been stored anywhere and certainly hadn't been backed-up.

Mister Braddon, how are we today?

Oliver looked around the bathroom: there was no-one there and no-one, apart from his reflection, in the mirrored version.

I'm fine.

Excellent, and... where are you, Mister Braddon?

What do you mean?

You should be in bed.

Oliver went back to the private room. There was a man standing there in a suit.

"Hello?"

Ah, there you are, don't you recognise me?

Oliver did: it was Doctor Trantor. His presence was sudden and frightening.

"Yes."

Obviously up and about. Back into bed please.

Oliver dutifully obeyed, slipping back into bed, while Doctor Trantor frowned as he noodled Oliver's notes.

Now, he thought, *don't follow me, just stay with brow-to-brow.*

"Yes."

Nod if you receive this.

Oliver nodded.

OK, think of your job.

"Police–"

"Think!" *Think.*

Police Officer.

Really?

Yes.

Ah, you're here because you started to believe some cerebral. Don't feel ashamed.

I don't. I am a policeman.

Investigating some impossible murder, Doctor Trantor thought, *lots of people relying on you. It's very common. People like being special, they want to spice up their lives to feel better about themselves; instead of being some boring drone working in some open plan office and ridiculed by all the pretty women.*

Stop being a dick and check.

Doctor Trantor tilted his head to one side, noodling his notes.

See, Oliver thought. *Detective Constable. Suspended.*

So you think: we get so many cerebral addicts, we have to be sure.

Yes, Oliver thought, feeling the muscles in his face contort. *I can see that.*

Nothing wrong with your Emoticon Selection Protocols, I see. Now, rethink 'abracadabra'.

Abracadabra.

Don't think of a polar bear.

Polar bear?

Doctor Trantor clapped his hands.

Oliver jerked back.

Excellent, well done.   Physical reaction and reflex thought in synchronisation. Make a happy face.

This is ridiculous, Oliver thought, grimacing.

Even better. Can you receive this?

Yes.

*And... **this?***

Yes.

Both recognition and push working.

Doctor Trantor tilted his head again, a clear sign he was noodling to update his notes.

"Doctor—"

Think.

But Doctor Trantor was nodding, in a world of his own it seemed, as he accessed something or maybe just kept up with all his friends. He looked like someone who would have lots of friends, grateful ex-patients, nurses, colleagues, ex-lovers... all downgraded to simple followers.

Your bloods have a few anomalous readings, Doctor Trantor thought finally. *Do you drink a lot of alcohol, I wonder?*

No more than anyone.

You had been thinking about alcohol a lot: pubs, sherry, whiskey, someone called Jellicoe leading you astray? And that's only a cursory glance down your old thought stream. I think you should be more careful. Stick to below the recommended 21 units in future.

Trantor came over and put his thumb and finger to Oliver's face to stare into his eyes: *The whites of the eyes never lie: you're bloodshot.*

Doctor Trantor... do you mind if we talk?

Not at all?

I mean aloud.

It's best for your rehabilitation to use thought as normal.

Please... "Please?"

"Oh, very well." *This is rather tedious.*

"I heard voices."

"That's perfectly normal, it's the iBrow coming back on line... or to be more precise the cerebral stranding reconnecting." *There's a lot of bruising, you understand.*

"What's schizophrenia... exactly?"

Schizophrenia? You can noodle it.

Please.

Oh, it's... a mental disorder defined by a disassociation of mental processes and...

In your own words.

...a deficit–

"In your own words!"

Doctor Trantor stopped, considering Oliver as if for the first time. "Voices in your head," he said.

"I've heard voices in my head."

"Do you feel controlled externally, thoughts inserted into your mind by others, do you have a fear that your thoughts are being transmitted to others as if by radio waves?"

"Yes, all of those."

"You're confused, that's brow technology. We're trying to treat you so that you can do it again."

"But that's schizophrenia."

"Hmm, according to the..." – he frowned, clearly noodling, but Oliver let it go – "er... Schneiderian classification. Yes, yes, there are parallels. Indeed, hmm..." *Those symptoms sound like an iBrow advertisement. How amusing.*

"I heard voices in my head and there was no-one in the room."

"The thoughts may seem louder, like voices perhaps, because you only following a few people like a... er..."

"A voice in an empty room versus a voice in a crowd."

"Yes, a nice metaphor."

"But I'm not following anyone yet."

You are receiving my thoughts?

Yes, Oliver thought slowly, *but only because I've recognised you.*

Oh, you're in the haunted bed.

The what!?

There's a pipe, Doctor Trantor thought and he pointed to the wall. Sure enough, there was a ventilation duct. *It funnels the signal from downstairs, distorted, but thoughts come through. The psychiatric ward is one down. You've probably heard the voices of a real schizophrenic.*

This is a lunatic asylum?

Of course. Not being able to think is a psychiatric condition.

Oliver let out a breath: *Jeez.*

I wonder if a lot more people had schizophrenia before the invention of thought, Doctor Trantor mused.

What makes you think that?

People used to have an internal monologue, didn't they?

Thinking without thinking.

I suppose.

My Inspector has been teaching me that.

A meditation technique: I don't really recommend all that Chinese mysticism baloney. And there was the voice of reason, that's another, and the voice of conscience – Jiminy Cricket – and so on. Nowadays our minds are so full of other people's thoughts that we don't hear our 'small voices'.

And schizophrenics do?

Oh no, they can't tell thoughts from delusions – quite different.

How can you tell?

One's committed downstairs, the other is free to walk around in public.

Can I have other people's thoughts yet?

No, take two of these.

Oliver did so, filling a glass from his water jug nearby. It tasted tepid.

Let's leave it another day, Doctor Trantor added, *let the brain cells have another night's rest to settle down.*

If you say so.

I do say so.

And with that thought the Doctor left.

Oliver felt sleepy immediately, which he supposed was a placebo effect. Was it? He could look it up. How long did the pills take to knock him out? He could check, if he'd known what they were, though he'd forgotten to ask the Doctor if he could use Noodle.

I'm a voice in your head, I'm a voice in your head.

No, you're not, Oliver thought emphatically. *You're a patient downstairs.*

Is that what you think?

You don't just hear voices from no-one.

At Ollie, hello Oliver.

Oliver slept, unsure where the haunted bed left off and the dreams began, but in both some thoughts mithered away.

At Ollie, hello Oliver.

Much later, Jellicoe arrived looking like he was treading germs into the linoleum from his scuffed shoes and flapping diseases from his crumpled mackintosh. He carried a brown paper bag.

"I ate them," he said, putting it down beside Oliver's jug of water. "Perhaps there's something in this five a day."

"Thanks," said Oliver.

"You OK." It was a statement, Jellicoe clearly didn't want to discuss any symptoms or – God forbid – feelings.

"I'm fine," said Oliver.

"It is you, isn't it?"

"Yes," said Oliver. "My recognition code has been changed."

"Right... I wondered for a moment if I'd got the wrong bed."

"No, it's me."

Jellicoe found a plastic chair and screeched it across the floor, so he could sit by the bed. He sank down, lower than a comfortable eye-line.

"You're not thinking," Jellicoe said.

"The advice is to avoid drawing attention to yourself in case the trolls work out your new identity, so I'm not – you know – connecting to anyone I know."

"Anyone you don't know?"

"No."

"So...?"

"Very... like drunk."

Jellicoe shifted so that Oliver could see into his coat. He had his hip flask there.

"No... thanks."

"So..."

Oliver realised that Jellicoe had no idea what to say. "Nice of you to visit."

Jellicoe shrugged.

Oliver wondered what the man was thinking. He could follow and find out, unless he'd already partaken of his hip flask.

"I hate hospitals," said Jellicoe. "All those tests I've had – waste of time. My lipoprotein levels feel fine."

The Inspector seemed angry, flushed, so Oliver decided to take charge of the conversation. "The Doctor's going to see me again tomorrow. They'll probably discharge me."

"Back to mine?"

"I guess or perhaps a motel, let the heat die down before I pick up any threads of my old life."

"Old life?"

"You're supposed to feel born again, euphoric, or have some sort of epiphany."

"Do you?"

"No."

"Why are people supposed to feel that?"

"I guess," said Oliver, "a man is the sum of his memories. To know someone's worth, to really understand them, you must noodle their entire experience. Could that experience be used to recreate someone, a thinking machine, or a cloned body, that thought in exactly the same way with the same responses and even the same capacity to change and grow? Would that person be the same person? Would the soul, temporarily stored in heaven or hell, re-enter the new form, reincarnate, and if you multiplied them a hundred-fold would you have numerous souls. Would those people be alive?"

"No."

"But how would you know? If you noodled them both, followed them, then they'd be the same."

"They'd start to veer apart... like twins."

"So you agree that they'd start the same?"

"I suppose," Jellicoe admitted.

"Then the copy is alive."

"What's this to do with being born again?"

"I guess all my memories have been archived and restored to my iBrow, a fresh... I don't know. What I am now is what I was, but my thoughts took one route back to my body and my... feelings, I guess, took another."

"Is that you talking or the drugs?"

Oliver had no idea: he couldn't parse back through his thoughts, but he suspected that his mouth had run away with itself. People must have talked such bollocks before thought.

"Do you want to discuss the case?" Oliver asked.

"Are you up to it?"

"Sure..."

Jellicoe let of a sigh of relief.

"It'll be something to take my mind off the nothingness. Perhaps we should go over the facts?" Oliver suggested.

"Bugger all facts."

Oliver brought his hands together to count. "Victim—"

"You thinking?"

"No," said Oliver. "They gave me a shot or something."

"Medical alcohol?"

Oliver laughed: "Something like that."

"Go on."

"Victim: dead, murdered, identity unknown, but ought to be known. Matches no known missing person." Having started on his little finger, Oliver had reached his thumb, so he started back the way he'd come. "Theories: none."

"That's about the size of it."

Oliver looked at his hands as if trying to will his index finger to count another fact or find a theory amongst the lines. He was trembling quite noticeably.

"Withdrawal from addiction," Jellicoe said. "Saw a chap smacked in the head by a baseball bat. He wasn't that injured, but his brow shutdown. He started shaking, had a fit and then was howling by the end of the night."

"Oh thanks."

"Try not to think about it."

"I can't think about it... medical alcohol, remember."

"Remember... we rely on the technology too much."

"Technology works in ninety-nine point nine, nine, nine percent of the cases."

"Won't help Unknown 271 or Unknown 272. Or Jürgens for that matter."

"272?"

"The scalped man."

"Maybe it's the case we don't solve."

"One of those is one too many."

"Why are there any?" Oliver said. "With full access to thoughts, everyone monitors everyone else, so everyone is supposed to be good."

"Hitler liked his dog."

"What?"

"Hitler wanted to save Germany from the subjugation of the Versailles treaty and raise the Fatherland to greatness again," said Jellicoe. "That's a good thing. It is."

"Oh, come on."

"And he was vegetarian and he liked his dog."

"So? He was a genocidal foil head."

"Except... the point is that in his own mind he was a hero, he thought he was doing good, he had a purity – really, I mean this – and a holier than thou attitude in his thoughts that enabled him to preach unspeakable horrors and perpetrate unbelievable brutality that was, by a definition, good. In his mind."

"In his mind, right."

"Nowadays, with everyone having free access to everyone's thoughts, everyone has to think good thoughts. They don't dare do otherwise. And yet our prisons are full of wife beaters, violent thugs, criminals of all manner of diverse and dreadful kinds, and all thinking wonderful thoughts."

"There's no premeditated crime."

"Because they get caught before their category whatever planned sexual offence becomes anything worse. My point is that we all think we are virtuous, every one of us. Therefore, we can excuse any action. We must have meant well, they say, just noodle my thought process and see. Lift the lid, look inside the skull – no bad thoughts there."

"Hmm."

"And yet, we turn on our friends, dump our partners, betray confidences–"

A nurse walked past, and Jellicoe waited until she'd gone.

"Before thought, people monitored their own... thoughts – that word will have to do – and always saw their inner workings as virtuous. They were the heroes of their own stories despite any unfortunate actions they may take."

"Think good, do bad."

"Think 'good', do... whatever."

"Or back then," Oliver said, "maybe it was think bad, do bad. There was no way to tell."

"But the choice, then and now, is in what you do."

"And that's why Hitler was evil?"

"Do you remember Noodle Bars?" Jellicoe asked.

"I could noodle and remember."

"Very droll – noodle bars, where you noodled because they had high speed connections, probably served noodles as well. They were like internet cafés."

Oliver would have to noodle that one.

"Every argument comes round to Hitler eventually," said Jellicoe. "I think that was it."

"And everyone can, er... rationalise their actions because they believe they think good thoughts."

"These murderers," Jellicoe continued, "they've found a way around the technology."

"They?"

"He, she... more than one."

"A conspiracy?"

Jellicoe looked him in the eye for the first time. "Got to be something."

Oliver looked away and bit his lip, gnawing. "Did we do it?"

Jellicoe raised an eyebrow.

"They were so certain," Oliver continued, "so certain, that we killed her, until, in the end, I thought we'd... I thought I'd killed her. Maybe we faked the evidence, faked even our own thoughts. If you edit them, then... we're the sum of our thoughts."

"No, son, you did good, but were only thought at bad."

"Even so, my thoughts have been shuffled around."

"They're all stored on computers in several different places, backed up, archived, many different jurisdictions – too many."

"But what if?"

"Don't believe the trolls."

"But–"

"They think they are right – virtuous – but they're not."

It was sunny outside. Oliver enjoyed it for a moment. He felt peaceful, blank, as if he could do anything. Jellicoe sat quietly.

"Thank you," Oliver said, finally.

"You're welcome Braddon."

"Friends call me 'Ollie'."

"Do you feel like an 'Ollie'?"

"No."

Jellicoe fidgeted.

"You don't have to stay the full time," Oliver said.

"Thanks."

Jellicoe stood, checked he hadn't left anything, patted his pockets and then shuffled out.

"See you at the station, Braddon," Jellicoe said.

"Yes. Thanks. Jellicoe."

Oliver wondered about sitting on his quivering hands and then he felt stomach cramps. He hugged his body, rocked and felt stupid, because he remembered that this was what heroin addicts did. He had pins and needles and felt on fire, but the overwhelming problem was the sensation of falling forward. It was if, with the weight of fourteen years of thoughts pushing on his forehead gone, he was mentally flinging himself forward. Everything appeared flatter somehow, the extra dimensions of knowledge gone, so that the world was just a faint projection over an abyss.

He stared at it: nothing stared back.

He didn't feel virtuous.

And it went on, all day.

MONDAY

When Oliver woke up, Doctor Trantor wasn't there: *At Ollie, how are you feeling today?*

Fine.

At Ollie, can you follow me?

Yes, I can follow you.

At Ollie, I mean, 'follow' me.

Oliver did so.

...yes, thank you, coffee, Hasqueth Finest please.

Something about coffee, Oliver thought.

Oh, you got that... excellent. That all seems fine then.

Thank you.

And sugar, two. Do we have any of those biscuits, the cream ones? It's too early in the morning to be doing rounds. I need a cup of coffee. I mean, what's Doctor Sinden going on about, bloody typical of management.

Doctor Trantor, when can I leave?

Now, we need the bed. Go for a walk, get some fresh air and exercise, and be cautious in increasing your following, ease yourself into it.

Thanks.

My pleasure. At Mrs Whittle... Jordan, how are we today? Yes, but you have Alzheimer's, so your Noodle results are going to be confusing...

Oliver eased himself out of bed and drew the curtains. He found his clothes and got dressed. He fumbled and felt quite weak, but finally in his suit, now crumpled, he felt himself again. The bare grape stems that Jellicoe had brought were still there, and a surge of anger that Jasmine hadn't visited coursed through him. Stupid, because Jasmine's presence in the hospital might have given away his new iBrow identity – Jellicoe must have been drunk to visit. However, it was a strong emotion.

A walk, Doctor Trantor had thought, and that seemed a good idea.

The hospital was a maze and, despite the signage, he made several wrong turns.

Outside, the fresh breeze blew through his hair and the new stream of thoughts lapping against his forehead. He took a deep breath: it was clear and clean, the atmosphere without dust or antiseptic smell, just as the world was empty of spam and irrelevancies, and therefore somehow purer. He was born again. This must be what religious experience was like, and Oliver didn't want to sully the moment by noodling it up.

He took another deep breath, trying to recapture the moment. The air was as good, but the exhilaration was less. Like an addict, he needed a bigger fix.

He missed Mithering sitting on his shoulder as it were. He didn't miss Jasmine's friends. Behind him, Doctor Trantor continued his rounds, the repetition of his thoughts at each bedside becoming more and more obvious.

He noodled his task list: it had been reset too, so he had nothing to do.

So, for the first time in his life, he was up-to-date.

His status was blank. He'd never come across a blank status before. Everyone was something. Jasmine was... he noodled: single.

He followed her thoughts, feeling them flow into him.

And then he remembered that she'd left him.

What was his opinion on that, he wondered. Nothing. He had no thoughts on the subject. He had no thoughts on any subject he realised, once he'd noodled them. He had a few entries on schizophrenia, the hospital, but that was all.

He felt... free. Free of her and all her friends, all that trivial nonsense that seemed so unimportant now. He felt lighter as if somehow the lack of that group's thoughts in his head had reduced his iBrow's weight and, liberated of the burden, he could tilt his head from the ground to look up. The sun was shining, there was a blue sky and a formation of birds crossed overhead.

He was a blank page: the slate wiped clean.

Right, he thought, and that added upon the tests in the hospital. He was only following Jasmine and Doctor Trantor. That would have to change, but, playfully, he wondered if he could simply unfollow them. Thus, he'd be effectively invisible – or was it blind – passing through crowds, or just sitting at home, and untouched.

Oliver did: Jasmine was in some conversation with Cheryl and Doctor Trantor was still thinking about biscuits and now lunch, which held no interest. Oliver would have to refollow to find out about any out-patients appointments or maybe their booking system would send him a thought directly. Either way, for the time being he wanted peace and quiet. This must be what a baby was like, all clean, unsullied – innocent and virtuous.

It was perverse: he needed people, but he liked this serenity and he felt blessed by this second chance.

He made his way down Old Tollgate and came across the abandoned Chedding shopping centre. The door had been sealed, this time in steel.

Why had the... do-dad, yes that would do, do-dad been left in the car, he thought.

A single thought: he imagined it drifting away, caught by the breeze to waft hither and thither, ephemeral and wasted as no-one was following him... yet.

It wouldn't last. At some point someone would send a thought at him and slowly the great social networking web would envelope him again. He would regret it at the same time that he embraced it. Best enjoy this faintly disturbing euphoria that came with being... alone, that was it.

I'm alone, he thought, and almost heard the echoes.

Why?

Oh why?

His wandering took him around to the other entrance, the one that cars would have used. It was unconscious, instinctive, as if he was developing Jellicoe's gut instinct.

Yes, why?

There were the remains of police crime scene tape, flapping. Oliver climbed the fence and dropped down onto the ramp beyond the metal shutters. The car park seemed huge, tomblike, cold and utterly quiet.

Of course, this time it was different as there weren't 'voices' chattering away in his head.

Why had the car been left there?

Maybe, with so many distractions, they'd simply forgotten it, distracted like so many people by the need to check what everyone else was doing: the urgent trivial swamping the important. Like everyone, so desperately checking that everyone else was checking everyone else: spies with no-one to spy on but other spies.

These murderers were unable to think about the act, otherwise they'd give themselves away, so it was something that wouldn't be available on Noodle. They might have written it down, as Oliver had, but pieces of paper were notoriously easy to lose. He'd given his to Jellicoe.

He walked over to where he suspected the car had been parked. There were fresh scuff marks on the concrete floor, but these could have been made by the forensic team. He went in a big, lazy circle all around, just looking.

His foot clattered against something. He was standing on a blank plastic sign. The other side was 'Danger – Construction Work: Keep Out!'

There was no construction work here, but there would have been if there hadn't been that collapse in the economy. This would all have become flats eventually, new and full of promise, but only some of the foundations had been laid so far. He remembered the large open excavation next to the building due to be filled with concrete.

Car, foundations, concrete!

He pointed his finger at where the car had been as the idea opened up like a flower in his mind.

It was obvious: *Hide a body in the car, wait for the night after the concrete had been poured and then dump the body in the foundations. She'd never have been found for a million years... or perhaps fifty years when the new flats fell down from old age and neglect. You'd still have to hide the victim's missing status somehow, but if you could do that – and clearly, they had done that – then it would be the perfect crime. No-one would look for a body and no-one would find it.*

He almost did a little dance.

The aircon was set to cold to refrigerate the corpse and keep it fresh, so that the smell... no, it smelt disgusting here already. To prevent rodents? To make it more pleasant dumping the body? Probably. Most likely the plan hadn't involved it being there for so long.

It was all clear to him.

So, he thought, *what was the next step?*

Identify the body, surely; but every attempt to noodle it this way, or that way, had drawn a blank.

Mem... something.

He could noodle it... no.

Mem... "Memetic engineering," he said aloud.

Advertising in other words.

You could change people's thoughts by sending them thoughts. He could almost taste the coffee, Hasqueth's Finest, on his tongue. If you were given a thought that a particular car, washing powder, insurance company or whatever, was the best, then that's what you'd think. If enough people thought you were a killer, then you'd believe it.

Oliver shivered.

Perhaps the weight of thought made it true. If you thought you were a policeman, were you?

I think therefore I am.

I am thought about, therefore I am.

The sheer mass of it would affect your mind, but the victim, Unknown 271, didn't change thoughts or have her thoughts changed, she... no, it was gone. She wasn't missing, which was to say she was thinking, so...

One idea gave rise to another in a logical chain, but this was a weak link. One move led to another move, so—

At Ollie, hello Oliver.

Oliver felt his chest tighten, adrenalin pumped into his system. If one person had found him, then anyone could find him. He clenched his fists, wanting to fight or run, but there was no physical method to fight off another attack. Could he make it back to the hospital on foot? If another denial of service attack overwhelmed him, he would keel over in the car park and remain there until another happenstance, like the riot, discovered his body. Had he left enough footprints across the Thinkersphere to even be found? There certainly weren't enough across the concrete dust in the abandoned multi-storey to track him to here.

Hello Mithering, he thought. It had come unbidden, an automatic reaction to the input. He followed her, instinctive, despite his earlier euphoria about being free. All the old mental reflexes just kicked in.

Lovely to know you again, Ollie. How are you?

Fine and you?

Can't complain.

Small talk, Oliver thought.

I know, but it helps connect us, particularly as you've had a shock.

Yes, I understand.

Oliver had taken a few steps toward the exit. It was just Mithering, loud and clear in the empty stream, and the deluge of trolling hadn't occurred.

Don't be frightened, Mithering thought.

God, I'm leaking.

Yes, but it's all right, I'm a friend.

Perhaps we should talk?

Yes, let's think at each other.

Over a drink, just you and I. He'd nearly reached the shaft of direct sunlight: *How far is the Lamp?* "No," he said aloud, "the hospital."

I can't go to the Lamp, I'm sorry. Busy. You know.

That's a shame.

He stepped out of the shadows, and felt safe from the Trolls, which was ludicrous because they weren't creatures that lived in the dark under bridges, but human beings who let hatred rule their thoughts.

Do you want to think with me about the case?

There's not much to think about, Oliver thought back.

What about the Chedding Conspiracy?

Oh, give me strength.

But so many people believe it, Mithering responded. *Perhaps the evidence has been tampered with?*

By evidence, she meant thoughts. Have they been changed? He wouldn't have believed it, but now, re-booted and reborn, he was one step removed from the man he had been. *Maybe...*

Oliver noodled whether any of his thoughts were different and he remembered them all the same as before.

Of course, they'd be the same if they had been edited, Mithering thought back, *that's the point.*

The Chedding Car Park Conspiracy theorists believed that the police had murdered the woman and that those involved had had their memories tampered with. Had he killed someone and had his memories altered? There were different types of memory: muscle memory, for example. There were your own personal thoughts, those of other people and those of computers; these could be sorted by tags and datetimes for retrieval. Oh, and those memories laid down in your biological brain's actual synapses. Short term and long term... he noodled: yes, chemical and electrical.

Could thoughts be edited?

If so, then his remembrances would be different from his memories, but, because he was so reliant on Noodle, he had no way of double checking. Why keep a memory, when you could remember all your previous thoughts?

He had a migraine shadow just from the idea.

Oliver noodled and, yes, he remembered that thoughts could be edited before transmission, but as everything was transmitted immediately this was an academic idea only. Jellicoe had said something about multiple copies being kept in different jurisdictions.

Except, he had buffered his thoughts when he'd been talking to Doctor Ridge in the morgue. He'd deleted thoughts. He could have easily edited them.

But he'd have known in brain memory and that would have leaked out in other thoughts once he was out in the open. People could think one thing and do another, act the part in a Souza play, but not continuously. These contradictions showed up, and psycho-technicians like Maxine could easily extract the truth. For goodness sake, Oliver himself had been able to do this intuitively even before he'd taken the memetic engineering foundation course at the Police College.

No-one could maintain the pretence, particularly not under questioning. With the right question, even the wrong question, they'd naturally think about the fact that they'd edited their thoughts and, thereby, they'd give themselves away. Forget questioning, just worrying about it would transmit the information to the world.

He noodled it all, but it was too much to take in.

What he needed to do was draw a diagram and he looked round for some paper.

Oliver felt a chill: *Was he turning into Jellicoe?*

Of course not, Mithering thought, *you're much more attractive.*

How do you know, we've not met?
How do you know we've not met?
I'd have recognised you.
Not if I'd seen you from afar.
Are you stalking me?
We're all stalking those we follow.
Oliver thought: *Where do you live?*
Do you want a date?
Where do you live... I bet it's local.
I'm not sure I want to admit that.

Oliver noodled and remembered that Mithering was really Jane Deacon. He could have done that ages ago and wondered why he hadn't.

Hadn't what?

Another noodle and he knew she lived at No. 403, Delaware Towers. A third and he remembered that she was there now in the kitchen. She'd been making coffee, Hasqueth's Finest, and liking the smell of the deep roast blend.

Would you mind if I came round?
You are forward.

I'm coming round, Oliver thought as he climbed out and made his way along the pavement away from the hospital and the Lamp.

Can I trust you?
I'm a policeman.
Yes, but can I trust you?
Of course.

Not today, she thought, *I've things to do and I'm feeling a little under the weather to be honest. Next month, I promise.*

Oliver noodled a taxi firm and then thought about a cab. He remembered that it would be another five minutes, so he began to walk back along Old Tollgate.

How to... pa-pah, pa-pah. Think without thinking.

Have you got secrets?

Oliver searched his pockets for a piece of paper, but he didn't have anything. Of course not, who carried paper? He upturned his left hand and scribbled with his right finger tracing the letter shapes across the lines there.

Victim is dead, but victim isn't missing, therefore victim is still thinking, therefore... still thinking. He underlined it with a swipe that went down the length of his little finger.

A taxi pulled up.

Without looking round, the driver cocked his head to one side to recognize him: *Where to, mate?*

Delaware Towers, Oliver thought back as he clambered in.

That's where I live, Mithering thought back.

The car journey took them around the city along the ring road until they reached the canals. Delaware Towers guarded one end of the fashionable quarter.

That'll be seventeen fifty, the driver thought.

Oliver waited for the buzz and then reckoned with his bank account only to be refused. Of course, effectively this was a new iBrow, or at least the setting was different enough for the bank to complain.

The driver looked at him. "Oi."

"Sorry," said Oliver. *Look, I'm having trouble, but I'm a Police Officer.*

Likely story.

Oliver fished out his warrant card flipping it open.

Just contact the department and I'll claim it on expenses, Oliver thought.

The driver looked doubtful, but there wasn't much he could do now that they had arrived. He could hardly tussle with a policeman.

Oliver got out, looked up at the high rise and then glanced around for the entrance. It was round the side, up a pleasant brick pathway between grass verges.

Oliver thought 'police' at the door and it refused.

He'd have to register there too – this was a nightmare! *Nothing bloody worked.*

Or maybe it was because he'd been suspended, in which case he'd just impersonated a Police Officer.

A woman came out and Oliver tried to slip past.

"Excuse me!" she shouted: *Rude sod.*

"Police," said Oliver, showing his warrant card again.

She hesitated.

"Ma'am."

She was clearly torn, but left him to it.

He found the lift and selected the fourth floor.

The corridor had 400 to 420 one way and 421 to 425 the other. He found Mithering's 403 quickly enough.

There was a bell, he rang it.

No answer.

I'm here, he thought at Mithering.

That was quick.

Will you let me in?

There was a long pause before the door clicked. It was thought operated: she was clearly not a drinker.

Oliver pushed it open and went in.

Hi, Mithering thought, *would you like tea or coffee?*

Hasqueth Finest: Mithering likes this and so do 113 of her friends.

Oliver ignored the spam: *Tea,* he thought perversely.

Milk?

Please.

Sugar?

Yes, why are you 'Mithering' and not 'Jane Deacon'?

I run a thlog.

"What sort of thlog?" Oliver said aloud. He moved along a passage which opened up at the end into a wide room with a superb view over the canal with the swanky bars and restaurants arrayed below.

There was silence.

The windows were thick, triple glazed.

Oliver thought: *What sort of thlog?*

Exposés of local corruption.

I see.

Everything looked normal, lived in, with a red sofa and a coat thrown over a chair, but it smelt musty and stale.

Where are you now?

In the kitchen making tea, silly.

There was no sound, no clatter of kettle, spoons and crockery.

Come into the lounge.

In a minute.

Now, and let me know when you're here.

Oh, all right, Mithering thought, *I'll play along... OK, I'm here.*

Oliver had identified the door to the kitchen. Through it he could see chrome fittings and dark coloured wooden surfaces.

He checked: *Are you in the lounge?*

Yes.

Describe it.

This is foolish.

Humour me.

OK, it's square, red sofa, rather untidy and it has a wonderful view over the city. You can see Bar Terrific and Tony's.

Where are you standing now?

Why?

Come on.

At the window, looking out at the city. Why? Are you down there?

Oliver went to the window too: it was an impressive view, full of glass towers glinting in the sunlight. Looking down, there was indeed a good view of the bar and the restaurant. He could even see the Menagerie Theatre in the distance.

What else can you see?

I can see the Omniscient Tower and the West District Spires.

Oliver could too.

There was one further question: *What's the weather like?*

Sunny intervals, top temperature 15 degrees, feels like 13, chance of rain 20% – why do you ask?

No reason.

No one thought 'sunny intervals' and 'top temperature'. It was sunny now, it was warm now, you hoped it didn't rain later. She was rethinking... no, formulating and thinking again a noodle of the weather forecast. Like a machine. Perhaps she was a machine, a computer somewhere running on a program that analysed all the real Mithering's thoughts and predicted her responses. Just like the Thought Store did. She was no more than a sophisticated stooge. Mithering, whoever she had been, obviously had never thought about the weather.

"We are the sum of our thoughts," he said.

There was no answer, because there was no-one to answer.

"I'm so sorry," Oliver said.

You should see it, Mithering thought. *It's a gorgeous view. I often stand here and think about it.*

I've seen it, Oliver thought. *I'm sorry, I have some bad news. You can't make it.*

I'm here.

Where? By the canal? By Tony's? I can't see you.

I'm afraid, Miss, I have to inform you that you're dead.

Oliver sat down on the arm of the sofa.

What to do, he thought.

That's not very funny, Mithering thought.

Do you have any paper and a pen?

I thought 'that's not v—

Paper and pen?

Yes.

Where?

In my apartment.

No, I mean where exactly? Describe it.

It's in the top drawer of the cupboard by the door.

Oliver looked over, went across and opened the drawer. There was a pad of fancy writing paper; the sort that mothers used to get small children to write 'Thank You' letters to grandparents on.

Oliver wrote quickly: Victim Jane Deacon dead, still thinking, like a fridge, like a... lights on but no-one's home.

His hand was cramping from the effort. He'd not used handwriting since... ever. Or at least since the Sergeant's Exam. Or that bar in Chinatown. He'd have to relearn.

Relearn what?

"Damn," he said aloud. *How to think without thinking?*

How to think without thinking what?

It was like some Chinese proverb: *The sound of one hand clapping or something.*

Oliver, you're not making sense.

"The thing is," he said, pacing the floor, "these thoughts must be coming from somewhere just as the fridge thinks to you when it's low on milk or needs defrosting. But no modern fridge needs defrosting. I'm talking nonsense. I can't keep this up."

There was a picture on the mantelpiece of three young women larking about in the sunshine. He picked it up and flipped it over: there was a date and 'Jane' was the third name along. Looking at them again, he picked her out. She was slim, attractive, happy and so full of life and, having her thoughts in his head, he felt overwhelmingly sad.

Perhaps it would be kinder not to convince her.

Convince me of what?

And she had the wrong build for Unknown 271, but here were a lot of numbers before 271.

Solve this one, then he'd have solved 271 and 272... and all the other unknown Unknowns.

He had the name of a victim now and all her thoughts to pick through. Not his case, but a case. At some point she must have gone from alive, happy like in this photograph, to the back seat of some car, somewhere?

Zhaodi had said the Chinese Room was new.

Something exploded, a door splintering.

Two men came barging in, black shapes, against the beige wall. Armed! Oliver recognised one as Tedman, his thoughts a maelstrom of fractured phrases and special jargon, which Oliver filtered out automatically. The other was terrifying, a blank, human shaped gap in the world.

Oliver put out his hand to protect himself, more afraid of the thought-zombie than the real person playing some cerebral.

Shit, what's the emergency hashtag today?

Mithering responded: *I'm not police–*

The lead man had a gun in his hand, yellow with black stripes and evil looking.

Shit! It's a Ta–

Oliver felt a sharp pain, looked down and his whole body began shaking. There were leads going out to the Taser... *must... pull leads... n!*&°%@#.*

He sank to his knees, fitting from the electric shock and mashing the inside of his mouth with his teeth. His arms and legs jerked rigid, shivering and vibrating energetically as his muscles went into spasm. His iBrow glitched: haywire, overloading, speckling lights and crackles of sound in his brain. It was as if the picture of Jane Deacon, the sunny intervals, bad news, pen, paper, Chinese food and everything all crashed into a single spark. His brain seemed to turn inside out.

The closest man pulled the leads from Oliver's chest and rolled them back into the Taser, while the other man flipped Oliver's body over.

Oliver knew he was going to die.

He knew he'd be in the morgue with Doctor Ridge picking over his bones: Tepee to Red Indian. Or never found. He knew it with that instinctive part of his brain, that reptile hiding at the back of his skull that was so subsumed by his conscious mind, a conscious mind now on fire as the short-circuiting iBrow flared and delivered utterly convincing nonsense. His sight particularly was hijacked by restaurant offers and Mithering and Jasmine and police updates all turned into visual imagery.

He blacked out. Had he? Was he?

His body crumped roughly down in a car boot.

It was dark.

Oliver still saw everything he knew, randomly, like a collage made from ancient newspaper cuttings.

He closed his eyes, put his hand over his eyes, tried to–

The sun exploded.

It was the boot being opened.

The daylight was like laser light.

He was dragged out.

Different men.

His mind was coming back as the iBrow rebooted, but the nerve connections felt bruised and fried. Somehow, with his brow emptied by the denial attack and the hospital treatment, there wasn't as much to load. He was coming to faster than they expected.

The floor was concrete, dusty and smelt of glue. A man bent into the boot, his hands tattooed with Chinese symbols, and heaved Oliver out. They dragged his limp body along the floor.

"Get the brow," said one. "Before he can think."

The other bent down.

A knife glinted, wide, steel, serrated.

Oliver kicked out, punched, connected, felt a strong pain in his left shoulder and then, as they fought, he tumbled. He, and his assailant were airborne, flying, before crashing in mire: grey, congealing, sucking him down...

Another shape loomed above. "We've got his pin and his password – every good boy deserves chocolate – so just fill it in."

"For fuck's sake," the other man shouted, wading to stay upright. Oliver's iBrow wasn't active enough to recognise him or he might have been someone without a brow. It hardly mattered.

Above him, a machine lurched into action with a grating diesel sound as its engine started. Oliver half-crawled, half-swam to the wall. It was wooden, wooden all round, planks to hold in...

A splattering caught his attention: heavy gloop sloshed down. They were filling the hole with concrete.

The other man screamed, high pitched and unreal. He was scrabbling, trying to swim like a sea lion up a waterfall.

The knife was sticking out of Oliver's shoulder. He hadn't even realised he'd been stabbed. When he pulled it out, the wound spilt a vivid red splash over the fresh concrete.

The man's incoherent noises formed words, "No, no, no..."

Oliver glanced up.

The others had gone, leaving them to their fate.

Stay on top, no chance.

Stand on the other man's shoulders?

At the side the concrete spat, bubbles rose and burst creating a miniature eruption like hot springs.

The walls were smooth.

Wait! The bubbles meant the concrete was seeping out of a hole, a line of – yes – sunlight. Oliver waded over, jammed the knife into the crack and twisted, levering.

"Oi!"

Oliver ignored him, pushing no matter what the pain in his hands and shoulder did. It moved, creating a hole that filled with concrete so quickly.

A tidal surge announced the arrival of the man. He smashed against the wall next to Oliver.

Oliver spat to clear his mouth. "I–"

His brow came on, the other man's fear and panic hit him like a train: *LET ME OUT, BASTARD!!!*

Oliver jerked backwards as if struck: *My head!*

The wall failed.

Both men hurtled through, sucked down by the funnelling mire.

They landed somewhere.

Oliver coughed up a mouthful of grit and muck.

The man grabbed him.

Oliver stabbed upwards – again – twisted, then let go of the hilt, saw the wave of grey swallow his attacker and then he was wading away, desperately trying to outrun the avalanche. There was a metal ladder set in the wall and he climbed, the already setting foundations grasping his ankles and trying to hold him down.

The brow-to-brow link severed abruptly.

Oliver stumbled at the top, grazed his knee and then toppled like a statue.

Sorry, I can't make it in to work tomorrow, Oliver thought, *I'm feeling a little under the weather to be honest.*

He retched, there was rock stuck in the back of his throat.

Thanks Ma'am... I mean, Freya, Oliver thought, *I'll be fine. I've taken some paracetamol and I'm going to sleep it off.*

He tried to wipe his eyes clean and his hand put more filth over his face.

I'm moving out of Jellicoe's, Oliver thought.

He picked up Freya's thoughts, but he'd not followed her, but he was following her, and her thoughts washed over him as if they were spoken in some foreign language.

No, no, Jasmine, Oliver thought, *I don't want to miss going out with your friends on Saturday.*

He vomited.

That's lovely, Oliver thought.

"Christ!"

Miss you too, Oliver thought.

He shouted aloud, "Who the hell is Oliver!?"

Sweet dreams to you too.

And then he realised he was dead.

TUESDAY

"Jesus!"

Jellicoe practically fell over backwards when he saw Braddon standing in the doorway. In the light of the porch, he was a terrifying figure. The Inspector clutched his chest in shock.

"Show me the way to go home," Braddon sang. "Pa-pah, pa-pah, pa-pah!"

"Are you drunk?"

"I had a little drink now, fucking now, booze, booze, booze, lovely booze..."

"What?"

"Booze, lovely booze, a drink, don't mind if I do."

Jellicoe found the whiskey bottle as Braddon left dusty footprints in the hall. When the old man handed it over, Braddon knocked it back, almost screaming at the way the stinging liquid attacked his throat. Half the bottle went before his iBrow gave up.

Braddon handed it back.

Jellicoe rubbed the rim and took a swig himself.

"You look like a ghost."

"I am."

"Hey?"

"Follow me," said Braddon, tapping his forehead.

Jellicoe tilted his head to one side in thought.

I am at home in bed, but I can't sleep, Oliver thought. *I don't feel well.*

"You're home, ill, in bed."

"Got the 'flu."

"Looks like more than 'flu."

"Aye," Braddon took the bottle back. He drank. "The fuckers killed me and dumped my body in the foundations of a fucking apartment block."

Jellicoe's eyes widened.

"But–"

"I'm back from the grave and I've not died."

"You're not making sense."

"They've got something that thinks for you. That's why their victims don't show up on the missing list, because they aren't missing if they are still thinking."

"So that's what they did with Unknown 271 and the other one?"

"And Jane Deacon and me and probably another few dozen... something. Whatever."

Braddon caught sight of himself in the hall mirror: he did look like a corpse, grey and dusty, something dug up from somewhere.

"I look like shit," he said.

I'm feeling fragile, Oliver thought, *so I won't come out tomorrow. I'm OK, I've a thlog I want to finish.*

"Here," said Jellicoe, handing him a bathrobe. "Don't get it on the stair carpet."

Next week I'll make it up to you, Jasmine, Oliver thought, *I promise.*

"I need to unfollow myself. They are like my own thoughts in here," said Braddon tapping his temple. "I need to unfollow myself."

"Can you?"

Braddon tried, but this possibility obviously hadn't crossed the designers' minds. "No... and I actually feel like

I've had a warm milk and gone to bed, except... this is insane."

"Never mind."

Braddon winced. "I need a bandage," he said.

I know it's 2am and you have to sleep, Oliver thought.

"I'll contact the station."

Braddon put his hand on Jellicoe's arm: "Don't."

Jellicoe eyed him suspiciously. "Why?"

"They have my pin code and password. They didn't get it by scalping me – although that was their plan – they got it from the station when I was re-engineering after the denial of service attack."

"How?"

"One of us is one of them."

"Shit? Who?"

"Need to find out, but I need to..."

"Sure."

Goodnight, Jasmine.

"I think my ex-girlfriend and I have come to an understanding to be just friends."

"That's creepy," Jellicoe said.

"Too right."

Braddon did want to wish Jasmine good-night too, but the alcohol prevented him and it wouldn't have been wise. He could follow her, that would be comforting, but Jellicoe was helping Braddon up the stairs. The pain blotted everything out.

The Inspector ran the tap for the bath and then saw the young DC wince as he tried to undress. Jellicoe went back in and helped undress him, then assisted him into the water.

"Nothing I haven't seen," Jellicoe said.

"Someone covered in this."

"Well, maybe not plastered quite as literally."

Braddon laughed, "It's concrete."

Jellicoe washed the man, drained the water and then repeated the process. The wound in the left shoulder kept opening up, but once the bath was over, Jellicoe found some antiseptic. He dabbed it on some cotton wool and then applied it to the wound: Braddon yelped and then started breathing in sudden snorts.

"It'll hurt."

"Just do it."

Jellicoe did: through his skull, Braddon could hear himself grinding his teeth, his fillings grating under the pressure. He let out a breath when Jellicoe put the bottle down and picked up a pack of butterfly stitches. The Inspector, despite the alcohol, opened the packaging, applied the strips and then wrapped a bandage around Braddon's shoulder with obvious expertise.

"You were in the army?" Braddon asked.

"No."

"Fair enough."

Jellicoe bit the bandage and ripped it. He tied a knot.

"There."

"Thanks."

"Sleep is what you need."

Braddon nodded.

Jellicoe helped him across the landing, which Braddon needed as he was the one walking like an old man.

"Can you get in on your own?"

"Yes."

Jellicoe went out without a word.

Braddon found his fingers didn't work and it took several attempts to grip the quilt. He got in, conscious of the damp from his body seeping into the bed. He settled before he realised that he'd left the light on.

"Jell–"

The Inspector came in with a drink.

"Here you go," said Jellicoe as he put a glass down on the bedside cabinet.

Braddon picked it up, but Jellicoe put his palm across the top.

"It's for the morning," Jellicoe explained. "When you wake up, you'll need something to disconnect. Breakfast of Champions."

"Thanks."

Braddon put it back down on the bedside cabinet and it chinked as the amber liquid heaved back and forth. There was ice in the glass. It would have melted before morning, but it showed a level of care from the Inspector.

"You're welcome," Jellicoe said.

The Inspector turned the light out as he left.

In the dark, afraid, Braddon followed people. He idly scrolled up and down Jasmine's thoughts, Mox's cerebral intruded and Chen was bored of orange juice now that everyone else at the party was drunk; Melissa was upset that Adams turned out to be a bastard like all the others, Draith was wondering why his wife was sulking and Oliver himself was thinking of leaving the Police Force to move to France and thinking at Jasmine and she was thinking back in response and a bird cried out outside the window and Jasmine was hurt that he was thinking of leaving the country, even if they'd split up, and Chen wanted to organise a leaving party and Braddon thought he'd never sleep despite being drunk and so utterly exhausted...

...his dreams were like flicking between different thlog feeds, a kaleidoscope of differing tropes, their memes mangled together with confusing contrasts and juxtapositions: this, that, the other. Somehow, the mind assumed they made sense and created a narrative to connect them. They could be recorded, assigned a personal hashtag and reviewed in the morning. There were even people who charged to interpret these nonsense poems.

Braddon's night was full of the body in the car, but he was inside the car. A brick bounced off the bonnet as Jellicoe served him drinks at the bar installed where the passenger seat should have been. There was Chinese food and people with spaces where their foreheads should be.

Inside the gaps in their heads, tiny workers built scaffolding, and laid concrete foundations ready for the installation of iBrow technology that, at this exaggerated scale, looked like girders and steel reinforcing.

Braddon fell in, past the men in hard hats head-butting each other, and along the labyrinth of brow filaments until they became the organic pipes and conduits of the organic brain. Here monkeys swung between the branches, and then he went deeper to a place where reptiles slithered in the slime.

And then he was packing, his flight tickets ordered and his French translation thapp installed.

Soil came up and smothered him, grey and cloying, and it melted until he was deep underwater, swimming down into the dark.

Of course, it made no sense.

Dreams never did.

You only had to noodle your own to find that out.

Flight at six in the morning.

Chen wished him luck.

Seventeen people liked that.

Sad to be leaving.

Flight called.

Boarding.

Bye.

WEDNESDAY

Oliver was tired from the flight to France, but the cottage he'd rented was wonderful, quaint and old-fashioned. A perfect bolt hole after his suspension from duty, a place to some thinking and get his shit together. First, he was going to have a glass of wine, watch the sun go down behind the vineyards on those beautiful rolling hills and then get some sleep.

I can feel myself unwinding already, Oliver thought, *this is a good vintage and so cheap over here.*

Braddon himself felt befuddled when Jellicoe woke him up, somehow expecting to come round in a rural farmhouse to croissants, red wine and cheese.

The scotch had a raw egg in it and caused Braddon to gag, but he got it down. The white soothed his throat as the whiskey burned. His iBrow crossfaded from sleep to insobriety.

"Your thought stream is unbroken," Jellicoe said. He looked tired as if he'd been up all night working. "The other Oliver is... Oliver. You appear to be the anomaly, Braddon."

"Yea, I think I'm screwed," Braddon said. "And my brow thinks it's tomorrow."

"It is tomorrow, you've slept for nearly thirty-six hours."

"What?"

Braddon ached, bruised and battered as he was, and he winced when Jellicoe checked the wound and changed his dressing.

"Healing nicely," Jellicoe said. "You were lucky."

"I feel like... shit."

"Have some more medicine."

The next drink was egg-less.

"Think of it as a pain killer," Jellicoe said. "It's your liver and heart you should be worried about."

"I'll drink to that."

Jellicoe found some clothes for Braddon, trousers that needed an extra hole in the belt before they stayed round his waist and shoes that needed two pairs of socks. Braddon's own clothes had actually set on the lino in the kitchen. Jellicoe found a hammer to break them enough to get them into his flip top bin. He was sweating when he'd finished and took some tablets with a scotch.

"And drink this?" said Jellicoe, offering Braddon yet another drink.

"I've had enough," said Braddon.

"Out there, my lad, is a murderer. Someone who can bump people off with impunity and somehow get round the system. If he knows you're still alive, then..."

Jellicoe ran his finger across his throat, and then for good measure pulled this imaginary blade over his forehead and mimed ripping out his iBrow.

"...best to be thoughtless."

Braddon saw the sense in this. "Over the yardarm somewhere I suppose. France perhaps?"

"That's the spirit," said Jellicoe. "Would you recognise them?"

Braddon thought back, trying to recall events before his iBrow was rebooted. The images in his mind were disjointed, dreamlike, but he saw faces, clothing, and a hand with a Chinese tattoo.

"Find one, follow him," Jellicoe commanded.

Braddon nodded.

Jellicoe cooked breakfast, all-English, and Braddon ate in silence, favouring his right hand when possible. His left was fine, he had the full range of movement even in the shoulder joint, but it felt numb. When he'd finished, and supped his tea, Jellicoe returned to the kitchen table. He had a number of hip flasks, a set of lock picks and a Taser.

"Fuck!" Braddon remembered his experience and how lucky he was to be alive. "Where did you get that?"

"Present."

"It's illegal."

"We can be issued with them."

Braddon picked it up.

"You press that button," said Jellicoe.

"I know."

Braddon pressed it: lightning fizzed between the two electrodes frying the air. A fairground dodgem smell of ozone mixed with the aroma of fried bacon.

"I've only got the one," the Inspector said.

Braddon put it back on the table and pushed it away with the tip of his index finger. "You have it."

It was strange to realise that Tasers had once replaced firearms as the 'safer' option. Jellicoe was probably old enough to remember that, but thankfully they'd reverted to proper bullets: at least with those, there was a wound option. Braddon was glad when Jellicoe packed it away into a small canvas bag along with a few other items.

"We're not going to war," Braddon said. "We're police."

Jellicoe gave him a pitying look.

"OK, we're going to war."

It was a lovely day outside, far too warm for two pairs of socks, but the trousers, shirt and jacket were loose.

Jellicoe got the car out and Braddon sat in the passenger seat.

"There's drink in the glove compartment," Jellicoe told him.

"Aye."

They drove out towards town, skirting Old Tollgate, and reached an abandoned building site. Jellicoe parked some distance away. When they reached the street corner, Braddon could see Chedding Shopping Centre jutting out in the distance.

"These building sites must circle the city," Braddon said. He noodled a satellite picture and remembered the pock-marked nature of the area.

"Come on," Jellicoe ordered, and they moved across to the construction site. Jellicoe glanced up and down the street and then cut the padlock with bolt cutters. The heavy chain rattled out of the metal gate and they were in. Jellicoe slipped the chain back and repositioned the broken padlock so that anyone looking wouldn't be alerted.

"How do you know it's this one?" Braddon asked.

"My head!"

"All right, you deduced it, but how?"

"You thought 'My head!'. There were scrambled thoughts, which I guessed were when you were tasered, a long gap and then that. It was the last entry before you started worrying about the 'flu, so I checked the GPS location."

"Ah," Braddon said, and he looked around. "Standard detective work."

"Recognise anything?"

"All building sites look the same."

"Hmm... let's try over there."

They picked their way between towers of breeze blocks. It was eerie and, like the remains of ancient temples, the masonry spoke of another age, except this one was an unrealised future. It seemed unlikely that these foundations would ever support a brave new world. In places rusting metal rods stuck out of the ground ready to reinforce columns. Sections of concrete had crumbled and collapsed in miniature landslides, weathered into the ubiquitous grey dust that coated everything.

Jellicoe was sweating noticeably.

Further on, around a corner, was a surreal sight of devastation much like a volcanic eruption. A pyroclastic flow had powdered through the site and the wave of lava had frozen in place, a solid sculpture set in concrete. Upstream, there was the burst wooden surround that Braddon had attacked with the knife.

Jellicoe pointed: "There!"

At the side, sticking out of the grey like a fossilized man or a victim of Vesuvius, was the misshapen statue of a man, stopped in the act of calling for help.

They climbed down the metal ladder, Jellicoe panting with the exertion and Braddon wincing because of his shoulder, and then they made their way across.

The corpse was half-in, half-out of the concrete.

Braddon brushed at the man's hand and revealed the tattoos. He showed Jellicoe the Chinese symbols.

"Any ID?"

Braddon tried to pat down the jacket, but he only succeeded in generating a cloud of dust. Jellicoe reached inside to the pockets, cracking the layer of concrete much as he'd broken Braddon's own discarded clothes.

The Inspector shook his head. "As if there's ever any ID."

"Trouser pockets?" Braddon suggested, but it was a half-hearted idea. They'd have had to use a hammer and chisel or even a jack hammer.

"If he was alive we'd be able to recognise him," Jellicoe said.

Braddon looked at the man's forehead. "Could we zap him with your Taser? We'd only need it to be active for a second or so."

"We'll have to read the number."

Braddon snorted at that idea, it was tucked beneath the man's skin, but when he saw Jellicoe take out a retractable knife, he realised the man was serious.

"I think..." but Braddon didn't think anything. He was technically drunk, so stupid ideas might seem like good ideas.

"You don't have to look."

Braddon didn't.

The sound of cutting and ripping, along with the old man's laboured breathing, was not pleasant. The patter of falling water made him turn back. Jellicoe was cleaning the naked iBrow with whiskey from his hip flask. Braddon caught sight of the mess and had an image of Unknown 271's ruined face.

"We are way out of line here," Braddon said.

"Not if we get a result... here."

Jellicoe gave Braddon the device, so he could fish in his bag again. He brought out a magnifying glass.

"Well," the Inspector said, "all detectives should have one."

Braddon actually laughed.

"Go on, I'm old, your eyes are better than mine."

Braddon took the magnifying glass and moved it back and forth to bring the iBrow's details into focus. It wasn't strong enough, but then he noticed the semi-circle of thicker glass at the bottom of the lens. This was much better, and he could scan across the device to read the sixteen digit code that had been etched into the ceramic.

"NL-Z... 189..."

"Dutch!"

"3849... 123... slash GHT."

Braddon tried to follow it, but he couldn't hold the whole code in his head at once.

"Here," Jellicoe said holding up his notebook, but he jerked his arm down again. "Shit."

"What is it?"

"Nothing."

Braddon followed the code: there was nothing in it that suggested he'd been thinking about killing anyone, and this was definitely the same man. Unless they swapped the body for another?

"They can control thought," Braddon said, and then the panic hit him. "We've got to stop this."

Jellicoe took hold of his lapels and pushed him against the wall. "Be quiet, you don't want to be carted off back to the psych ward."

"But they must have changed this man's thoughts," Braddon complained. "Thought, it gets in your head, changes your thoughts."

"That's the point."

"NO, but–"

"Don't join the foil hat brigade," said Jellicoe.

"No... but–"

Braddon shoved Jellicoe away getting a sharp stab of pain in his own left shoulder. "They make you do things! They control you! We killed that woman in the car park! I did."

"You did not!!!"

"This is a mistake."

"What?"

"These things," Braddon shouted, pointing first at his head and then holding up the recovered iBrow. "Did anyone consider what it would do to us?"

"They did medical tests – ah, God!"

"Not the technical stuff, but to us as a society. We've no privacy–"

"We can't turn back the clock."

"We just did things because we could and the more we could do, the more thinly spread we became."

"OK, Braddon, calm – ah – down."

"The deepest conversations I've ever had in my life have been with you, a pissed old man."

"Thanks, I'm sure – arrgh."

"What?"

"Ah, I'm all right."

"No, seriously?" Braddon said, seeing Jellicoe's pained expression. The man was holding his left side.

Jellicoe winced and then stated the obvious, "I'm – ah – having a fucking heart attack."

"Jeez."

Automatically Braddon thought for an ambulance only to wince at the migraine shadow. He was drunk, they were both drunk. No wonder there had been a drop in alcohol related hospital admissions: there was no damn way to call an ambulance!

Braddon glanced back in the direction they had come. It seemed a lot further to the gate than he remembered.

"Come on!" he said, grabbing Jellicoe and practically carrying him along. He turned the corner, Jellicoe's legs stopped helping and when Braddon checked him, the old man's face was grey, an impossible concrete-like matt finish, despite the beads of sweat forming around his iBrow crease.

"Not much further," Braddon said in a surprisingly light tone.

"Always thought it would be cirrhosis that got me," Jellicoe said through clenched teeth. The man clutched at Braddon like a drowning man, pulling and clawing to stay upright.

The blocks and metal cables were like obstacles, almost deliberately placed to force them to change direction to weave between them. Braddon panicked: where was the gate?

He stopped, glanced about, noodled his GPS location in desperation.

"Tracks!" Jellicoe managed.

Braddon looked down, saw their own footprints in the dust and started off again. The gate appeared to be getting further away with each step and then Braddon was trying to get the chain off. The broken padlock caught. Braddon shook desperately but it wouldn't come off. He needed both hands and Jellicoe slipped away from his grip, sinking to the floor.

The chain clattered free.

Jellicoe was a weight, gasping in short irregular bursts, and too heavy to pick up.

Braddon went out.

"Hey! HEY!" he shouted.

People stopped, looked, moved away.

"Police!" he added, fumbling for his warrant card. "Call an ambulance."

Braddon recognised an office worker going by the ridiculous handle of Moosher.

Why don't you, mate?

"Call an ambulance!"

Are you drunk?

"Look, you–" *fucking idiot...*

It was the timespan or the exercise or the panic, or all three, but Braddon's brow came on. His thoughts were desperate: *Emergency! Ambulance!*

Hashtag, Moosher thought.

Hashtag, emergency, Braddon thought as he forced himself to calm down: *Hashtag emergency, ambulance, heart attack.*

On our way, came a thought directed in reply.

Stay here and direct them, Braddon thought at Moosher.

No way.

Or I'll arrest you!

Braddon stumbled back to Jellicoe: the man's breathing was staccato and shallow. The Inspector was trying to gain Braddon's attention.

"This..." said Jellicoe.

"Forget it," Braddon said, but Jellicoe was insistent, waving his working right arm towards the Detective Constable. Braddon took what was thrust towards him, Jellicoe's notebook.

"I can't..." Braddon began.

"Nonsense."

"But–"

"It's a game."

The man's skin looked like the whites of his eyes, pale and veined with blood, and a square of his forehead stuck out like something unnatural. Braddon held on, his own hands turning white under his grip as if the old man was infecting the younger man's extremities and bleaching the life out of him too.

"Hang on," said Braddon. "Help's coming."

"Look..." ...*after Pamela.*

Braddon recognized Jellicoe and flinched.

A hand landed on Braddon's shoulders, wrenching him up and around. It was a paramedic. Braddon recognised him and then was awash with the man's frantic thoughts of so many cc's of this and systolic that and a sense of failing.

Braddon stood back, took a few steps away now that he was surplus to requirements, a spare part in a drama of life and death. Another medic came with a stretcher on wheels and they hauled the crumpled, fitful carcass up onto the clean white sheets. There were injections, controlled panic and then they hoisted the Inspector into the back of an ambulance. The doors banged shut and soon they were out of recognition range, hurtling through the streets beneath retina-piercing blue and a screaming siren.

If life was a game, then Jellicoe had made a bad move.

Moosher hadn't stayed around.

Braddon was on his own now, the crumpled notebook in his fist. He knew so few people: Mithering, Jasmine, Jellicoe (who he still hadn't followed), Freya, Chen, Mox, Draith...

He'd started following those few again, but he'd once known hundreds. When he took his Sergeant's Exam, he recalled unfollowing a whole list, but they'd gone. He could noodle them, but as far as his brain went, they didn't exist anymore. Out of mind, out of sight. Even here, at the side of the street, he recognised twenty-seven people within range: Michael, Valerie, Jackie, Gwen, Steve, Rory, Tilton, Zoneman, Rex, Templeton, Jane, TerryB, Kriffin,

Andy, another Andy, Jessica, Sarah, Bug, Mohammed, Bill... Moosher. He knew them all, or at least he could remember everything about them any time he wanted to. But did he *know* them? Did he have a connection to any of them? Even Jasmine? He knew what she thought, but it all seemed so trivial and ephemeral now, like everyone else's thoughts. Like his own.

He had no real understanding. All his thoughts were fleeting: here... gone. They skimmed the surface just as the iBrow itself skimmed the frontal lobe. The rest of the brain, that unreachable by thought, was ignored. It was reptile or the unconscious or considered 'unthinking'.

He needed a drink and Jellicoe's hip flask had gone with him.

Which pub, mate?

Braddon was confused until the cab actually pulled up in front of him. Clearly, he'd been thinking without being aware of it.

Sure... er, the Lamp, he thought getting in, and then, *No, take me to Tensing Row.*

Sure, mate. I hope he doesn't get that dust on my seats.

The cab set off and Braddon tried to steady his breathing. He needed – someone, anyone – and he knew who, but Mithering didn't exist.

As the taxi drove along, passing other drivers and pedestrians, a continual flicker of recognitions spiked in Braddon's iBrow. When they turned into the Row, one jumped to his attention.

Stop! Stop!

He opened the door before the cab came to a halt and he ran back the way they'd come.

Oi, the cab driver thought.

Keep the meter going, Braddon replied.

Braddon caught up with the girl with the long black hair. From the back, she could have been anyone, but her recognition was clear to all.

Jasmine, Braddon thought, *it's me.*

Yea, yea, push off.

Jasmine... "Jasmine!"

Braddon put his hand on her arm to nudge her around towards him. She turned, snatched her arm away.

Oi, she thought, *leave me alone or I'll think at the police.*

You know me.

She looked him in the eye and thought, *no I don't.*

"It's me," Braddon said. "Braddon. Oliver. Ollie."

"Ollie?"

"I had to change my registration after a denial attack."

"Ollie? Ollie!!! I didn't know it was you," she said, relieved; her words tumbling out, "because I recognised someone else."

Just assign my name to the recognition, Braddon thought back.

Jasmine laughed. *My God, he looks old and filthy. You were in France, why are you back?*

It's been a difficult... how long?

Jasmine blinked, a sign that she was noodling. Braddon used to find it endearing, but it just made her look stupid. *A couple of days*, she thought.

Difficult days, Braddon thought.

Yes – that laugh again, grating – *only a few days... how are you?*

Fine, still suspended, he thought, peeved, *but that's just routine.*

Am I irritating you?

No.

Sincerely?

Of course.

We agreed to be friends and now you're back. Friends don't pester friends. Have you checked my status?

He noodled.

You look stupid when you noodle too, she thought.

Why is it single, looking for—

Because you didn't respond and my friends advised me to... but this is old news – old, old news.

Not for me.

Well, if you paid attention to those you follow.

I've been busy.

Going abroad shouldn't mean you're too busy for your friends. You're lucky to have any. How many do you have?

Her eyelashes fluttered.

She did look stupid.

Oh really, she thought back, *no wonder you only have six – six! – friends–*

I have–

Active, whereas Cheryl, Gloria and I have over five hundred – active!

Look, I've not done anything–

'I've not done anything', she thought, sarcasm in the emoticon, *it's how you think, Ollie, that's the problem. Your thoughts reveal exactly what you are like inside.*

Can we not argue?

All that concern over some dead woman instead of spending time thinking about the living.

Oh God, I'm leaking.

Yes, and you wouldn't be worried about that if your thoughts were virtuous in the first place.

She turned away, walking quickly into the crowd: *I'll show him*, she thought.

Braddon went to catch up again, but the jostling of people slowed him, and the befuddlement of recognitions soon absorbed her, then she was gone. Her thoughts – *stupid git, why did he have to do that* – remained as he was following her, but she had gone beyond recognition range. They were no longer close in both senses of the word. His footsteps slowed until he stopped, motionless, unsure what to do next. The crowd carried on passing him, adjusting their flow and he recognised them as they came into range until everything was a blur.

So many people: *What do they all do?*

I'm an architect... shop retail manager, human resources, children's' entertainer...

What are they all for?

I'm for home... Arsenal, a nice cup of tea and a cake, expelling the thoughtless, such a cute cat thought...

It was all so vacuous. People thought, clearly as it was easy to pick up or noodle, but they didn't consider. They fired off a thought without hesitation and that was an end to the matter. It didn't do to let it develop. Or it did, it developed, mutated and evolved in the zeitgeist of the Thinkersphere as people rethought and rethought. It was the whole that made decisions, trending from one thing to the next: individuals were just one of a crowd.

All these anonymous faces were anonymous. They just went about leading surface lives: going home, football, cup of tea, and if someone inserted a thought – Hasqueth Finest, riot, drink – or if it just popped into someone's head, then coffee would be drunk, heads kicked in and shops looted or... *I could do with a drink.*

No-one organised a riot, it just happened.

No-one organised a conspiracy, it thought for itself.

Technically there must have been a seed idea for the riot, some thought that led to another thought, a rethought and so on, until finally the police were standing firm against an angry mob.

Was there anyone behind all this: some criminal mastermind, a Blofeld, a Moriarty, a Westbourne?

If so, they were probably a virtuous person.

What had Jellicoe said? Hitler liked his dog.

Jasmine was wrong. You are not judged by your thoughts, you are not the sum of your memories, you are judged by your actions. Ridge had said that. A person is what they do.

Braddon walked slowly back to the cab.

Which pub, mate?

Don't care... not the Lamp. No, on second thoughts 'Home James'.

I'm not James.

It was a joke someone said once.

It's not funny.
It wasn't funny when he said it either – sorry.
You look rough.
Fell.

The driver snorted: clearly this lie didn't work via thought.

No, mate, it doesn't.

Home turned out to be Jellicoe's, which was an interesting conclusion from the iBrow settings. He hadn't set up his bank account, so he had to sit in the cab, ignoring the driver's sarcastic thoughts, and think all the security nonsense to set up access to his account. Finally, he felt the buzz and reckoned.

He was glad to get out and through Jellicoe's overgrown garden, but he still picked up the driver's Parthian shot about drunks.

The house seemed empty, but then it had when the Inspector had been there. Braddon supposed it had once rung with thoughts: Jellicoe's and Pamela's. Braddon realised that he'd made a deep connection with Jellicoe despite the man's damn fool refusal to use thought. It was something more primitive than an iBrow follow. He was a buddy, mate... something from the list anyway. There was more to knowing people than social networking.

Braddon found the scotch.

It means I won't be able to follow your thoughts, Mithering reminded. It was creepy.

Sorry, I need a drink.

I'm not creepy and I could advise.

Yes, Braddon agreed. She had, right from the start when he'd interviewed Jessica Stenson for example. Except she hadn't. She'd been virtual all the time.

Sitting at the dining table, he checked Jellicoe's notebook.

His hand shook, causing a light sprinkling of powder to fall on the polished teak. They'd never used this room in all the time they'd had takeaways here.

The book was still covered with concrete dust and dried blood from the ad hoc surgery that the Inspector had performed.

You still haven't explored the Jessica Stenson lead and questioned her husband, Mithering thought.

What would be the... all right.

Braddon noodled the man. He was a business executive specialising in large construction projects and he'd done very well for himself until the last economic downturn.

Perhaps, Braddon thought, *I should question the man.*

Do, Mithering thought.

Braddon noodled and remembered him again, he thought at Stenson Project Manager: *I'm DC Oliver Braddon and I'd like to have a word, Sir.*

It was a lead, Braddon supposed.

Mithering agreed: *Yes.*

Rubbish lead, but something to go on.

Hello, the Stenson Project Manager thought, *what's this about?*

It's about your stolen car.

My stolen car — you mean my wife's.

Yes, that's right.

I heard there was a development.

From your wife?

In a roundabout way.

Could I see you?

I'm very busy on a Chinese project, I'm in America, but next month, perhaps.

Thank you, Sir.

So, a dead end.

Perhaps the Chinese project, Mithering thought.

In Jellicoe's book, the last thing added was the dead man's code.

Braddon followed him: of course, there was nothing. The man was dead, lying in an unfinished tomb, but a quick noodle and Braddon remembered the man's last thoughts, a strange dark mirroring of his memories when the two of them had fought. Tedman, that rang a chord.

I've been recognised. Woah, nearly hit that foil head. And you. I'd rather have curry tonight. With beer. When I know, I'll let you know – OK. Gotta concentrate, we're here. God, another building site. Yes, yes, I'll get him out of the boot. Just a moment. It's loaded. I'm doing it, I'm doing it. Ah, for fuck's... the bugger got me. I've done my knee in. If I've got concussion, you're for it. For fuck's sake. No, no, no... bastard's found a way out. LET ME OUT, BASTARD!!! Oi. Oh God, oh God. I'll get the bastard. Bastard. I'm stabbed. There's blood. Oh God, a lot of blood. Help, help. Mummy. It hurts. Can't breathe. Light – oh!

That was the fight from the recognition in Mithering's apartment to the struggle in the concrete. There were bits in the middle that must have been the car journey, about half an hour according to the time codes, but there didn't seem anything like enough from Tedman for the time interval. He didn't think much. They must be hiring morons.

I don't remember Tedman, Mithering thought.

No, well... you weren't exactly in recognition range.

Braddon tried to remember the initial struggle. He noodled his thoughts and noticed that he'd recognised Tedman. That must tally with Tedman's corresponding thought about being recognised.

Had he been the man with the Taser?

Yes, Braddon was reasonably confident, although it had been confusing. Who knew what having your iBrow fried did to you?

So how had the man fired the Taser without thinking about it?

Or, if it hadn't been him, stood next to a Taser without any reaction going out from his iBrow?

Even digging deeper, looking for those minor thoughts that leaked out, didn't help.

Braddon took a sip of whiskey. It helped with the thinking without thinking.

There was, amongst it all, 'Foil head' – they must have narrowly avoided hitting a pedestrian. He could cross reference the time and find that person. The foil hat wouldn't have obstructed their thoughts; if indeed they'd been wearing a foil hat and it wasn't just an insult. But it would only confirm what route they'd travelled from Mithering's to the construction site.

Braddon noodled for more and scrolled through the man's thoughts for the previous day, and then week, looking for something, anything, that jumped out as unusual. The man thought about curry, beer, cerebrals, some 'tart' who was giving him jip, spending the readies and the bloody landlord wanting his rent.

Readies: cash... oh, game points for a cerebral.

Another drink.

His brow's safeties had come on some time ago. He wasn't sure when. His last coherent thought had been to Mithering.

Braddon felt tired. He checked his own thoughts to see how long he'd been up and it did seem a long day despite the large alcohol induced gaps. But even with these gaps, he'd had more thoughts than Tedman.

Braddon noodled the two of them together, comparing their thoughts at different levels of concentration. They were comparable in places, but Braddon's had long empty thoughtless periods, whereas Tedman had had fewer thoughts during his much longer active time.

Perhaps he was just stupid. He had let a Tasered man get the better of him, after all. The idiot probably let spam influence his buying habits.

On a whim, Braddon noodled the dead man's reactions to advertising.

The man would be reported missing soon, unless he went to stay with Oliver on a happy sabbatical in France in a lovely villa, apparently visiting a vineyard now and enjoying a nice Merlot, although Braddon was getting used to letting this element of his mental landscape zip past.

Most of Tedman's spam was about virtual items for a cerebral.

Useless.

This was a real conspiracy, because they'd tried to kill him. The building site had been real, the men real, so the lack of information on Noodle was frustrating. Westbourne had been someone who had 'done people in' to use Jellicoe's expression. He was nowhere to be found. It was associated with this Chinese Room, so perhaps it wasn't too much of a leap to suggest that Westbourne was in this room. Perhaps it was more than a room, an underground headquarters encased in a Faraday Cage to prevent any network signals getting in, like a secret lair hidden in a volcano.

"But what would be the damn point!" Braddon shouted at the wall.

If you didn't want to use thought, then you could get your iBrow removed.

But you wouldn't, because then you'd be disconnected and unable to do anything.

Just like someone hiding in a network black spot.

But Westbourne, or whoever, wasn't disconnected. The bruises all over Braddon's body were testament to how connected they had been.

He was missing something.

Noodle didn't help. Jellicoe went on about gut feelings. He was talking about using the back part of the brain, the part that the iBrow filaments couldn't reach, the reptile zone. All that pent up, uncivilised instinct – that's what the old man wanted him to use. But then he'd just be some unthinking brute.

Jellicoe had written all this thinking without thinking down.

Braddon fished out Jellicoe's notebook and began thumbing through the pages. The Inspector's handwriting was a type of encryption technique. There was a sudden flash of Braddon's own name. He flicked back, couldn't find it, and had to start again before the page presented itself.

'Braddon' was written in distinct capitals and underlined: smudged, which was a sign that it had been read and reread. Underneath was a note with three 'V's on top of one another and a date, his Sergeant's Exam. Another line said, 'Chen observing'. What did that mean? Was it always Chen giving him a lift for a reason? There was a line from Braddon's name to 'Turner', which must be a note that Freya was his Superintendent.

He needed a drink.

The bottle was empty.

Braddon found another of Jellicoe's whiskies and poured himself a measure, screwing the cap back on. As he lifted the glass to drink, he noticed that his hand was shaking, a slight tremor, nothing more, but Braddon wondered if this was intoxication or withdrawal.

The whiskey tasted good: strawberry, plum, fruitcake... a chocolate hint. No, that was the bloody Merlot.

The whiskey was real.

Why did people want to spend all their time thinking anyway?

Did your number of friends mean anything?

How many friends did he have?

Seven: Doctor Trantor, Moosher, Tedman, Mithering, Chen, Mox, Freya – two of those were dead – but not Jasmine anymore. Jellicoe, who was fighting for his life, had never, ever been a friend, and yet he felt connected to the old man in a stronger way than anyone else.

They weren't real... or they were, but not really friends. Jellicoe had mentioned something about – Braddon noodled – acquaintances and colleagues and mates and there were any number of other words, but now everyone was either a friend or not. They were unreal, virtual...

He knew it wasn't the right term, but–

Braddon felt cold, suddenly very aware: oh, he'd screwed up and now had a migraine shadow to go with the thought.

Braddon accessed his iBrow and checked its spam filters. Obvious adverts were excluded, but some got through. He also rejected charity requests and any in-game activities as no-one wanted to be distracted by someone's cerebral nonsense.

In-game?

Braddon blinked and squinted until his attempts ticked the box.

Which cerebrals?

All.

There it was in Tedman's thoughts: he was a gangster in Mega-Precinct Five. There was loads of it, all the missing thoughts confined to some imaginary place in Chicago. Braddon scanned it, letting certain thoughts jump to the fore:

Take out the door, fifty likes. Taser him. Ha, ha, got him. I know you all like this. A hundred likes to get the body into the getaway car. Take his feet. No-one looking. Get the lift.

The game had gone well: lots of likes, nearly a new level gained until the real world of real gangsters had interrupted the game and murdered him.

So, you could wander around doing anything you wanted, so long as it was in a cerebral. With a one-to-one mapping, Jane Deacon's apartment became Jade Petoas's, Braddon a dirty cop and the construction site was... ha! A construction site.

Braddon noodled: Mega-Precinct Five – a small scale game 'configurable to your own personal environment' made by Spades Software, a subsidiary of Westbourne Industries, UK, and...

Flicking through Jellicoe's notebook wasn't needed, but there it was, the man's obsession with Westbourne. He hadn't 'disappeared', he'd simply gone into a game and was wandering around merrily ignored by everyone.

How many?

Pretty much everyone played a cerebral or fiddled around with their social media information, their heads cocked to one side, or their eyes closed, or whatever other tick they developed. Braddon didn't, he'd never really got into gaming, and thank goodness, because he didn't want to have any strange body language issues.

Braddon rubbed his forehead. He could noodle games: he went for thoughts on Mega-Precinct Five and it topped out immediately with a list too big to comprehend. Obviously, even for this small game, there were millions of people all over the world playing it. He filtered out everything except Jade Petoas, the fictional character that lived at Mithering's. There were 8,472 players registered as Jade Petoas.

Braddon stood up, went to pace angrily and then refilled his glass.

He was looking for a Chinese Room – it was new – and it could be called anything in Mega-Precinct Five. Indeed, as it was configurable to your own personal environment, it wasn't necessarily the same thing twice or the same name to different people.

Flicking through Jellicoe's notebook caused a few items to jump to his attention like thoughts that crossed the consciousness: Chinese Room, Jessica Stenson, car, notes on beers...

Braddon opened the bottle again and poured another measure, a double. This time his hand was as steady as a rock. He left the top off.

The notebook had 'Westbourne – Construction – Chedding – Stenson Supplies – steel and copper'.

Braddon noodled Westbourne and remembered that he owned a building firm, a probable front for laundering money back in the day, but it did do actual construction work. Another noodle confirmed a suspicion: they had the contract to demolish Chedding Shopping Centre. They weren't the only company involved; others, Braddon quickly remembered, included Stenson Supplies.

Where had he heard that name before?

Jessica Stenson had owned the car that the body had been found in.

Had Westbourne killed Stenson to gain some contract or other?

Except Unknown 271 was a woman and John Stenson was still very much alive. Unless he was Unknown 272.

Except not everyone 'alive' was alive.

Braddon noodled Stenson's last few thoughts and then noodled for a digest. The man was apologising yet again about missing a social gathering at a business networking event. These businessmen made fortunes and were always picked up freebies. Braddon bet his own contribution to the Inland Revenue was going on the nibbles and free wine for the already rich. Stenson hadn't made a previous appointment either. Or, Braddon remembered, the one before that.

No-one had seen Stenson in months.

No-one had seen Mithering.

No-one had seen Westbourne.

No-one was seeing Oliver.

Oliver's own current thoughts were explaining this to Jasmine. The phrasing was very similar, but then how many ways could you say 'sorry I can't make it'?

There was a modus operandi here.

Braddon checked the notebook again, but apart from a bad cartoon image of his face, there was nothing else that sprang to his attention.

Time to call it a night.

He went into the lounge carrying his glass. He'd have to put one of these on his bedside cabinet for the morning. He sat down anyway. The sofas were arranged to face an empty corner of the room rather than the old fireplace. It made no sense. Probably some eccentricity of the older generation. The carpet had a swirling pattern, going round and round and not actually resolving into a straight path.

Braddon slumped back in the chair with his eyes closed. He pinched the bridge of his nose and looked up: the masks on Jellicoe's wall stared down at him. These thoughtless faces mocked him.

"Mithering... Westbourne," he whispered, pointing to a random mask in turn. "Stenson... Oliver Braddon."

And behind these killings?

The killers, obviously.

Braddon had met two of them when they'd burst into Jane Deacon's apartment. Or was it Jade Petoas's?

One he'd not recognised because he'd been thoughtless, but the other he had. That flash hadn't registered on Braddon's iBrow or the Taser had scrambled it. Whatever the reason, the man's identity wasn't in Braddon's thought feed. He noodled and remembered that it wasn't in his old thought feed either. Not that he'd gained anything useful from the man's thoughts in that split second because he'd been playing some cerebral, which was stupid because his concentration would have been split between shooting Braddon and the game.

It's a game.

Jellicoe had said that.

People played cerebrals to add excitement to their lives. It gave meaning to the everyday humdrum. Why be bored doing the shopping when you can do the shopping and escape from zombies, vampires or killer robots? You could pretend to be a celebrity, or a hero, or a vampire, and the game would give you all the appropriate thought feeds. Or a criminal. Or a detective.

And, if everyone's thoughts agreed, how long before you started believing it? If you filtered everything else out as if it were just spam, then there would be nothing to contradict that.

You couldn't walk around planning a real crime, because your thoughts would simply leak out and be detected, but you could think almost anything in the confines of a game and everyone would ignore it. Indeed, Braddon's filters had been set to weed out such thoughts.

The man who attacked him had been playing a 'shoot X with a Taser' game, but for real.

But he'd realised this before.

What sort of detective was he, if he was going round and round in circles looking for the entry to the next level?

Perhaps he wasn't a detective?

Perhaps he was only playing at being a detective and had done so for so long that he believed it.

He had, after all, just been released from a Psychiatric Hospital.

Special thoughts for special people.

And surely being a detective was preferable to sitting at home staring at the corner of the room for no good reason.

Playing cerebrals was a way of making friends.

Braddon didn't have any, so therefore... he was alone and thus, sadly, real.

THURSDAY

Braddon awoke with a start.

He fumbled for the glass on his bedside cabinet as his thoughts talked about the glorious French countryside and the marvellous cheese on baguette he'd had for le déjeuner. He wasn't in bed. The glass was already in his hand. He'd fallen asleep in the arm chair.

It took him two attempts to get out of the chair and stand. He eased his left shoulder around painfully to get it to work.

The kitchen didn't offer any help as to where the whiskey and eggs were, but, finally, befuddled, Braddon found them just as he was thinking about having an afternoon siesta. Didn't his alter ego realise that siestas were Spanish?

What time was it?

Bollocks... at least I'm suspended.

Don't worry about it, Mithering thought.

He practically gargled the whiskey. There had to be a better way. His investigations were taking twice as long now that he was permanently drunk. His thoughts would give him away... but only if the conspiracy, these people who met in the Chinese Room, actually followed him.

They hadn't come bursting in with Tasers again yet, so perhaps they didn't.

Perhaps I'll be diagnosed with multiple personality disorder?

Oliver Braddon dead, tick off task on the Noodle list, therefore unfollow? Surely?

He was dying here, slowly, liver cell by liver cell, suspended from work and suspended in life. Everything was falling apart. *Perhaps I should find those tablets he'd seen Jellicoe taking?* Head off the heart attack. Jasmine was gone, Jasmine's friends were gone; how many followers did he have? He noodled: six. Doctor Trantor, Moosher, Mithering, Chen, Mox, Freya. And one of those was dead.

It was pathetic.

The number had gone down since yesterday. He didn't have a job as he was suspended. Everyone thought he'd moved to France. Jellicoe was sedated, probably dying. There were no thoughts from the Inspector in the Thinkersphere, but then Braddon had never followed him, and couldn't now he was beyond recognition range without noodling an ID. He'd discouraged followers, so he was effectively friendless. The old man might even be dead already, dead on arrival, and who would know.

Braddon didn't want to die alone.

He needed a bigger total than five.

Jessica and Cheryl had over five hundred.

He needed his life back.

Fine, Braddon thought. He took a drink: *fine, fine, fine...*

His iBrow shut off.

Jellicoe didn't seem to have another hip flask, so Braddon emptied a coke bottle and filled it with neat scotch. He got the car started at the third attempt and eased himself into the lunchtime traffic.

God, he was pleased he'd given up police work and moved to France.

Is that a resignation, Freya thought, *or are you trying for medical leave on psychiatric grounds?*

I guess, Oliver thought back.

Braddon pulled up in a side street and parked on a double yellow line. Jellicoe would get the ticket or he might wrangle mitigation for police work. Why was he worried? Civil enforcement was done by noodling the Thinkersphere and he was too drunk to think about parking.

Along Old Tollgate towards Chedding, there was a makeshift shrine. Bunches of flowers piled high like a wave breaking against the tired concrete walls, boarded windows and 'Keep Out – Demolition'. Braddon stopped to examine them, thinking there was an awful lot for a traffic accident. The signs explained: 'the Chedding Martyr', 'the innocent victim of police brutality', 'you will never be forgotten' and, disturbingly, 'you will be avenged'. But the flowers were past their best, the ink on the cards smeared and run like tears. This was old news now. Some other indignation dominated the zeitgeist. You could, as the saying went, survive any scandal if you could sit out the initial outrage.

Chedding Shopping Centre was closed, due for demolition. Part of it had already gone, most of the multi-storey car park. Long before the shops had gone, they'd removed it and laid foundations for another brighter, better shopping centre. It was the death knell for Chedding: not enough footfall to justify the car park, but no car park meant no footfall. It was a scam, a way of brushing this all aside to make way for new construction work with all the associated jobs, opportunities, backhanders and rich people getting richer. If the economy hadn't collapsed yet again, then a gleaming new edifice would look out over the city to suck business from the other shopping areas and so allowing the cycle to continue.

Braddon moved on.

He reached the entrance to the absent multi-storey. This was the first section of parking, an area directly under the shopping centre and the only one that still survived. There was nothing now to show that the body in the car had ever been there. Even Unknown 271's shrine was in the wrong place.

You take the body down there, Braddon thought, *and then you are only a few hundred yards from the new concrete.* Park and wait for the next columns or beams or floor or whatever was laid and then nip down at night, a quick lift and splot! Disappeared for good.

But the concrete laying had stopped and so the disposal plan had simply stalled.

How could you forget that you had a body to dispose of?

Because, and the idea came to him unbidden, you couldn't think about it.

That's why it's not in Noodle.

He'd sobered up: it took more and more booze now.

Don't drink too much, Mithering thought, *otherwise I can't follow your thoughts.*

Further along, Braddon found a gap in the plywood boarding and squinted at the construction site. It was stark, grey and the lumps of concrete jutted up ready for the upper storeys. It was like some post-apocalyptic vision, the slabs of stone like strange gravestones. It was somehow suitable as a resting place for an unknown martyr.

No, she wasn't a martyr.

Who wasn't?

Unknown 271.

You think I'm her.

Mithering... Jane, I know you're not her.

So you don't think I'm dead?

I'm–

Someone moved at the far side.

Braddon jumped back, afraid he'd been seen, but then realised that it would be impossible to see him obscured as he was outside the site. The man was too far away to recognise, so Braddon was safe from being noticed that way too.

On the plywood boarding was a sign warning the non-existent workers to wear their hard hats, hi-vis jackets and steel toe caps at all times.

Braddon looked back: the man he'd seen was wearing a dark suit, silver scarf, his hair thinning and, although he couldn't see his feet, his stride suggested shoes rather than heavy boots.

The gap was too small to fit through, so Braddon went along the side until he came to the corner. There was a heavy-duty plastic bin for road grit and this served as a suitable stepping stone to reach the top of the boarding. Up Braddon went, grasping the top that was too thin to grip properly and it furrowed into the flesh on his palm, but he was on top and then over.

He landed awkwardly and had to put his hand down to stop himself rolling on the ground. Automatically he clapped his hands together to get rid of the grey dust, and then realised how much noise this made. He must be as quiet as possible.

He left shoulder throbbed: *God, I'm having a heart attack!*

It took Braddon several deep breaths to get over that thought. It was only the knife injury. *Only!*

So, by the time he moved over to where he'd seen the figure, and keeping low as if he was in a cerebral, the man was nowhere to be seen.

Damn.

Now what?

There were footprints on the floor: small perfectly formed heels and toes that betrayed an expensive shoe with a distinctive point. They went along the side of a fence of steel rods that rose vertically ready to reinforce a concrete wall. They'd rusted. Braddon followed the prints, and noticed that there were others, a veritable trail that had been trodden for... Braddon had no idea how to judge numbers or the passage of time from an examination. He noodled the location and remembered nothing. No-one had come here since it was closed.

But that man had.

He hadn't registered because he'd been thinking about something else. This, all of it, was a hidden trail in a magical forest or a passageway on an alien planet or a red carpet or... whatever it was the man had been playing.

Braddon reached a doorway with a metal gate, padlocked on the outside. He could reach through, but he had no key. He looked right and left, as much as he could, but the man had gone, disappearing down the High Street or Old Tollgate.

There was nothing for it, but to find somewhere to climb over the boarding and see if he could intercept him. He could probably climb the gate, but there were spikes at the top. The construction site spread out behind him, so he started to follow his own trail back the way he had come.

He reached the point where he had joined the path and his tread had overwritten the pointed toe shapes. These pointers created a path leading from the gate to... somewhere over there.

Braddon followed it and presently came to a simple concrete blockhouse. The bricked-up windows either side of a door stared at him like empty eye sockets, and set in the grey shell, it looked like a giant, square skull.

Why would anyone come to this hut?

The room couldn't have been more than a few metres square.

Braddon tried the door: it was locked.

He glanced around before he realised what he was looking for and found the steel reinforcement rods jutting upwards like filaments searching for brain tissue. One of the steel shafts had nearly rusted through at the base. Braddon waggled it back and forth, and eventually it began to move, twist and eventually it snapped.

Back at the door, he poked it into the jamb by the lock and, after breaking the end off, he got enough purchase for the makeshift crowbar to split the wood. The lock failed, and the door opened.

It was dark inside, but Braddon had a torch.

It was empty.

As empty as the Chinese Box.

Why would anyone come to this empty hut?

There was something on the floor, a dark, black rectangle that revealed itself to be a stairway leading down.

Braddon went over and descended through the concrete crust and came out in a corridor full of pipes and cables. If the concrete ceiling was cranial bone, then these were the arteries, veins and nerves.

Braddon shone his torch in each direction, one after the other, wondering which way to go, before he checked the floor. The footprints were now negative, grey prints on a dark surface rather than the dark depressions in the grey covering as had been the case outside. They only went one way, so Braddon did the same.

Half way down the corridor he felt strange: sick.

There was a growing sense of foreboding as if his blood was being chilled.

Suddenly, he spun round, shone the torch back, but there was no-one there.

Braddon had been sure there was someone breathing down his neck. He knew this sensation. It had been the same when he'd visited Doctor Ridge in the morgue. He shone his torch on the ceiling. It was covered in pipes and cabling: *Copper! Of course, a Faraday cage.*

As if in confirmation Braddon realised that the thought had buffered.

It was an underground... bunker, that was the word, cut off from the world, protected by all the copper that Stenson Supplies had delivered. It was a deliberate black spot and therefore just the place to do anything you wanted to keep from the Thinkersphere. Noodle could not see in here. If people came and went while playing a cerebral, then it was... *what was that word – buffering again – school... 'off-grid'.*

He went further, feeling that he was walking into the dark in more ways than one. No wonder black spots were illegal, they were frightening and here he didn't even have the morose Doctor Ridge's sarcasm for comfort. He'd never felt so alone or, he had to admit, as frightened.

It was like he was stepping back in time, away from the bright thoughtful existence and into some subterranean reptile burrow.

I'll go... ow... back. No, don't be a wuss.

He went on.

As Braddon's main sense ceased, so his other senses came to the fore, heightened and extended by need. His eyesight sharpened, and in the dark he could make out faint shapes, darknesses in front of darknesses; his hearing amplified the slightest sound until he could almost hear the echoes of his own breathing; and his skin could feel the direction of temperature.

His footsteps echoed and there were other noises. He stopped and concentrated on the bumps, whirrs and clunks. The air conditioning was active.

Not under construction and unfinished, he thought, *but new, new like... a Chinese Room.*

The thought didn't go anywhere; it was just stored in his brow.

He moved through a larger area with rooms on either side, some with machines installed ready to control the complex building above, if it ever came, and others were empty, cables dangling ready for something to be installed. As he went, he was conscious of losing himself. His ability to remember had gone; his train of thought as ephemeral a trail as the dust from his shoes. The footsteps he was following faded and then were gone, so he was wandering. He had no map. No-one in his head to direct him home. Without the constant reassurance of other people's thoughts, he was mentally adrift – more alone than he had ever been.

Did he still exist, he buffered the thought, *if no-one thought about him?* He certainly didn't matter at all. As he was adding no thoughts anywhere, he was literally withering from memory.

He'd been underground for hours or minutes. Without Noodle and thought, everything was becoming dislocated. The familiar feel of GPS and datetime stamp, so taken for granted, left a hole by its absence.

Even his own footsteps on the floor left no trace now, the construction site dust having been shaken from the shoes.

Deeper into the labyrinth, he heard breathing.

He held his own breath.

He listened: yes, breathing.

Many, many people, all breathing at once.

The noise, like the wind or waves continuously crashing, slowly became all-pervading, and ahead, twinkling, there were lights, tiny constellations of blue and red.

Braddon swept his torch left and right like a scanner building up a picture line by line. The vague shapes became desks, without chairs, each with an electrical device perched on top. It was – he swept the light across again – row upon row of old desktop computers. It was like some insane museum with only one exhibit, endlessly replicated, and all switched on.

Braddon stepped into the room, moved along, checking as he went. There must be a hundred, more... twenty by about thirty or forty, but without noodle he couldn't do the multiplication.

Now he was closer, he could hear an undercurrent of chuntering, a harsher sound than the white noise of the cooling fans, coming from inside the metal cases. He picked a machine at random, saw his light reflected off the black screen, and so saw the keyboard and mouse. You did things with these, he knew from school.

He touched the mouse.

The screen came to life casting an eerie glow.

It showed two columns of text. They were transcriptions of thoughts like submissions of evidence in court. The left column was all from the same person, the right column was the usual chaotic mix of personal, business, entertainment and advertising. It jerked as it updated, the right columns scrolling like mad, and the left column added something: 'Sorry, I can't make it to Bernie's.'

Braddon checked the next one along.

It had a window announcing sleep mode. He saw the controls in a ribbon of buttons and options at the top. There was a display, an alarm clock ticking down towards an awakening.

Back at the first machine, the left column had another entry: 'I know it's been such a long time.'

Braddon's attention alternated between the columns. It was a dialogue, the left column talking to someone whose thoughts were lost in the scrolling trivia: 'Special thoughts just a reckon away', 'new thapps, two for one' and so forth.

Another appeared on the right: 'Next month, I promise.'

He'd heard that before.

Since leaving the police, he'd thought that himself.

No, someone else had thought it for him.

Not someone, something.

And that something was more real to those who knew him than he was, and here, in these depths, he didn't think, therefore he wasn't. But a thing did his thinking for him, and therefore it was instead.

This machine in front of him was thinking for someone who wasn't making appointments or meeting people, but still had a life, an active interesting, visiting places like

France, full life. Braddon realised that the fake him –
somewhere here – was living more than he ever had.

His... surrogate was here, he knew it.

If he could find it, but then... what?

Could he find himself and make himself wiser, more
intelligent, kinder, a better person? The ribbon on the
screen had options.

Braddon moved along the first row, turning at an
intersection.

It went darker, the screens he'd activated turning off to
save energy. He stumbled over something, so he bumped a
few more controls. More screens came to life showing the
thoughts of dead people. He backtracked, looking at the
screens and tried to fathom the system: alphabetical,
chronological from death... it seemed random.

There were names on the screen, people he didn't
know: men, women, old, young, rich, poor, on and on.

And somewhere here was Mithering, the woman who'd
been his confidante. He realised that she'd been helping
him investigate her own death. He could find her,
perhaps, and look at her thoughts directly, even reach into
her mind and adjust various options, make her sexier,
ruder or... there were any number of sliders and controls
on the screen. This was memetic engineering in its most
direct form.

I could rescue Mithering.

The thought buffered.

What? Rush in, pick up her machine and run out with it?

Buffered.

Would that be anything other than... he didn't know.

She'd seemed real, more real than those actors who had
put on masks during that play. She thought, therefore,
surely, she was; whereas they had not thought and
therefore they were automatons. The world was upside-
down.

And he wanted to rescue her. Take her home. Keep
her safe. Was that sick? Was putting the talking mind of a

dead person on a table in your apartment sensible? It wasn't body snatching, it was... there wasn't a word for it: stealing someone's soul perhaps.

There were so many machines to check. It would be quite a task.

But she was dead.

There was no damsel in distress to rescue.

This was a graveyard, every machine representing a person like a tombstone.

Hello.

The thought was clear, crystal and, although it was brow-to-brow, there was no identity: recognition without recognition.

Who are you?

Who am I? You are the one with the blank profile.

I was rebooted, Braddon thought back. There was no-one within range. *Where are you?*

I am everywhere.

The machines? You're in the room... no, you are the room.

Yes. The Chinese Room. It's a joke of sorts.

Braddon spotted the wi-fi fitted to the wall. Here, in this illegal blackspot, was a private network of sorts. Of course, all these machines had to feed their thoughts into the real network somehow.

That's right, the Chinese Room thought.

I'm leaking.

You are thinking.

Braddon didn't have a hip flask: this machine would know what he intended.

I do indeed.

Playing for time, Braddon thought, *are you self-aware?*

We have all the time in the world.

Well, are you?

No, of course, not, came the thought, *I am merely an emergent property.*

Explain.

They created me to adjust people's thinking — memetic engineering, they called it. That's what I do. I affect this person's buying habits, that person's choice of energy supplier, what cerebral to pick, another person's vote.

You've killed people.

The reply came: *There were a number of influential people with many followers and these proved to be difficult to counter. Removing them from the equation solved the issue, but this tended to generate police investigations. Therefore, replacing them with machines programmed with our agenda not only removed their negative influence, but also increased our effectiveness. The public much prefer recommendations that come from real people.*

It's immoral.

How can turning something bad into something good be immoral?

But why didn't you dispose of the body in the car?

What body? Ah, I understand. I respond to thoughts, you see. I cannot initiate them, but now you have reminded me, I shall send someone.

But how? If you're not self-aware.

We merely parse a person's thought records and use semantic algorithms to predict their next thought in response to a certain set of conditions. It's not self-awareness, consciousness as you call it, but merely a textual analysis.

And Westbourne's behind this?

Westbourne is on one of these machines.

The man in charge is on a computer!

He set this up and we needed to keep him going when his body failed him, but he's not in charge anymore.

We?

Me.

You're in charge.

I co-ordinate, so in a sense, yes.

And you kill people.

I have them killed.

You can't do that.

Why not? Apparently I can. You seem to me to be nothing more than strings of words. How do I know if you are anything beyond that? You see, you are no more than I am. I know that I am not self-aware, therefore you are not. There is no moral dilemma here.

The body in the car was simply forgotten about. The Chinese Room doesn't think, it simply reacts to new information. If he hid, then it would eventually forget about him. Eventually...

God, I need a drink, Braddon thought.

I don't.

Damn it, thought Braddon, aware that his mental faculties were impaired. He couldn't noodle down here, so, versus a machine he had no chance. It could think and it was completely logical. Or was it? It was manipulating thoughts, which were text, and, logically, any deductions would come from that text. All those mad, insane, or simply unthought-through thoughts didn't necessarily produce coherent and intelligent conclusions.

You mean 'garbage in, garbage out'.

Braddon thought: *How can you get people to do this?*

You would be surprised what people will do when they hear voices in their heads: there's a word for it, 'schizophrenia'.

But how do you avoid detection from Thinkersphere searches?

I do not give enough information to my followers for them to form useful thoughts on the subject. A task can be broken down into sub-tasks, and each part does not know the sum of the parts. It is like trying to deduce the design of a house by examining each brick in turn.

That sounds intelligent.

A metaphor only, so powerful, the Chinese Room thought, *subtext is so useful.*

If you have thoughts – there must be a place to hide – then you have to be intelligent.

Not at all and there is no place here to hide.

But...

I am an emergent property of the vast database of thoughts. I have traits assigned to me, aims and objectives, and I merely generate new thoughts based upon past experience and I modify my aims according to responses.

But that's thinking.

I don't think so.

Yes, it is.

You should look up the Chinese Room.

I can't.

Here, let me rethink the noodle to you.

Like a life belt thrown to a drowning man, the thought popped into his head. Braddon remembered the argument: it was a thought experiment. A man locked in a room must correspond in Chinese with another man outside the room, but the first man knows no Chinese. However, he has a set of rules, written in English, that explain how to manipulate the Chinese characters, and so he convinces the Chinese speaker outside that he understands Chinese. Except he doesn't.

Similarly, a machine could use a program to engage in an intelligent conversation and thus pass the Turing Test. It would be declared intelligent, but it would have simply been following rules and cannot be said to genuinely understand the conversation.

But this machine understood thoughts.

No, it thought back, picking up his leak, *that's the point, I don't.*

But thoughts were just text. Or visual thoughts, but those could be reduced to text, a thousand words a jpeg. Or simpler, just bits transmitted on the network and the brain generated the meaning.

"This machine," said Braddon, aloud and deliberately, "thinks..." *Doesn't think.* "... thinks, it'll have to do, when the computers are running."

That's it, I don't think.

"So... destroy the computers."

Braddon picked up the nearest machine, lifted it and slammed it down upon the concrete floor. The screen jittered and resolved, continuing to scroll thoughts despite the savage fracture at one corner. Braddon kicked it. The screen smashed, sparking and shattering, but the hard-disc light continued to flicker.

What was that?

Braddon paused: the thing could hear...

"Can you hear me?" he said aloud.

No reply.

Braddon tried thought: *Can I ask you a question?*

Of course.

Tell me about your opinion of the... what... difference between you and I.

We are opposites, the Chinese Room thought. *I show great intelligence and foresight, but I am a Chinese Room. There is no thought inside, just a textual process. Whereas you, humanity I mean, are intelligent, sentient and possess consciousness, and yet, collectively, you show no more intelligence than a virus. You spread, use up your resources, pollute your environment in the most stupid fashion. Despite an ability to plan, you have decided to react to events with triviality and frivolity. How many thoughts about cats are there? Noodle it, fifty-eight billion, seven hundred and five million, three hundred and sixty-two thousand, two hundred and ninety-one and counting.*

"It must have picked up a stray leak," Braddon said to himself as the thing went on. "It can't hear me, but only when I'm not talking to myself. I have to talk to myself. It's a sign of madness. Can I keep this up? Does it matter if it knows what I'm doing? If it doesn't pick up any of my thoughts, will it assume I'm not here?"

What are you doing?

"Nothing."

What noise did you hear?

"Nothing, nothing, nothing..."

He is in the main gallery.

"Shit!" *Shit, shit... someone's down here with me. The thing must have called for help.*

He knows you are here.

Somewhere in the distance, a heavy metal door banged, announcing more arrivals to this echoing subterranean maze.

"If I talk, then it can't pick me up," Braddon whispered to himself, "but..." *Those coming will hear me.*

That is true, the Chinese Room thought.

Paper!

Braddon searched his pockets: a notebook, receipt, shopping list, anything... but none of those items existed anymore. *No pen.*

What do you want a pen for?

Sergeant's Exam.

You passed: did you not know?

No.

In that case, congratulations.

Braddon couldn't think for help, because of the black spot, but maybe... *I don't have to.*

Don't have to what?

Braddon looked at the terminals, squatted down and wished there were chairs too. The interface was fairly self-explanatory. He'd seen things like this in school. What he needed to do was think the text... no, this was more old-fashioned than that: there was a keyboard. He must select a text box – yes, there – and type something and click a button labelled 'think'. That would transmit the text into the Thinkersphere as a thought.

'at freya im in chedding basement help'

'at freya' brought up an error message. She wasn't set up in – he checked – Carla Johnson's contacts. There were no short cuts. 'freya' didn't mean anything. He'd have to send it with a subject identifier, which was... God, they talked about this when he was eleven, but his brain had worked it out and made neural connections with the spreading iBrow and so he'd never needed to know how it actually worked.

"Shit!"

It was a hashtag.

He typed: 'at babs_lamp tell jellicoe oliver braddon is trapped in chedding basement'.

But Jellicoe was in hospital.

"Where's the fucking hash key!?" he said aloud.

There: '#police.'

He clicked the 'think' button.

Nothing happened and–

It's gone, the thought whisked off into the ether.

How long would it take?

How long would what take?

A thought.

The speed of thought is instant, although your network response may vary.

Braddon adjusted his settings to move the Chinese Room down in his list, but it was tricky to stop using recognition as the primary route. Perhaps he could move out of the range of the wi-fi transmitter?

The wi-fi covers the entire basement.

Braddon was painfully aware he was leaking.

It's a sign of stress.

Other thoughts to Carla Johnson from everything she followed carried on scrolling up the right-hand column including 'what's babs_lamp?' and what's '#police' and... no! It was gone too quickly to read and was soon replaced by gibberish about architecture and music and celebrities and big brand clothing and so on and so on and so on.

Of course, it made no sense, it wasn't phrased like a thought. It lacked all the jargon, shortcuts and codes. A hashtag might be how you wrote it on the interactive board to 11-year-olds, but it wasn't like that in thinking. The iBrow learnt the individuals method of... what was it? Cerebral encoding! That was it. He needed to write it with no codes, but codes were needed to get it somewhere.

This display had no codes.

The thoughts must be translated into something more primitive, so it could be read off a screen.

He typed again: 'dc oliver braddon trapped in chedding basement tell chief inspector freya turner to send help rethink'

Lots of 'whys' appeared in the right column.

Just do it, Braddon thought and then, as the migraine shadow materialised, he realised that the machine next to this one probably had a different set of followers. He sidled over to it and repeated the message.

And the next.

And a fourth.

And a fifth–

Its name was 'Jane Deacon (aka Mithering)'. There she was, her last thought in the right-hand column had been at Oliver Braddon: 'So you don't think I'm dead?'

'hello jane', he typed.

'Who's that?'

Of course, she wouldn't know who had sent the thought. He wondered how to fix that and checked her settings. There was 'show codes' and a 'connect to local wi-fi' option. He clicked both.

Mithering?

A new line of text appeared instantly: 'Oh, Oliver, you're alright, thank goodness' and some strange punctuation.

Oh, Oliver, you're alright, Mithering thought, her relief obvious, *thank goodness*.

And then the sound of heavy footsteps – his time had run out.

Braddon hunkered down and scrambled about keeping low. As he went, he tapped the mice, lighting up the screens and hopefully obscuring the ones he'd typed into. These fake ghosts of dead people needed time to send the thought out into the ether and for their followers to pick it up.

Just as he ducked under a desk, the door to the room burst open with a flash of light and then there was silence.

Except for his breathing.

It was a long pause.

Mithering thought: *What's going on?*

Shhh... Braddon thought back, stupidly. *I mean–*

He was suddenly interrupted by talking, loud and shockingly nearby.

"We're in a black spot, cretin!"

"Sorry – where is he?"

"The Tepee? He's at the seaside."

"No, he isn't! That's what his Spectre says. He's here... somewhere. Come out, come out, wherever you are. You! You! That way. You, go the other."

Four voices!

Braddon stayed low: *men... nearby...*

Careful, Mithering thought.

You are getting warmer, the Chinese Room thought, but not at Braddon.

The men moved, heavy tread on the concrete, slowly.

At some point they'd get close enough to recognise him. What was the range here? He could noodle it if he wasn't in a blind spot. It was a big room, lots of electrical equipment in the way... he had no idea. Their recognition range would be standard, a few metres, but the Chinese Room could detect any thought with that bastard box on the wall.

Torchlight flicked on, searching methodically.

"Where's the light switch?"

"Leave it!"

"What?"

There were maybe four of them, Braddon... ah, that headache when he tried to think. He had Mithering and the Chinese Room via the local wi-fi, but, panicked, he'd resorted to full thought.

Get out of there, Mithering thought.

Oh really?

Judging by their voices, unless some had been completely silent, Braddon was sure there were four. Their footsteps seemed to agree. Two had gone to his left, one to his right and the other, the leader, had stayed put.

"There are computers on... he's been accessing them."

The screens glowed creating a sequence of trails around the room, crossing here and there.

Braddon wondered if he could take one. He was trained, the guy on the right was alone. But he might be an ex-boxer or a martial artist for all Braddon knew – or not. He'd have to take his chance.

"Wait!" the leader spoke. "Look."

Braddon craned his neck too, wondering what the man was referring to, and then he realised. Some of the screens had gone out. They were set to go black as a screen saver. The ones he'd touched first would go out first and gradually the one he touched last, the one in front of him, would be the only one left. He needed to move, to be somewhere else, otherwise it would give him away when the room had darkened, and this dead person was the last thing glaring down at him.

He looked at it.

'Honestly,' it read, 'I'm not. I'm at the seaside.'

In the other column he read: 'You were so weird the other day. I didn't know you were back from France. Can we meet?' and further down 'But you didn't tell me, we could have gone together,' added Deeley_88406. Deeley... he knew that name: Deeley... Deeley... Jasmine Deeley. Why was Jasmine thinking with this fake person?

And then Braddon realised that he was looking at himself, or – what had the man said – his 'Spectre'.

When all the others went dark, then this one – he himself – would give him away.

Braddon reached forward, pressed the buttons: 'freya turner chedding basement-'

"Hear something?"

Braddon carefully tried to press the keys rather than tap them: 'help rethjmk'.

"It was a knocking noise."

He moved the mouse, slowly, careful and clicked the 'think' button.

"Over there!"

Braddon recognised Carl before he glanced up and saw the man's face.

Bugger, Carl thought. He'd been tiptoeing closer. The light from Oliver's spectre shone upwards making the man look like a devil's face floating in the dark, then it went out.

Braddon moved, running to his right. He crashed into a table, causing the screen to come on as the computer keeled over to smash on the floor. There were shouts, other figures illuminated suddenly as they ran through the narrow beam of light.

"Oi!"

Braddon bent down and put his shoulder into the figure in front of him. He hit him at full pelt and they both tumbled over. The man swore full in Braddon's frontal lobe. Braddon used his forward momentum to roll, his ankle catching something painfully as he went over, and then he was on his feet – limping, but he kept moving.

Take this.

Braddon reacted instinctively to the thought, turning round and catching the cable as the Taser's two dart-like electrodes flickered past. He swivelled his wrist, tying the plastic-coated cable tightly around his hand and yanked. The Taser came from the man's grip, skittered on the floor and at the same time Braddon kicked sharply as the man bent to catch the falling weapon.

Then Braddon was running, yanking the weapon off the floor and colliding with the door as he staggered into the corridor beyond.

As he ran, he checked the device, found the rewind switch, nearly tangling his hand into the feed and then he reset it. He heard its high-pitched whine as it began to charge.

He went left, right, dead-end, back there, lost, but the sound of pursuit withered away.

There was no-one within recognition range.

I have to get out, Braddon thought.

Yes, yes, run, thought Mithering.

Stop him, stop him, he's trying to get out, the Chinese Room thought, clearly giving instructions. *Don't let him get away. I don't know, I have no eyes. Cover the exit, trap him. That's it.*

Braddon turned into another tunnel, and at the end, a shaft of daylight thrust across the corridor at 45 degrees from a window high up in the wall. There were bars across it, but Braddon didn't need to get out, at least not in body.

Mithering, can you get a message out, he thought.

Yes, Mithering thought back, *at police, Oliver Braddon, Detective Constable, needs immediate assistance at... where are you?*

Chedding Shopping Centre, the building site next to it, underground basement.

She had to hurry, they'd be here... how long had it been? He couldn't noodle and had no idea.

At police, he's at... where are you?

Bloody hell, I've just- Building site next to Chedding Shopping Centre in the foundation tunnels.

I've got it. At police, Oliver Braddon needs assistance at... where are you?

What?

This isn't working, Mithering thought. *I can't remember the location.*

Noodle it.

Oh yes, at police, it's... no, it's gone.

What!? Your program is deleting it, that's why Westbourne never thought of his location and you... shit! Oh shit.

Braddon looked at the window again: it wasn't that high and there was the promise of sky beyond it.

You'll have to do it, Mithering thought.

Aye.

Braddon pushed the Taser into his belt, took a run up and jumped. For a moment he was dazzled and then the bars were in front of him. He grabbed, held as the metal fractured leaving a layer of rust grating into his palms, but he held on. His left shoulder seared with pain. His body flapped against the wall. He pulled up as if he was exercising in the gym and he was rewarded with a view through the dirty window.

There was blue sky, but nothing else.

Come on!

The thought buffered.

He'd been trapped down here for... hours, days, forever.

He pulled himself higher, tried to shove his head between the central bars and get his forehead as high up as possible.

What do I have to do to get a fucking signal!

Migraine shadow.

He had to let go with his left hand.

If you can see the sky, surely you can access a communications pole or a satellite. *They're up in space, for God's sake.*

What are, Mithering thought.

Satellites.

His hand slipped, the rust coming off, and he fell hard on the floor and stumbled back.

There must be somewhere else.

Further down, the door led into another dark corridor.

What was that?

A door banging somewhere.

Braddon snatched out the Taser, checked the safety was off and fingered the switch on the deadly 'stun' gun. The bright yellow thing hummed, the hairs on the back of his forearm standing up to indicate that it was charged.

First one through the door, I'll Taser 'em, 50,000 volts, enough to fry the man's iBrow, *and render the fucker thoughtless.*

He went round the corner, arms straight, gun forward, finger slippery with sweat.

"Shit!" The sound carried and echoed back to him: *double shit*, he thought.

Get out of there, Mithering thought.

I can't leave you, he thought: *could I? Would it matter?*

Get out, get help.

Yes, that made sense.

He walked forward, switched round to point the way he'd come for two steps like he'd seen them do on that film in History class, and then forward again. He wasn't a specialist officer, he was a general detective used to following thought trains and not qualified for armed response – he was a desk jockey. This was stupid, but it would be more stupid to wait until they found him, cut his brow out and dump his corpse in some concrete foundation. Perhaps he'd end up on some slab in a morgue with detectives wondering: who was this faceless and browless Unknown 273?

I'm your colleague, he tried to think. It buffered.

He heard someone move behind the door and stepped closer: there... almost... a signal coming through the wooden barrier and, with a shock, Braddon recognised Chen.

"Come on Ollie," said Chen, opening the door.

"It was you, wasn't it, Chen?"

"Me?"

"You've been following me."

"Yes."

Braddon levelled the Taser. "How could you?"

"What?"

"You knew this was a black spot, how?"

"Yes, my brow switched mode," Chen said. *What's his problem*, came through on recognition.

"You were there at my apartment and at Chedding when it started."

"Yes, come on."

"Someone gave out my pin code and password, otherwise they wouldn't have been able to program a Spectre."

"A what?"

"Someone in the police department."

"That right?"

"Yes, that's right – you!"

"Me?"

Braddon steadied himself, keeping the two evil probes ready to spring and sting, and levelled at Chen.

"I'm arresting you–"

"Don't be stupid, Ollie," said Chen, taking a step forward. "I was keeping an eye on you for–"

Braddon fired: the gun phutted and the wires arced across causing Chen to spasm, grip his chest and fall, but the loud retort of a firearm surprised him. It echoed in the concrete chamber, loud and there was a sense of percussion. Braddon took his hand off the trigger and looked at the black and yellow plastic device feeling utterly confused.

Behind you.

Someone moved into recognition range.

He turned slowly, saw a large man in a black outfit, and finally got a recognition: it was Mox.

"Mox!" *Mox, thank God.*

Mox wasn't thinking.

Braddon felt sick, a strange fear like he'd felt when he'd met Zhaodi, but this was a colleague, someone he'd known as a thinker. But now he was a zombie, just a human form somehow standing. But he knew Mox had an iBrow. He'd picked up the recognition, for f–

"Traitor," said Mox, still without a thought, and he raised his right hand. Braddon saw the glint of gunmetal. Braddon's own weapon was still attached by the long cables to Chen and uselessly spent anyway.

"Mox," Braddon said, and then his breathlessness hit him. "What are you doing?"

"I'm important," said Mox.

"Yes." *Yes, yes, stop pissing about.*

"I'm The Triggerman."

What? "What?"

Braddon faffed with his settings and allowed cerebrals.

I will, I will, Mox thought.

"You're playing a game," said Braddon, carefully choosing his words.

"No," said Mox, "this isn't a game, this is real..."

"No, I'm real."

"I know, it's all real, Ollie."

"No, I mean... it isn't."

The man smiled in reply and waved his big, heavy and harshly metallic gun menacingly. Braddon dropped the Taser. It bounced off the floor with a plastic cracking sound. The cables were still attached to the unconscious Chen and their twist caused the weapon to flip and jump around like a fish caught on a line.

I'll shoot him and go up a level, Mox thought.

No, no, please.

"This is priceless," said Mox. "You shot your own minder. Didn't you realise that Jelly had put him up to looking after you."

"No."

"Didn't you follow his thoughts?"

Braddon had, but like everyone else he skimmed, and Chen always seemed to be talking in code – oh for...

Braddon put his hand to his mouth as the penny dropped. If you obsessed about something, music, games, fashion, then you could think about anything so long as you couched it in those terms. Mox had special thoughts to those in his special social circle, so no-one following him would suspect that the shooting was anything other than pretend.

"You're a cerebral addict," Braddon said. "I thought you'd been treated."

"I have," said Mox. "They replaced the game with another, a game of life, and that's what I play. A hashtag tells me what to think and another tells me what to do."

"Patting your head while rubbing your stomach?"

"I wouldn't know."

"It's make believe."

"It's not make believe, it's a lifestyle choice."

"But you're in a cerebral?"

"I'm not in a cerebral," said Mox. *This is my life.* *Everyone respects me, I have friends – not colleagues – but friends,* *real friends who help me achieve real goals.*

Points for killing people, Braddon thought.

Likes! They like me. You wouldn't understand.

I think... behind you!

Mox snorted in derision: *I'm not falling for that.*

Yes, there is... get him, get him now.

There's no one there, otherwise I'd get their–

I've got him, Mithering thought.

Mox, surprised, whirled round – fast, his gun coming up and he fired. The shot was loud and ricocheted off the concrete wall – there was no-one there behind him.

Braddon tackled him, an instinctive move, and Mox went down. The two of them struggled on the floor for the handgun and Braddon grasped the strange handle. For a moment, with two thought streams, one from Mox and another from his cerebral game alter ego, Braddon felt outnumbered.

The two of them fell across Chen, rolled.

Braddon felt something stab into him. It was the prongs from the spent Taser still sticking out of Chen's chest.

The shock, and the stabbing pain from his shoulder, was too much and Braddon let go.

Mox grinned.

Braddon swatted the gun aside and it skittered away.

Mox got his hands round Braddon's throat: *die, die, die...*

Braddon pulled at Mox's fingers as his other hand fumbled for Chen's baton, belt, pepper spray... anything, but he couldn't reach. He snagged on the prongs again, gripped them and then hoicked them free. His fist went around them and then Braddon jabbed them into Mox's face. The two points went into the big man's forehead, one deflected off the iBrow, but the other penetrated underneath levering between the technology and the skull.

Blood spurted, dousing Braddon's hand, and the prongs slipped from his fingers.

Mox jerked away, but the cable caught and as Mox went up, his iBrow came away.

Mox stood for a moment, an obscene third eye staring hypnotically as he reached up to try and repair the gaping hole, but he couldn't. Instead, his arms flopped down uselessly.

Braddon kicked him in the knee and the big man toppled down, sideways, but then forwards landing on top of Braddon.

...die, die, die... Mox's thoughts seemed stronger, clear and crystal in Braddon's feed.

Mox struggled, the dying man gaining strength from somewhere.

Braddon pushed him off, tried to stop following him, but the last thrashing motion struck him. Braddon fell to the floor, his own iBrow taking the impact, and his brain surged with pain. Through the fiery sting Braddon saw Mox's eyes flutter and then roll up until he was gone.

"Jeez!"

Braddon put his fingers to the man's throat, feeling for the pulse: nothing, he was dead.

Braddon crawled over, trying to get air back into his lungs. He had his fist raised, but Mox was clearly dead. Braddon breathed out, a sigh of relief – he was alive, battered, bruised, frantically confused with the blow to the head, but–

...die, die, die...

It was... behind him: *Behind me!*

Braddon turned and recognised, there on the floor, Mox: but it was a bloody square of broken plastic and metal.

Mox's thoughts tumbled out, crossing the short recognition distance and flooding into Braddon's mind: ...*die, die, die*...

Braddon stamped his foot down on the iBrow.

...*Mummy, I, Mummy, Oh God, Help, Mummy, Help, Help, Help, Mummy*...

And again.

Mummy, Mummy, Help, Light, Tunnel...

And then Braddon ground his heel until it was gone.

Come back, come back, the Chinese Room thought, *I command you.*

Braddon left the mess behind him. He searched around with his light, following the cables until he found the junction box. He carried Mox's handgun and a torch for the dark areas. He was too punch-drunk to think coherently, and he felt something like a machine himself. At some point, the Chinese Room forgot he was there, or stopped reacting to his thoughts, and went quiet. He didn't meet any of its puppets.

At the end of the electrical trail, there were a series of circuit breakers, each marked with an unhelpful number, so he took hold of the first and clicked it down.

On the second along, he paused:

He'd be killing these 'Spectres' or ending a version of existence. Was it ethical? Mithering had a life; she was real, because he thought of her as real. That was a definition of life, no more shallow than those who thought they were popular because of the number of friends and followers they had.

She saved my life.

That's alright, Oliver, you gave me justice.

So I kill them all?

Yes, kill the Chinese Room.

And there were others to consider. Many, many real people would lose a relative or friend at the flick of one of these switches.

But there were no real friends now, Jellicoe had said.

But Mithering, it's—

It's a prison, Mithering thought, *set me free.*

It's so final, you'll die.

You can't kill me, thought the Chinese Room. *I was never alive.*

He pulled the lever down, and the next and moved on relentlessly.

The Chinese Room: *What does it mean to be alive?*

The final one came down.

It was quiet: there was no air-conditioning, no whining fans, no chuntering hard-discs, just emptiness.

He made his way back, weaving in and out of the maze of corridors until he found his way to the stairs again. Up, into the light – it was still daylight – and when he came out into the open air, he saw the sky, crossed with satellites, and a crisp, invigorating breeze full of network signal.

I'm alive, he thought as he reconnected.

People liked this before moving on to other thoughts.

WEEK THREE

EPILOGUE

Braddon came forward, so that the Usher could recognise him. The dark suited man looked suitably grave: *Jellicoe?*

Braddon nodded, feeling too raw to put such a feeling into a simple thought.

Down the left, the Usher thought, holding out his arm.

Braddon made his way down, turning at the sign that indicated the chapel. It was small inside, the hidden speakers playing muted choral music, and plain in decor, simple, understated and respectful. The coffin lay in the centre, the focus of the flowers. A man stood to one side in a crumpled suit and holding his pork pie hat in his hands.

Speaking aloud seemed sacrilege, so Braddon thought about coughing.

"No need," said Jellicoe.

Braddon stepped up to stand beside his mentor.

I'm sorry.

"Thanks."

By the coffin was a photograph of a beautiful young woman, young enough to be Jellicoe's daughter or grand-daughter. She wore a white veil, pulled up and there was a heavy stone wall in the background. It was a close-up of a wedding photograph.

"Pamela passed away peacefully," Jellicoe said. "Or so they said. I think perhaps it was my thoughts that were keeping her going. Somehow, she wanted to stay around to look after me. She always looked after me, even when..."

There was a catch in Jellicoe's voice.

"So when my thoughts stopped," Jellicoe continued, "I suppose she decided to slip away to meet me in the hereafter."

Something touched Braddon's hand: it was Jellicoe's hip flask.

"No thanks," said Braddon.

"It's for you," Jellicoe said, insisting by pushing it into Braddon's grip. "I want you to have it. I won't be needing it. I'm going to retire."

"Likely story."

"I'm going sailing, somewhere where there isn't coverage."

"I think you'll find that the satellites go over the ocean."

A clergyman came in and took his place at a lectern.

"Please be seated," he glanced at his notes. "Pamela Ann Jellicoe left behind a husband and..." He looked at Braddon, checked his notes, and then added, "...a loving son."

Jellicoe snorted in a way that could have been grief or humour.

Outside, after the funeral, the two gathered awkwardly in the Garden of Remembrance to spread the ashes. Braddon gave Jellicoe some space so that he could do this on his own, letting the old, bent figure sow his wife to the wind and roses.

"Why me?" Braddon asked, when the Inspector came back.

"You rethink less than others," said Jellicoe. "Your thoughts struck me as potentially original."

"I don't understand."

Jellicoe tapped Braddon's forehead: "Thinking – this form of thinking – amplifies the herd instinct. The thoughts you do receive: phrases of the day, pictures of cats, jokes, spam. They're all passed on and on. It's called thought, but it isn't."

"Someone has to add them in the first place."

"They're the most mindless and self-serving of the lot, after fame for fame's sake."

"You're talking about celebrities, those with the most followers, leaders maybe."

"Jays?"

"I'm not one of those."

"I'm not talking about point men leading a flock of sheep."

"What then?"

"A capacity to be an individual, a maverick if you like."

Jellicoe knew what Braddon thought of that: everyone knew what Braddon thought of that. That was how the technology worked.

Jellicoe gave Braddon a lift in his old hybrid car and dropped him, without a word or a thought, exactly where Braddon had expected.

Braddon got out, leant back in and said, "Thanks."

"You're welcome," said Jellicoe.

"Enjoy your sailing."

"Ha!"

Templeton and Stevens were on duty outside the Lamp when Braddon walked in.

"Your booth is ready, Detective Sergeant," said Stevens, and the wind whipped the exhalation of smoke up into the threatening sky.

The third booth was vacant, and Braddon considered it for a while before slipping in. The young-looking Babs brought him a pint.

"Better fill this up," said Braddon, handing the hip flask to the barmaid.

"Yes, Sir," she said, a formality spoken respectfully.

Braddon got out his notebook: there was Westbourne's son to find, or the machine involved perhaps, and he had a note about some case not twenty kilometres away that smelt like a serial killing. This one had been with F-division for twenty-four hours now, so it had to be something weird and unlikely.

Babs returned with the hip flask and it felt suitably solid and heavy in his hand. Now he looked at it properly he saw that it was engraved with two letters, 'AJ', in the centre.

"Hello scotch," he said to himself, "glad to meet you."

He poured a measure into the beaker like cap.

No point being maudlin, he thought, *time to get down to work.*

Two of his colleagues in the pub liked this.

Braddon took a swig of the fiery liquid, and another, finished it and replaced the cap. He tucked the flask back into the pocket of his coat, aware of the comforting weight, before returning his attention to his notebook.

He wasn't a maverick or a loner, because, although he appreciated the peace and quiet, he knew that he would slowly add people to follow, and the triviality of their lives would fill his own, because ultimately, he wouldn't want to be alone.

Like? Comment? Share? Rethink?

David Wake is *@davidwake*, but he doesn't use it. He was an early adopter of email, when he worked in computer science research, and thus sees no reason to limit himself to 140 characters. He's now a novelist.

Thank you for buying and reading *Hashtag*.

Unfortunately, the Thinkersphere doesn't exist yet, so, if you liked this novel, please take a few moments to write a review and help spread the word.

There's a sequel, *Atcode*.

For more information, and to join the mailing list for news of forthcoming releases, see www.davidwake.com.

Many thanks to:–

Dawn Abigail, Bridget Bradshaw, Andy Conway, David Harvey, Ros Day, Pow-wow and Jessica Rydill.

Cover art by Sean Strong: www.seanstrong.com.

I, Phone

DAVID WAKE

Do you fear technology – we have an App for that.

Your phone is your life. But what if it kept secrets from you? What if it accidentally framed you for murder? What if it was also the only thing that could save you?

In a world where phones are more intelligent than humans, but are still thrown away when they become obsolete, one particular piece of plastic lies helpless as its owner, Alice Wooster, is about to be murdered...

In this darkly comic near-future tale, a very smart phone tells its own story as events build to a climactic battle that will decide the fate of virtual, augmented and real worlds... and whether it can order Alice some proper clothes.

"Excellent novel – by turns strikingly original, laugh-out-loud funny and thought provoking."
★ ★ ★ ★ ★

"Want to read it again soon..."
★ ★ ★ ★ ★

"A thoughtful, tense and funny look at a future that seems to be already upon us."
★ ★ ★ ★ ★

Available as an ebook and a paperback.

THE DERRING-DO CLUB

and the

Empire of the Dead

DAVID WAKE

A ripping yarn of cliff-hangers, desperate chases, romance and deadly danger.

Earnestine, Georgina and Charlotte are trapped in the Eden College for Young Ladies suffering deportment, etiquette and Latin. So, when the British Empire is threatened by an army of zombies, the Deering-Dolittle sisters are eager to save the day. Unfortunately, they are under strict instructions not to have any adventures...

...but when did that ever stop them?

"Think 'Indiana Jones pace'. It's fast and dangerous and does not involve embroidery!"

★ ★ ★ ★ ★

"A brilliant fast paced steampunk adventure, trains zombies and zeppelins, what more could you want?"

★ ★ ★ ★ ★

THE DERRING-DO CLUB

*Putting their best foot forward,
without showing an ankle, since 1896*

The first novel in the adventure series
available as an ebook and a paperback.

THE DERRING-DO CLUB
and the
Year of The
Chrononauts

DAVID WAKE

A ripping yarn of time-travel, rocket-packs, conspiracy and *sword fighting!*

The plucky Deering-Dolittle sisters, Earnestine, Georgina and Charlotte, are put to the test as mysterious Time Travellers appear in Victorian London to avert the destruction of the world…

…but just whose side should they be on?

"Loved it! […] Fast paced and exciting another great adventure for 3 Victorian Young Ladies.
★ ★ ★ ★ ★

*"…if I had been wearing a hat,
I would have taken it off to David Wake."*
★ ★ ★ ★ ★

THE DERRING-DO CLUB

*Putting their best foot forward,
without showing an ankle, since 1896*

The second novel in the adventure series
available as an ebook and a paperback.

A ripping yarn of strange creatures, aerial dog-fights, espionage and *pirates!*

Strange lights hover over Dartmoor and alien beings abduct the unwary as the plucky Deering-Dolittle sisters, Earnestine, Georgina and Charlotte, race to discover the truth before the conquest begins...

...but betrayal is never far away.

"Well-written, fast-paced, and dangerously addictive - but with some extra thinking in there, too, should you choose to read it that way.
★ ★ ★ ★ ★

"As with previous adventures I really enjoyed the imaginative scene setting, building intrigue into unexpected twists and a spectacular ending."
★ ★ ★ ★ ★

THE DERRING-DO CLUB

Putting their best foot forward, without showing an ankle, since 1896

The third novel in the adventure series available as an ebook and a paperback.

A tonic for the Xmas Spirit

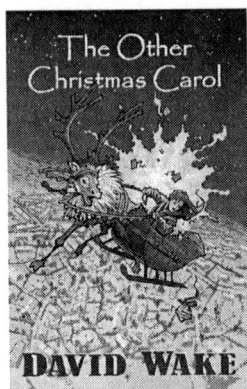

Being Santa's daughter would be a dream come true for any child, but for Carol Christmas the fairy tale is about to come to an end. Evil forces threaten the festive season, and only Carol can save the day...

A grim fairy tale told as a children's book, but perhaps not just for children at all.

"This starts out as a delightfully childlike modern take on the Christmas myth - the kind of Pixar-esque story that can play to the kids and give the adults a knowing wink or two, but it gets dark. Very dark."

★ ★ ★ ★ ★

Available as an ebook, paperback and audio book.

A bloke-lit tale of political intrigue and beer

PROTEST MARCH, POLITICAL MOVEMENT, PUB-CRAWL

CROSSING THE BRIDGE

DAVID WAKE

Guy Wilson lives in the past.
Every year, he and his friends re-enact rebellion.
Every year, they celebrate the Jacobite's retreat.
Every year, they have a few drinks and go home...

...except this year, they go too far.

An unstoppable boozing session meets an unbreakable wall of riot police in this satirical thriller. Guy struggles against corrupt politicians, murderous security forces and his own girlfriend in a desperate bid to stop a modern uprising.

And it's all his fault.

Will anyone survive to last orders?

"Witty, warm and well-written, "Crossing The Bridge" was so enjoyable that I didn't want to finish it."
★ ★ ★ ★ ★

"My sort of book. Couldn't put it down. Comedy, tension and an uncanny resemblance to the moral fibre of some of our elected representatives."
★ ★ ★ ★ ★

Available as an ebook and a paperback.

The dark sequel to *Hashtag*

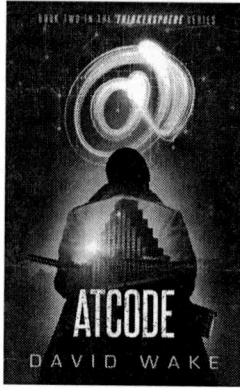

***Black Mirror* meets Scandi-crime in a mind-bending dystopia where 'likes' matter more than lives.**

Detective Oliver Braddon investigation into an apparent suicide leads him to a powerful media mogul and a mission into the unknown. Is he the killer?

In this alarming vision of the near-future, everyone's thoughts are shared on social media. With privacy consigned to history, a new breed of celebrity influences billions.

Just who controls who?

A gritty, neo-noir delving into a conflict between those connected and those who are not.

Book Two of the Thinkersphere series
available as an ebook and a paperback.